The Mill House Murder

J.S. Fletcher

Originally published 1937
London, U.K.

This edition published 2023 by

OREON

an imprint of

The Oleander Press
16 Orchard Street
Cambridge
CB1 1JT

www.oleanderpress.com

ISBN: 9781915475275

Sign up to our infrequent newsletter
to **receive a free ePub** of
Fatality in Fleet Street
by Christopher St John Sprigg and get
news of new titles, discounts and give-aways!

www.oleanderpress.com/golden-age-crime

A CIP catalogue record for the book
is available from the British Library.

Cover design, typesetting & ebook: neorelix

Contents

1

MRS. JOHN MARTENROYDE

It was in the winter following the resumption of my associations with my old firm (formerly called Camberwell & Chaney, but now styled Chaney & Chippendale) that on walking into our Jermyn Street office one January morning I found Chaney knitting his brows over a letter which he presently passed across to me.

"This seems to be something in your line, Camberwell," he remarked. "Perhaps you'll attend to it? The gentleman appears to want us to do some work for him in London, but to go all the way to Yorkshire for instructions. I can't go, nor can Chippendale. You're the travelling man – you take it on."

I sat down at my desk and read the letter, which was written on a big sheet of letter paper in a bold, masculine hand of a somewhat rudimentary sort – my idea was that the writer was not much given to the use of his pen. And this is what I read:

Todmanhawe Grange
Shipton, Yorkshire
Jan. 24th, 19 –

Messrs. Chaney & Chippendale
Jermyn St., W. 1

Dear Sirs, – I have some business that I want attending to in London; business of a very private and confidential nature, and having had your firm highly recommended to me by a London friend, I should be glad if you could undertake said business. As I shall not be able to go to London at present, and the business is urgent, I shall be obliged if you can send one of your firm down here to take my instructions, as soon as possible after your receipt of this letter. For your information I had better tell you how to reach this place. If your representative would take the 12 o'clock train from St. Pancras Station, London, to Leeds, he would arrive there at 3.52, and after changing would catch the 4.07 to Shipton, where my car would meet him at 4.43. As already said, I should like to see your representative as soon as possible and to offer him every hospitality during his visit here.

Yours truly,
James Martenroyde

Then followed a characteristic addition.

PS. As you may not know my name, I may state that I am the sole proprietor of Todmanhawe Mills, and that my bankers are the Shipton Old Bank, Ltd. My London office is 59a, Gresham Street, E.C.

It was not the way of our firm to make delay in anything, and after sending off a telegram to Mr. James Martenroyde, informing him that Mr. Ronald Camberwell, of Chaney & Chippendale, would be at Shipton at 4.43 that afternoon, I picked up the suitcase which I always kept ready packed for any emergency and set off to St. Pancras. And some five hours later I stepped out of a warm first-class carriage on to the windswept platform of Shipton station and shivered in recognition of the wintry landscape of which for the last twenty miles I had been getting glimpses in the rapidly gathering dusk.

A smartly liveried young chauffeur came along the platform, eyeing the various passengers who had left the train. He spotted me and my suitcase and came forward.

"Mr. Camberwell, sir? From Mr. Martenroyde, sir. This way, sir – the car's outside."

Seizing my suitcase, he led the way over a bridge and down the opposite platform to the exit from the station. There stood a handsome limousine, one of the most expensive of the luxury makes – capacious enough to carry a small family. Opening one of the doors, the chauffeur ushered me inside, installed me in a thickly cushioned corner, and drew a rug over my knees.

"Beg your pardon, sir, but you won't mind if we give Mr. Martenroyde's sister-in-law a lift back?" he asked as he tucked me up. "Mrs. John Martenroyde, sir. She's in the town and as she lives close by our place—"

"Oh, of course," I replied. "By all means. Is the lady here?"

"No, sir – pick her up in the market place. All right, sir?"

I assured him that I was very comfortable, and after switching on the electric light above my head, he mounted his seat and drove off. It was now almost dark, and I could see little of the town through which we drove – there was a long street, flanked on one side by great buildings which I took to be mills or workshops, all brilliantly lighted, and at the end of it a long, wide space which I set down as the market square of which my driver had just spoken. There were crowds of people on the pavements there, and between the pavements and the roadway were rows of canopied stalls on which all sorts of merchandise lay displayed – this, I concluded, must be a market day at Shipton. Halfway along the square, the car drew up before the front of an old-fashioned, bow-windowed hotel, the lower casements of which were veiled by red blinds. The chauffeur dismounted and walked into the open door; following his movements along the wide hall within, I saw him turn into one of the rooms. But he was out again at once, and turning into another; evidently he knew where to look for the lady he was expecting. Presently he came out to the car and opened the door.

"Not here yet, sir," he said. "Doing a bit of shopping, I expect. I'll just look round for her, sir – I know where she's likely to be."

He turned off towards a row of shops, and thinking that he might be some time in finding my prospective fellow traveller, I got out of the car and looked about me. I had never been in that part of the country before – this, I concluded, was doubtless a typical Dale town. That it was in the heart of the pastoral country which lies between the Yorkshire hills and the Lancashire border I knew; that I was a couple of hundred miles from London I soon recognised by hearing the speech of the folk who passed me or gathered about the stalls. I was taking all this in when the chauffeur came back, alone.

"Can't see her yet, sir," he said. "But she can't be long. Sorry to keep you waiting, sir."

"Oh, that's all right," I said. "I'm in no hurry. You're not a Yorkshireman, I think?"

"Londoner, sir," he answered. "Mr. Martenroyde brought me up here when he bought this car at the show at Olympia, two years ago."

"Like these people?" I asked.

He smiled at the question.

"They're all right, sir – when you get to know them," he answered. "Bit queer, sir – to us southerners, at first. Couldn't understand their lingo when I first came here, but I know it pretty well now. Here's Mrs. John, sir."

I turned – to see a tall, finely built woman, warmly wrapped in a magnificent fur coat, bearing down upon us. In the glow of light from the street lamps and from the naphtha flares which hung above the stalls, I had a good view of her as she came up. She was apparently between fifty and sixty years of age, still uncommonly good-looking and with much of the fire of youth still shining from her dark, keen eyes; and from the sharp, questioning look which she gave me, taking me all in as she drew near, I saw that she was a woman of perception and character.

"Good evening," she said, as I drew aside from the open door of the car and raised my hat. "I'm sorry to keep you waiting. Orris," she continued, turning to the chauffeur, "just stop at Simpson's, top of the market place, and go in and ask for a parcel for Mrs. John Martenroyde – you can put it in the front seat. And that's all."

She stepped into the car, and I followed; Orris spread the rugs over our knees, and we moved off. At the top of the square Orris pulled up again and vanished into a dry-goods shop; presently he came out carrying a bulky parcel. Mrs. John Martenroyde leaned forward and watched its disposal on the front seat. Then as we set off again, she settled herself in her corner and tucked her share of the big fur-lined rug round her plump person.

"A cold evening," she remarked. "You'll no doubt feel it. You'll be from London, I expect? Orris, he said there was a gentleman from London expected."

"I am from London – yes," I assented. "But it was very cold in London this morning."

She received this news in silence, as if slightly incredulous of it.

"I never was in London but once in all my life," she said after a pause. "Me and my husband, John Martenroyde, once went there, for a week, not so long after we were wed. But eh, I was glad to get home again! I couldn't stand the crowds in the streets and the noise of the traffic. I was rare and pleased to see Todmanhawe again, Mister – I don't know your name."

"My name is Camberwell, Mrs. Martenroyde," I said. "I heard yours from the chauffeur."

"Mrs. John Martenroyde," she remarked. "My husband – dead some years now, Mr. Camberwell – being younger brother to Mr. James Martenroyde that you're going to see. And very quiet you'll find it, our way, after London."

"Todmanhawe is a quiet place, then?" I suggested.

"Last place God ever made, some of them say that lives in it," she answered. "Out of the world, you see. Of course it isn't so bad, what there is of it. There's five hundred people employed at my brother-in-law's mill, and there's others in the place, and there's a few private residents, and there's Todmanhawe Grange, where James lives, and the Mill House, where me and my two sons live, so it isn't a desert. But, of course, one of my sons, Mr. Sugden Martenroyde, he's not at home now – he's his uncle's manager, or representative, as they term it, in London – perhaps you know him?"

"No," I said. "I haven't that pleasure, Mrs. Martenroyde."

"Well, of course London's a big place, and there's a deal of people in it," she said. "You couldn't be expected to know everybody, same as you do here. But Sugden, he's been in London two years now, and he likes it – I expect there's things in London that appeal to young people. However, he's just been home for a fortnight – gone back this afternoon. I like him to come home now and then – it's not right for young men to forget their home-tree. Now, my other son, Mr. Ramsden Martenroyde, he's always at home, always has been. He's a real home-bird, Ramsden. But then, you see, Ramsden's work is at home – he's manager of his uncle's mill. A good, steady businessman, is Ramsden – I often say that I don't know what James Martenroyde and Todmanhawe Mill would do without him."

"Is Mr. James Martenroyde married?" I ventured to ask. "Shall I find a Mrs. Martenroyde at Todmanhawe Grange?"

It seemed to me that my companion stiffened. She drew herself up in her corner, and when she replied, there was a new note in her tone.

"Nay, you won't!" she said. "James Martenroyde is a single man yet. But if you'd come a bit later on in the year, you'd have found a Mrs. Martenroyde there – if you understand what I mean, Mr. Camberwell."

"Oh!" I said. "Mr. Martenroyde's going to be married?"

"That's what's arranged," she answered. "Of course, a wilful man must have his own way. They say us women are wilful, but I consider men far worse."

"You – you don't approve of Mr. James Martenroyde's marriage?" I suggested.

She gave me a look full of meaning and shook her head.

"No need to say owt," she answered. "But I don't approve of elderly men marrying girls young enough to be their granddaughters."

I allowed myself to laugh – quietly.

"Well, as you say, Mrs. Martenroyde, we men are very wilful," I said. "I suppose Mr. Martenroyde must have his way."

"Oh, he'll have that, mister, don't you make any mistake," she said. "There's nobody has ever crossed James Martenroyde in owt he wanted to do, I can tell you. A masterful man – that's what James is. But of course you know him?"

This was a question which I had rather not have answered. But Mrs. Martenroyde was not the sort of person one can put off with silence or evasion.

"I can't say that I do – yet," I replied. "Mr. Martenroyde sent for me on a matter of business – I've never met him before."

"Eh, well," she remarked, "you'll meet a fine man, as far as looks go. I'll say that for James – he's a good man to set your eyes on. But you know, Mr. Camberwell, a man of sixty years of age didn't ought to wed a young girl of two-and-twenty! Why, Lord bless us, when she's at her best he'll be a doddering old fellow of eighty, if he's alive. Nay, in my view of things, like should wed with like, mister – I never could bring myself to approve of old men marrying young women!"

I was saved from offering an opinion on this thorny subject by the sudden turning of the car from the shadow of a thick belt of trees into a clearer space from which I got an equally sudden view of a great building, lying in a valley, far down below us, its long ranges of windows blazing with light. Behind it I made out against the darkening sky the irregular lines of a ridge of high hills, on the sides of which, dotted here and there, were other lights, betokening the presence of farmsteads or cottages. But the great mill was the conspicuous object in this suddenly revealed panorama, and as we drew nearer I saw that it was a building of six storeys and that lights shone in the windows of each.

"Yon's Todmanhawe Mill," remarked Mrs. John Martenroyde complacently. "The electric light makes a good show, doesn't it, mister? – lights all Scarthdale up."

"This, then, that we see before us is Scarthdale, is it?" I inquired.

"Scarthdale it is," she answered. "Yon's Scarth Fell at the back – when you see it tomorrow morning, you'll find that it's covered with snow. And, as I say, that's Todmanhawe Mill, or if you look up the hillside where there's a big house lighted up, that's Todmanhawe Grange, where you're going – the river runs between the grange and the mill, deep down in the valley. My house is near the mill, on this side of the river; I can see a light in one of its windows, but you won't – it's a small place compared with the grange. We're going down into the valley now, Mr. Camberwell, and I hope this young fellow will be careful – it's a one-in-three business hereabouts, my son Ramsden tells me, and there's two of these hairpin bends before you get to the bottom."

Orris took us safely down a winding road which, dark as it was by that time, I realised to be of a precipitous sort. The great mill and its blaze of light drew nearer and nearer; finally, having reached the level of the river, the car stopped at a house which stood at the angle of a narrow lane leading to the mill, and Mrs. John Martenroyde announced that she was safely home. She bade me a polite goodnight, hoped she had not incommoded me by her presence, and, Orris carrying her parcels for her, made for her door.

As I waited for the chauffeur to return, I became aware of three distinct sounds. Somewhere, close by, I heard the swish of water. Somewhere, farther off, there was the roar of water rushing over rocks. And as an accompaniment to these sounds I heard the steady throb of machinery. I gathered from all this that we were now close to the river Scarth, that somewhere not far away the river ran through a defile or over a weir – the hum of machinery, of course, came from the big mill whose lighted windows were now high above my head.

Orris came back; again we moved forward and were presently crossing a long bridge of stone – so long that I reckoned it must be of seven or eight arches. Then we began to climb again. Cottages and small houses appeared on either side of the road; this I took to be Todmanhawe, or a part of it. Still we were climbing and continued to climb until the cottages were left behind. Then came a turn to the right into a narrower road, and then presently into a carriage drive, bordered by trees and shrubs. The car pulled up before the front door of a big house, and dismounting from it, I found myself standing on a terrace that overlooked the valley. Once more the great mill and its long ranges of lighted windows lay far below me.

The door of the house opened and a blaze of light and breath of warm air greeted me. So, too, did an elderly, cheery-looking woman who held the door wide open and motioned me to enter.

"Come your ways in, sir," she cried. "Mr. Camberwell, isn't it? I'm Mrs. Haines, Mr. Martenroyde's housekeeper, sir. Mr. Martenroyde, sir, his compliments, and will you excuse his not being here to welcome you? He'll be kept down at the mill till six o'clock or so. But I can look after you, sir. Now, perhaps you'd like to take something after your cold ride? A drop of whisky, now, or maybe a cup of tea – dinner won't be till seven o'clock, sir?"

She had bustled me into the hall as she talked, and through an open door I had a glimpse of a big, inviting dining room, with bottles and decanters on its sideboard, a centre table already laid for dinner, and in the wide fireplace a great fire of logs. Towards these comforts the good woman stretched a hospitable hand.

"No, thank you, Mrs. Haines – not at present," I said. "What I want more than anything is a good wash – I'd tea on the train, just before I left it."

"Then I'll take you up to your room, sir," she said. "There's a grand fire up there, for I saw to it myself. Orris, you bring Mr. Camberwell's luggage up – you know which room he's in. This way, sir."

She led me up a thickly carpeted stair, the walls of which were covered with old engravings, and presently inducted me into a big bedroom wherein a fire was piled halfway up the grate. And there, after pointing out various features of the room and telling me that there was a bathroom next door, she left me. Evidently Mr. James Martenroyde believed in having his guests well looked after!

I went to one of the four windows of the room and, drawing the heavy curtain, looked out, to find that I was facing the valley and that the big mill and its rows of lighted windows lay almost in front, deep down beyond the river, stretches of which I could see glittering in the shafts of light from the mill. Somehow, that mill and its blazing lights fascinated me – I imagined the hundreds of workers there, finishing their day's toil amidst the hum of the machinery. I opened the window and leaned out, thinking to hear that steady, monotonous hum myself. But all I heard was a rising wind among the trees and shrubberies of Mr. Martenroyde's gardens, and through that the rushing of the river over its rocky bed.

I made my toilet and went downstairs again, and into the room in which I had seen the cheery fire. It was a big room filled with old-fashioned furniture, and there were old pictures on the walls, and in an alcove on one side of the fireplace two or three shelves of old books. Something in its atmosphere suggested the old bachelor, and I was wondering what sort of man I should find Mr. Martenroyde to be when I heard the front door opened and closed, a firm, heavy step in the hall, a loud voice demanding Mrs. Haines's presence; and, a few moments later, I found myself confronting the man who had commissioned my services.

2

THE MILL OWNER

IT WAS A BIG, burly man, clean-shaven, fresh-complexioned, active in movement, alert of eye, who came striding into the room, gave me a quick, all-embracing glance, and held out a strong, firm hand, with a smile which denoted a genuine desire to make me welcome to his hearth.

"Mr. Camberwell?" he said. "How do you do, sir? I must ask your pardon for not being on the spot when you arrived, but us poor mill owners, you know, we have to keep our eyes on things in these hard times – it's all we can do to make a living, Mr. Camberwell, nowadays. However," he went on, with a sly glance which developed into an unmistakable wink of his right eyelid, "there's still bite and sup to be had – what'll you take after that long, cold journey and before your dinner? I've some rare fine old brown sherry here – or perhaps you'd prefer a drop of whisky? These newfangled cocktail drinks I know nothing about, nor even how to mix 'em. Say the word, sir."

"You're very kind, Mr. Martenroyde," I answered. "Sherry, please."

He turned to the sideboard, found the decanter he wanted, and filled two glasses. Pressing one into my hand, he lifted the other.

"Here's your very good health, sir," he said. "Nay, we'll put it in Yorkshire talk – you may never have heard this before –

'Here's to thee and to me and to all on us, and may we never want nowt, noän on us!' A fine sentiment, Mr. Camberwell! But sit you down till dinner's ready. Have you ever been in this part of the country before?"

"Not quite hereabouts, Mr. Martenroyde," I replied. "But I've been within a few miles of you, to the northeast, in the next dale."

He gave me a comprehending look and nodded.

"Ah!" he exclaimed. "I remember now – it was you that was in that Middlesmoor murder case. Ay – just so! Well, I don't want to introduce you to any job of that sort, not I! – mine's a private business affair. But we'll leave it be till we've had our dinners. Never talk business on an empty stomach – that's one of my mottoes, Mr. Camberwell. My chauffeur brought you home all right and comfortable?"

"I've never travelled in greater luxury, Mr. Martenroyde," I replied. "That's a magnificent car of yours."

"Ay, it's a good car," he said, almost indifferently, "but I shall be getting a better very soon – I've had that two year. And you see" – he half-paused, giving me a half-shy, half-sly glance " – you see, I'm going to what they call alter my condition – I'm going to be wed!"

"I congratulate you, Mr. Martenroyde," I said.

"You'll congratulate me again when you see the lady," he answered, with a confident nod of his head. "A lass in a thousand, she is, sir! But there – if I can't show her in the flesh, I can show you her picture. I hope you're a good judge, Mr. Camberwell?"

"Expert, Mr. Martenroyde!" I answered, entering into his humour. "You can trust my judgment."

He laughed at that, and going over to a desk in one of the alcoves, unlocked a drawer and took out a portfolio. Coming back to me at the fireside, he handed me a large photograph – the work of a fashionable Bond Street photographer.

"There!" he said. "What do you think of that? Full-face, that is."

The photograph was that of a young woman whose charm lay not so much in absolute beauty as in the signs of intelligence manifested in her large expressive eyes and firm, well-cut lips: good sense and good temper were there in all the lines and contours. Before I could express an opinion, he handed me another portrait.

"Side-face," he remarked. "And this" – giving me another – "full-length. Now you've got her at all angles, as one might say."

The full-length view showed the young lady to be tall, well developed, a typical out-of-doors girl – well matched with the big man lingering at my elbow.

"You're a lucky man, Mr. Martenroyde!" I said. "A very handsome young lady. May one know her name?"

"You may," he answered. "Mary Houston's the name. She's the only daughter – only child, as a fact – of my friend Colonel Houston. He comes here every year fishing and always brings Mary with him, so you see she and I are old pals. And last year – well, we fixed things up. A grand lass, sir!"

"And the happy event, Mr. Martenroyde? – when's that to be?" I asked.

"First week in March – in London," he answered. "They live in London – Bayswater. You shall have an invitation to the wedding if you'd care to come."

"I should be delighted," I replied. "And I shall congratulate the bride as heartily as I congratulate you."

He laughed as he took the photographs from my hands and put them back in the desk. Then he shook his head and made a grimace.

"Ay, well," he said, "I've a right to please myself, and it's nobody's concern but mine, but there's always folks who criticise, and I've relations that are none so pleased that I should wed at what they call my time of life. Time of life! – I'm at my best!"

"I shouldn't think there's much doubt of that, Mr. Martenroyde," I said. "You look uncommonly fit."

"I am," he said. "Never been fitter in my life. But come this way, Mr. Camberwell – I'll show you a bit of preparation I've been making. When you're going to be married to a young London lady, you know, you have to do a bit of smartening up. Take a look at this, now."

He led me across the room to a door on its farther side and, opening this and switching on the electric light inside, pushed me gently into what appeared to be a blaze of white and gold.

"Drawing room," he said complacently. "A young lady must have a drawing room. I'll tell you what I did. I found out which was the best furnishing company in London – a real, slap up-to-date firm. I told 'em to send a man down here. I showed him this room – you see its windows look out on my flower-gardens. 'Now,' I said, 'furnish, fit, ornament this room in the very best style – expense no object,' I said. And here's the result. Fit for a queen – what?"

"A beautiful room!" I agreed. "I should like to see it when the sunlight's on it. Excellent taste, too, Mr. Martenroyde – excellent!"

"Ah!" he said. "I told 'em it had all got to be of the best. Pretty penny it cost, too! – they don't do things for nowt, firms like that."

"No," I said. "You'd have a pretty fine old bill. But," I added, slyly, "it shows that you've still got a shot or two in the locker."

"Ah, you have me there!" he replied, laughing. "Ay, well, of course I've done well in my time, and if things aren't quite what they used to be in my trade, we can keep on – we can keep on, Mr. Camberwell. But you must be getting hungry – where's our dinner?"

He led me back to the dining room, pressed more sherry on me, and kept up a flow of talk about one thing and another, until a smart, red-cheeked damsel appeared with the first signs of dinner. Thereupon my host bade me pull a chair in and fall to – and for the greater part of the next hour showed himself a good trencherman, an accomplished judge of sound wine, and the most assiduous of men in taking pains to make a guest at home.

I had formed a very good impression of Mr. Martenroyde by the time dinner was over – I thought him a good-natured, frank, open-hearted fellow, full of humour and essentially sociable and friendly. But when the rosy-cheeked servant had cleared the table and he and I were comfortably installed in a couple of easy chairs by the crackling fire, each with a fine cigar between his lips, I was to learn more of him.

"Now we'll talk a bit of business, Mr. Camberwell," he said. "As I remarked before, mine isn't a case of murder nor owt like it – it'll seem tame enough to you, no doubt. But am I right in thinking that your firm undertakes private inquiry?"

"Quite right, Mr. Martenroyde," I replied. "That's our business. We're private inquiry agents. Of course, the term is a wide one. As a matter of fact, we do a great deal of detective work."

"I understood so," he said. "Well, now, I'll tell you what I want, in confidence. You must know, to start with, that I'm sole proprietor of the business known as Todmanhawe Mill. I made that business, Mr. Camberwell. I've built it up from the start, my own self. Never had one stretch of a helping hand with or in it, sir – all my own unaided self – I'm a self-made man, and proud of it. Never mind how I started in life – it was in a very humble way, I can assure you. But I did get a start – and here I am, what they call a warm man. Well, now, I had a brother – he and I were the only two children our parents ever had – my brother John, a year or two younger than me. John never made owt – I don't know how it was – or happen I do know – but the more I prospered, the more he went downhill. I had to do a lot for him, and in the end he left a widow and two young lads, and I had to provide for them, for John left nowt! I sent the lads to school, put their mother in a good house in the village, and paid the piper for the lot. When the lads got to the right age I took 'em into my business, and they're in it today. The eldest lad, Ramsden, is my manager here, and his brother,

Sugden, is my representative in London, where I have an office in Gresham Street. And their mother – and them – lives at Mill House, down by the bridge yonder. You'll be seeing 'em."

"I've seen Mrs. John Martenroyde already," I said, thinking it best to let him know of this fact. "Your chauffeur gave her a ride back from Shipton, when he went there to meet me."

He gave me a look of surprise which changed to one of sly inquiry.

"Oh!" he exclaimed. "He did, did he? Quite right – so you rode home with Mrs. John, did you? Well, you'd hear her tongue, I'll bet!"

"She certainly talked," I assented.

"I'll lay she did!" he said, chuckling. "Never does owt else – powerful gift of the gab, has Mrs. John. She'd say something about me getting wed, no doubt?"

"Well, a word or two, Mr. Martenroyde," I answered. "In confidence, you know."

"Oh, you needn't repeat what she said," he chuckled. "I've a pretty good idea – I told you I'd relations that weren't best pleased that I'm going to be a wed man. Never mind 'em – let's go back to business. And that's about my nephew Sugden. I told you just now that Sugden's my man in London – been there two years. Now Sugden's been home lately for a two or three weeks' holiday; he only went back to London this very afternoon. And while he was at home I got a letter about him – from London. It's about that letter that I want to consult you and to engage your services."

"An anonymous letter, Mr. Martenroyde?" I inquired.

"Nay, it isn't," he replied. "No – if it had been, it would have gone into the fire, unread; I never have owt to do with letters of that sort. No, it's from a man that I know well enough – old employee of mine, William Heggus. He's a Todmanhawe man; I sent him to London, as warehouseman, when I started my office there."

"And he's written to you about Mr. Sugden?" I asked. "A private letter, of course?"

"Ay, it's so marked," he answered, "and it came registered. But here it is, and I want you to read it and then we'll discuss it."

He took a pocket-book from inside his lounge coat and presently found among numerous other papers a letter which he unfolded and passed across to me. The handwriting was a plain commercial copperplate style, and I had soon mastered the contents. There was really not a great deal in it. The writer, evidently an old-fashioned man, appeared to be uneasy about the way in which Mr. Sugden Martenroyde was living in London – he seemed to fear that the young gentleman was living rather a fast life among companions of a sort and quality he had not been accustomed to in Todmanhawe. Also he feared that Sugden was inclined to neglect his uncle's business – he was not at the offices sometimes when there was urgent need of his presence, and the writer had reason to believe that he frequented the races and had transactions with bookmakers. Finally, though disclaiming any accurate knowledge, he suggested to Mr. Martenroyde that it was not a desirable thing to let the account-books of the London office go so long unexamined – Mr. Sugden had full control of them and of the banking account, and so on and so on. I read the letter twice over and proceeded to restore it to its envelope.

"Well, what do you make of it?" demanded Mr. Martenroyde.

"The writer is evidently anxious," I said. "He may, of course, be all wrong. But tell me – did you show this letter to Mr. Sugden while he was here?"

"Eh, bless you, no!" he exclaimed. "Private – and confidential!"

"Nor mention it to him?" I asked.

"Not a word!" he said. "Not I!"

"Did you ask him any questions which suggested themselves to you after you'd read this letter?" I continued.

"Not a question," he answered. "I said nowt. Not my way. My way is to find out things for myself."

"Then Mr. Sugden," I said, "has gone back to London quite unaware that you have had this letter and that you are wanting to know something about his mode of life there?"

"Exactly," he assented. "I said nowt to Sugden, except that I should be in London myself in about a fortnight, and that I'd go through the books of the London office with him."

"Oh, you told him that, did you?" I asked. "Did that seem to take him aback?"

"Nay, I don't know that it did," he replied. "He's a pretty cool customer, is Sugden. No, he made no remark."

I passed the letter over to him, but he waved it back.

"You keep it," he said. "You might have to see Heggus about it."

I put the letter in my own pocket-book.

"What do you wish us to do, Mr. Martenroyde?" I asked.

He hesitated a moment, looking at the end of his cigar.

"Eh, well," he replied at last, "I don't like spying or eaves-dropping, but I know William Heggus well enough to know that he wouldn't have written that letter unless he felt that he'd good reason. What I'd like is that you could just find out what Sugden really does with himself there in London. Of course, he's only a young chap, and London's full of temptations. You could find out, I suppose?"

"Nothing easier, Mr. Martenroyde," I answered. "Give me Mr. Sugden's private address in London – I have his business address – and in a very short time we'll tell you everything about him, at any rate as regards how he spends his time. We'll tell you what time he goes to business and what time he leaves it; where he spends his evenings; if he goes to the races; what he does on Sundays; what sort of companions he has, male and female. One thing, of course, we can't deal with."

"Ay – and what's that?" he asked inquisitively.

"Money matters," I said. "We can't examine your books at Gresham Street."

"Now, you can leave all that to me," he replied. "I shall see to that when I come up. Of course," he continued, his tone altering somewhat, "if I found that Sugden had been monkeying with money matters, it would be serious. I'm not the sort of man to stand owt of that sort, Mr. Camberwell – Sugden would catch it from me if I found owt wrong! I'm particular – What is it?" he asked, breaking off and looking at me. "Hear something?"

"For the last quarter of an hour," I said, pointing to a door which stood very slightly ajar in one corner of the big room, "I've heard slight sounds from behind that door – just rustlings. You haven't any ghosts, Mr. Martenroyde?"

"Nay, I haven't noticed any," he replied, dryly. "It's one of our cats you hear. There's a conservatory behind that door, and there's a broken pane or two which my gardener's always forgetting to mend, and our cats – we've three or four of 'em about – they walk in and out; I hear 'em myself, but I take no notice till they knock a plant-pot down and then I go for 'em. Well, as I was saying, Mr. Camberwell, I should be – but I'll not pursue that subject. I hope there's nowt wrong with Sugden. But – I must know if there's owt in that letter."

"Leave it to me," I said. "You shall have a full and accurate report very quickly. Say in three weeks, or a month anyway."

"Well, I'm going up to town myself in about that," he remarked. "Have it ready for me then. You've a good staff, I suppose, Mr. Camberwell?"

"An excellent staff, Mr. Martenroyde," I replied. "Both men and women. They're chiefly young. And they're all keen and enthusiastic."

"Women, too?" he said. "Young women? Where do you get 'em from, then? Are they trained to it – like bloodhounds?"

"Well, scarcely that," I replied, smiling. "They do get some training after we take them in hand, certainly. But they're usually young people who appear to have a natural aptitude for that sort of thing. The cleverest woman assistant we have, Mr. Martenroyde, was a girl clerk. We've another who was a milliner's assistant; a third who was a nursery governess."

"And they're all good at this sort of thing, watching and tracking folks?" he asked. "Stick to 'em like leeches – what?"

"Leeches is a good word," I agreed. "Leeches – or limpets."

"Well, well!" he said. "Strange things in this life, aren't there? Let's have a drop of whisky."

We had a drop of whisky, and we went on talking about one thing or another until the time drew near to ten o'clock. Pleading sleepiness after my long journey, I asked permission to retire, and he took me up to my room and looked round as if to see that I had everything I needed.

"No bed for me yet," he said as we shook hands. "Every night, wet or fine, summer or winter, I walk round my mill. Done it ever since the mill was built – regular habit now. Well – sleep sound, sir. See you at breakfast-time tomorrow."

He went off and soon afterwards I heard the front door close with a bang, and his firm steps on the gravel of the carriage drive. They died away, and a few moments later I was in bed and asleep. And I was sleeping soundly when, two hours later, a hand came thumping heavily and insistently on the panels of my bedroom door.

3

THE MILL WEIR

When my slowly awakening senses fairly realised that this thunderous summoning was intended for me, I jumped out of bed, turned on the light, and reached for a dressing-gown. As I slipped into it I saw, by a side-glance at my watch, that the time was twenty minutes past midnight: I had been in bed and asleep two hours.

I flung open the door. There, in the garments in which I had last seen them – thereby proving that they had not been to bed – stood the housekeeper and the chauffeur. And eager as they had been to rouse me, neither of them, now that they had roused me, seemed capable of speech. They stood, wide-eyed, staring.

"What's the matter?" I demanded. "Something wrong?"

Mrs. Haines moistened her lips and spoke.

"It's the master, sir," she said, "Mr. Martenroyde. He's never come home."

It was my turn to stare. But I found my tongue.

"Never – come home?" I exclaimed. "Why – what time does he usually come home?"

"He's never out more than half an hour," said Orris. "Just walks round by the mill and back. Half an hour does it, sir. But – he's been out over two hours this time."

"Half past ten's his bedtime," said Mrs. Haines. "We always sit up for him, me and Orris here, in case he wants owt or has any orders to give for morning. I've never once in all these years known him to be out at this time. There's something wrong."

Pausing for a moment to reflect on the next thing to be done, I was conscious that since I had gone to bed the weather had changed. I had left one of my bedroom windows fairly wide open, and now as I stood there between it and the door I became aware that a high, rough wind had arisen – I could hear it tearing through the trees in the grounds outside. I could also hear the river foaming along over its rocky bed in the valley. Was it possible that Mr. Martenroyde –

"How does your master get across the river?" I asked. "Does he go round by the road to the mill, or how?"

"He goes over the weir bridge, a footbridge, near the mill," replied the chauffeur. "It's a narrow plank bridge, sir – dangerous on a night like this."

I hesitated no longer – Mr. Martenroyde must be looked for.

"Go down and get some lanterns, Orris," I said. "Find some that won't get blown out. I'll be with you in a few minutes."

"I'm sure something's wrong," repeated Mrs. Haines as they turned away from my door. "Many and many a year he's gone out for that last look round, but this is the first time he's failed to come back. Something's happened to him!"

I dressed hurriedly and went down to the front hall, to find Orris awaiting me with a couple of lanterns, and Mrs. Haines still bemoaning her master's unaccountable absence.

"Now," I said as I got into my overcoat, "just tell me – is there any house at which Mr. Martenroyde may have called and where he may have stopped talking or been detained?"

"Eh, no, mister," she answered in surprise. "He'd never call anywhere this time of night! – I never knew him do such a thing. He just walks round by the mill and back again – it's not likely he'd call anywhere. If he did, it would only be if there was something wrong at the mill, and we should have heard before now."

"But supposing he found something wrong at the mill," I said, "where would he call?"

"Why, I can't think of anywhere but at the Mill House," she answered. "Mr. Ramsden Martenroyde, his nephew – he's manager – he has the keys. Orris knows where that is."

Orris and I went out, each carrying a lantern. The wind was blowing hard round the corners of the house – a keen, sharp wind from the north-west – and I could hear the rushing of the river as an undertone to the sweeping blasts.

"Now," I said, "take the way by which your master goes every night – I suppose you know it?"

"Every yard of it, sir," he answered. "This way, sir – to the left."

He led me along the carriage drive to a gate which admitted us to the kitchen gardens; passing through these we came to another gate beyond which lay the hillside that sloped down to the river. There was a path there, on the left-hand side of which rose a plantation of fir and pine; on the right there was open land. As we followed the path, drawing nearer to the bank of the river, I began, getting used to the darkness, to make out the spume of the surging waters – evidently there was a great press of water coming down from the upper reaches of the valley.

"Does this river ever get in flood?" I asked.

"Yes, sir – comes right over the banks, often," replied Orris. "There's a row of stepping-stones a bit farther along, sir, near the bridge over the weir – I should say they'll be covered tonight, those stones. In dry weather Mr. Martenroyde always goes across them, but he'd have to take the bridge this time. I've seen the water cover that, too, more than once."

Presently we reached the riverbank; the path was alongside it for some distance. Flashing the light of my lantern over the swirling waters, I saw that they were racing along in considerable volume. It was a shallow river, that, and its bed was unusually rocky – great boulders stood up here and there, breaking the face of the stream and sending up clouds of spume and froth. My companion suddenly stopped.

"The stepping-stones, sir," he said, turning his lantern towards the river. "They're just about covered."

I turned my lantern to where he pointed, and saw that except for one or two massive blocks, higher than the rest, the stones were already under water. A few yards farther and we came to our end of the bridge, and I saw that the river was nearly up to its planks. A bridge it was, but not one that I cared about crossing on a wild night like that and with all that mass of water pouring down under it. Not more than a yard wide, it had no protection save a mere handrail on its right-hand side – and on the left the river looked black and deep.

I paused, looking about me. Across the river I could just make out the great bulk of the mill on the opposite bank. There was no light in it now, of course, and none in the cottages or buildings near it. But behind us, high above the bank down which we had just made our way, I saw a light twinkling in the upper room of a house whose roof and chimneys I could just see outlined against the grey sky.

"Whose house is that – where the light is?" I asked.

"Mr. Heggus's, sir," replied Orris. "He's an invalid – been ill a long time, sir. I expect his wife's up with him – he's often bad at nights."

"You don't think Mr. Martenroyde may have called there?" I suggested.

"Shouldn't think so, sir – never heard of him doing so, this time of night," he replied.

"Well, show the way across the bridge," I said. "Be careful."

A few steps along the bridge showed me that it had been built almost over a weir, above which the river was now rushing with tremendous force. It struck me at once that if anybody slipped from the narrow planking of the bridge into those swirling waters he would have very little chance of escaping from their steady sweep. And the planking was wet and slimy; I had to cling to the rail with one hand while managing the lantern with the other.

We crawled rather than walked along that bridge; here and there, as an extra forceful gust of wind came, the water swept over it. It was some eighty yards across. But at last we came to the end, and the great mill rose up almost immediately in front of us.

What happened to us there was startling in its suddenness. I had been prepared all along for the unexpected; I thought it highly probable that Mr. Martenroyde had met with an accident. But I was not prepared for what we found as we stepped off the end of the bridge on to a sort of landing-place paved with stone. There, lying half in, half out of the water which lapped the shelving bank of the river, lay the man we were seeking. I saw at once that he was dead.

4

FOUL PLAY

IN THE COURSE OF my now somewhat lengthy experience I have seen a good many sights which roused me to feelings of loathing and horror, but I have never seen one that so excited my indignation as that which now met my eyes. For as Orris and I drew near the dead man – a man from whom I had parted only two hours before when he was full of all the zest of life! – from where he lay, half-submerged in the edge of the water, I saw that here was no accidental death, but a case of murder. On the right-hand side of his forehead there was a terrible, livid, incised bruise, from which still ran a slight trickle of blood. Some hand had struck him down as he left the last step of the bridge, and the blow had been a fearsome one. For a moment I thought he might have slipped, fallen from the bridge, and dashed his head against the edge of a sharp rock, but a mere glance at the surroundings showed me that this could not have been so. There were no rocks and no stones there – the body had fallen across the soft, waterlogged turf of the bank.

I turned to the chauffeur. At first sight of his master's dead body he had begun to moan and cry; now he was sobbing unrestrainedly.

"Pull yourself together, my lad!" I said. "We've got to act now – there's been foul play here. Your master's been struck down by somebody. Now, where are the nearest houses or cottages?"

"There's some round the corner of the mill," he blubbered. "They'll all be in bed—"

"Go there and rouse them out – tell the men to come here," I said. "Then go to the Mill House and get Mr. Ramsden up. And now – where does the village policeman live?"

"Halfway to the bridge," he answered. "He's generally out on his rounds at this time."

"Get at him, somehow," I said. "Tell him to get on the telephone to his inspector or to the Superintendent. And listen – are there any friends of Mr. Martenroyde's living anywhere about here – on this side of the river?"

"Mr. Eddison, his solicitor, lives just beyond the mill," he replied. "And there's Dr. Ponsford; he lives near Mr. Eddison."

"Go to their houses and ask both to come here at once," I said. "Now keep your head, and remember what I tell you. First some workmen; then the Mill House; then the policeman; then the two gentlemen you've mentioned. I want them all here – quick!"

He hurried away, still weeping, and after covering the dead man's face with a muffler which I had twisted about my neck on leaving the grange, I stood there looking down at the still figure and wondering what enemy had robbed him of life in this vile and dastardly fashion. He had been so lively, so full of animation all the evening, talking, laughing, full of humour even when he was talking business, that I could scarcely comprehend the fact that he lay there at my feet – dead. Yet dead he was, and, I felt sure, murdered. Somebody had lain in wait for him at that end of the bridge, somebody armed with a heavy weapon. I had a long experience of wounds, and I had seen enough of the terrible bruise on James Martenroyde's forehead and temple to know that the blow which had caused it had driven the life out of him there and then. A blow like that could not be anything but fatal – and he had received it and died. Into which quarter of the black night, the roar of the river in his ears, the wind howling reproaches at him, had the murderer fled?

As I waited, I began to reflect on my own position. It was not a pleasant one, quite apart from the horror of this apparently planned and callous murder. I was unknown to any of the people who would presently come, except to Mrs. John Martenroyde, and all that she would know would be that I had come to Todmanhawe to see her brother-in-law on business. I could not tell anybody what that business was – and yet it suddenly flashed across my mind that there might be – was it possible? – some connection between it and this tragedy. In that case – but all that was something to be considered later on.

Hurrying footsteps and low voices behind me caused me to turn towards the corner of the mill. Out of the darkness came three or four men, two of them carrying lanterns, all of them showing signs of having dressed in haste. The foremost made up to where I stood, gave me a glance of keen inquiry, and dropping on his knees at the dead man's side, uncovered his face. The next instant he was on his feet, and the other men were ringing him and the body round.

"Nay, nay, nay!" he exclaimed. "Here's foul work – some devil or other's had a hand in that – he's been struck down!" He turned on me, again inspecting me with sharp questioning glances. "Who may you be, mister?" he demanded. "You're not one from our parts."

"No," I replied. "I came to see Mr. Martenroyde on business. When I went to bed he set out to walk round his mill. At midnight he hadn't returned and his servants called me up. His chauffeur and I came out to look for him, and we found him – as you see."

"Ay, we see!" he said grimly. "And a nice sight it is, and all! You found him where he is, mister?"

I showed him the exact position on the riverbank in which we had found the body lying. Silently, each made an inspection of it.

"Somebody's laid in wait for him there," said one.

"That's it," agreed another. "Felled him – and then he's fallen off this here bridge. A foul job!"

"Hadn't we better carry the body into one of your cottages?" I suggested. "Or couldn't we take it into the mill? Can one of you get admission to the mill?"

They made no reply for a minute or two, during which they continued to look at the dead man. Then the man who had first arrived spoke.

"If you take my advice, mister, you'll do nowt till the police come," he said. "The police – even if it be nowt but a village constable – like to have first say in these matters. And I should let the Mill House folk see him, and all. We can shift his body later."

"Here's Mrs. John coming," observed one of the others. "But I don't see Ramsden."

Mrs. John Martenroyde came hurrying along, some more workmen with her. She pushed through the group which surrounded her dead brother-in-law and looked down.

"What's all this?" she demanded. "Who's done it? Dead? – are you sure he's dead? Who found him?"

I stepped forward and again explained matters. She stared at me as if half-incredulous of my statement.

"He must have fallen off that bridge," she said. "We've warned him many a time about crossing it on nights like this. The wind's blown him off, of course." She turned abruptly on the men. "You've heard him warned, haven't you?" she demanded. "Mr. Ramsden's often warned him."

The men made no answer; instead they looked at me.

"I'm afraid Mr. Martenroyde did not come by his death in that way, Mrs. Martenroyde," I said. "He was struck down – by someone."

She turned on me almost fiercely.

"Struck down?" she exclaimed. "Who should strike him down? Well, if he was – but now then, you men, why don't you get him up and carry him under cover somewhere? You can't leave him lying there."

"We're waiting till the policeman comes," said a man, "and Mr. Ramsden ought to see him, too, before he's moved."

"Mr. Ramsden can't see him, then," retorted Mrs. Martenroyde. "Mr. Ramsden's staying the night in Shipton – he went to a dinner there. Get that mill open, some of you, and carry your master in there at once."

But none of the men – of whom there were by that time some twelve to twenty assembled – showed any signs of obeying these orders. They stood staring, waiting; one or two exchanged whispers.

"Here's the policeman," said someone. "And Mr. Eddison and the doctor."

Once more, when these three arrived, I had to explain my presence and the search for and finding of the dead man. Mr. Eddison, an elderly man, drew me aside.

"James Martenroyde told me yesterday afternoon that he was expecting you, Mr. Camberwell," he said. "He didn't tell me why he wanted to enlist your services. Now, did he tell you anything that has any relation to – this?"

I found it difficult to reply to that question: I was already beginning to have some doubts or suspicions – vague and uncertain – of my own.

"May we leave that over for the moment, Mr. Eddison?" I said. "I shall have to tell you or the police, or both, a good deal, I'm afraid."

"You think this is murder?" he asked. "Not accident?"

I pointed to the doctor, who, by the light of the lanterns, was bending over the body.

"Let us hear what the doctor says," I answered. "I know what my own opinion is."

But at that juncture the doctor said nothing except to ask if the dead man could not be carried into the mill. By that time more of the mill-hands had arrived; one was able to open the doors, and presently the body was carried inside and laid on a table in the office. And there Dr. Ponsford made a more careful examination while the rest of us stood about, waiting. At last he turned to where Mr. Eddison, Mrs. John Martenroyde, myself, and two or three of the leading workmen stood near the door.

"Mr. Martenroyde has been struck down by some heavy weapon," he said. "A loaded stick or something of that sort. Two blows – either of them sufficient to cause death."

There was a moment's silence. Then Mrs. John spoke, glancing at the sea of faces in the doorway and in the entrance hall of the mill. Her voice, rasping and provocative, sounded a note of something very like aggression.

"That'll be the work of some of you lot!" she declared. "He had his enemies among you, I know!"

A low murmur among the waiting crowd swelled to a deep growl. One man separated himself from the rest and stepped forward.

"You've no call to say owt like that, missis," he said earnestly. "It's a foul libel on innocent folk! There isn't a man in all Todmanhawe that would have laid a finger on Mr. Martenroyde – he was too much respected for that. And you know it, and your sons know it, and all!"

"Ay, well, and I wonder who you are to answer me back?" demanded Mrs. John. "Somebody's done that, and you've had quarrels with him, some of you, more than once, and you're none such white hens at any time. And you keep your tongue to yourself or I'll set our Ramsden to talk to you, and he'll—"

Mr. Eddison laid a hand on the angry woman's arm, at the same time motioning the men to silence.

"Come, come, Mrs. Martenroyde!" he said. "This isn't the time or place for that sort of thing. Where are your sons? Where's Ramsden? Isn't he at home? And Sugden? They ought to be here."

"They can't be where they aren't, then," retorted Mrs. John. "Our Ramsden's staying the night in Shipton, Mr. Eddison;

he went to a lodge dinner there, and he's spending the night with friends instead of coming home. And as for our Sugden, he went back to London yesterday afternoon."

I saw the man who had protested against Mrs. John's accusation, and who in obedience to Mr. Eddison had been drawing back to join the others, suddenly stop, staring at Mrs. John as if something she had said had caused him surprise. He looked from her to Mr. Eddison, back again to her, and he was evidently about to speak when a commotion arose at the door of the mill, and glancing in that direction, I saw the headlights of a big car.

"Here's the Superintendent!" exclaimed somebody in the crowd. "Superintendent Beverley, from Shipton."

I knew Beverley. Before his appointment to his present post he had been an inspector in another part of the county in which I had once had a case to deal with, and he and I had worked together for some weeks. Accordingly it was to me that he turned as he came hurrying in.

"No idea I should find you here, Camberwell," he said. "What is it?"

"You shall know why I'm here later on," I replied. "What you're fetched for at present is that Mr. James Martenroyde has been found dead – I found him – on the riverbank close by this mill, and in my opinion he's been murdered. See the doctor, and then I'll show you where I found the body."

He turned to Dr. Ponsford, but before they could go into the room where the dead man lay, Mrs. John stepped forward.

"I want my son Ramsden here," she said. "Now that his uncle's gone, Ramsden's master in this place. Mr. Beverley, couldn't you send your car back to Shipton to fetch our Ramsden? He's stopping at Mr. Marriner's – your man'll know where Mr. Marriner lives."

"Yes, I'll do that for you, Mrs. Martenroyde," assented Beverley. "That'll not take long." He went out to the road, sent his car off, and, coming back, passed into the inner room with the doctor. They were not long in there, and when they came out,

Beverley motioned me to follow him outside. "Show me where you found him, Camberwell," he said. "And tell me all about it – this is a case of murder, without a doubt, from what Ponsford says."

"I'll tell you all I know later on, Beverley," I replied. "At present let's confine ourselves to the finding of him and how he came to be there. When we've attended to that, I should like to tell you and Mr. Eddison how I come to be here at all."

"I was surprised to see you," he said. "Mr. Martenroyde sent for you?"

"He sent for me," I replied.

"Some private business?" he asked.

"Very private business – that's what I'm going to tell you about," I said. "I'm already suspecting – I don't know what."

I took him down to the end of the weir bridge and to the place on the riverbank at which we had found the body. For some little time we remained there, examining the immediate surroundings by the light of our lanterns. Eventually we went back to the mill. Ramsden Martenroyde had just arrived, a big, strapping, taciturn man of apparently thirty years of age; he, his mother, and Mr. Eddison were discussing the removal of the body to the grange. Presently some of the workmen were called, a bier was improvised, and the removal began; Mrs. John, Ramsden, and Dr. Ponsford accompanied the men carrying the bier. And when they had gone, Mr. Eddison, who was talking quietly to another elderly man who appeared to have dressed hurriedly and had just arrived, signed to Beverley and myself to join him and his companion, whom he presently introduced as Mr. Halstead, a personal friend of James Martenroyde.

"Now let us hear what you have to say, Mr. Camberwell," he said. "We'll go into the private office."

He opened a door close by and switched on the electric light. But before we could enter, the man who had shown his surprise when Mrs. John said that her son Sugden had left for London the previous afternoon came up, evidently anxious to speak.

"Can I have a word or two with you gentlemen?" he said. "It's important."

5

SUSPICION

MR. EDDISON MOTIONED THE man to precede us into the room. But he hung back, pointing to a fellow-workman who stood a little apart, watching us.

"He's in it with me," said the first man. "We've both a word to say. What I have to say, you see, Mr. Eddison, he can back up."

"Come in, both of you," replied the solicitor. He ushered us all into the room and closed the door. "Now, my lad," he went on, "what is it?"

The first man looked round at the rest of us. Something in his attitude suggested his desire for secrecy, and when he spoke, it was in hushed tones.

"You know me, Mr. Eddison," he said. "Outwin – worked in this mill, boy and man, a good thirty years. And," he continued, pointing to the other man, "you know Guest here, too – he's been here very near as long as what I have. And we're neither of us given to telling lies. And what we've got to tell you is Gospel truth. We don't want to make no trouble – but you ought to know, Mr. Eddison, what me and Guest knows."

"Well," said Mr. Eddison, "go on, Outwin."

Outwin drew a long breath and once more looked from one to another of us.

"You heard what Mrs. John said just now, Mr. Eddison, when you asked her where her sons were?" he said. "She said that Mr.

Sugden went off to London yesterday afternoon. That's not true. Sugden was here, at Todmanhawe, last night."

"Close at hand, anyway," said Guest.

Mr. Eddison looked at Beverley.

"You'll want to know about this?" he asked. "Mrs. John Martenroyde certainly said that her son Sugden had gone off to London yesterday afternoon."

"He was here last night," said Outwin, doggedly. "Me and Guest knows he was."

Beverley turned to me, whispering.

"Has this anything to do with what you have to tell, Camberwell?" he asked.

"It may have," I answered. "Hear what they have to say."

"Which afternoon – and night – do you mean, Outwin?" said Beverley, turning to the men. "These that are just past – it's morning now, getting on to four o'clock. You mean last night – this last evening?"

"That's what I mean, Superintendent," replied Outwin. "This is Tuesday morning. I mean Monday evening – last night. And Mrs. John meant Monday afternoon – yesterday afternoon. She said Sugden set off for London yesterday – that's Monday – afternoon. Whether he did or not, he was in this neighbourhood last night – of that I'm willing to take my Bible oath. And so," he added, turning to his companion, "so is Guest he re."

"Ay!" said Guest. "For why? I saw him!"

"Let's be clear about this, now, my lads," said Beverley. "Where did you see Mr. Sugden Martenroyde last night? But first of all, was he supposed to have set off for London yesterday afternoon? Did you know that he'd set off? Or that he was supposed to have set off?"

"I didn't," replied Outwin.

"Nor me," said Guest.

"I knew that he was said to have set off," I remarked.

"You?" exclaimed Beverley, in surprise. "How did you know, Camberwell?"

"Mrs. John Martenroyde told me," I said. "She rode with me in her brother-in-law's car from Shipton, and she mentioned that her son Sugden, who, she told me, was his uncle's representative in London, had been down here for a while and had gone back that afternoon – yesterday afternoon."

Beverley turned to the two workmen again.

"Where did you see Mr. Sugden?" he asked abruptly.

"In Hartwick village – this end of the street," replied Outwin.

"What time was that?"

"All about half past seven."

"What was he doing?"

"Walking as fast as ever he could go towards Todmanhawe."

"You mean," said Beverley, "you saw him on the road that runs from Hartwick to Todmanhawe village and passes just behind Todmanhawe Grange?"

"That's it. But he was in Hartwick – this end of Hartwick."

"What were you doing up there, Outwin, at that time?"

"Me and Guest here had gone up there to see Boothroyd, the blacksmith, about a bit of a job I wanted doing. We were in his shed, outside the smithy, when Sugden passed. It was raining, pretty smartly. He'd a mackintosh on, with the collar turned up."

"How could you recognise him, to be sure of him, at that time of the evening – quite dark?" asked Beverley.

"Easy enough – he walked right in front of Boothroyd's house, and there were strong lights in the windows. It was Sugden right enough!"

"No doubt of that," said Guest. "We've both of us known Sugden ever since he was the height of two pennyworth of coppers!"

"And you say he was walking sharply towards Todmanhawe?" asked Beverley.

"Well, as you know, Superintendent, that road leads nowhere else," replied Outwin. "After you leave Hartwick village end – town-end as us fellows calls it – there is nowt till you come to Todmanhawe. Leastways, there's nowt much. There's Dakin Heggus's house, on the hillside, and there's Todmanhawe Grange, and then there's nowt till you come to Todmanhawe. He was walking – as hard as he could go – in the direction of Todmanhawe."

"Last night – about seven thirty," said Beverley. He had been making a note or two in his pocket-book, and now he closed and put it away. "Very well, my lads – now then, just keep all that to yourselves till I ask you to speak. You know the importance of silence."

"Nobody'll hear owt from me," said Outwin.

"Nor from me," said Guest. "But we thought you ought to know."

"Quite right," agreed Beverley. "Now, just a word before you go. If Mr. Sugden set off for London yesterday afternoon, which station would he go to and how would he get to it?"

"He'd go from Abbeyside," replied Outwin promptly. "And he'd go there in Ramsden's car – Ramsden's man would drive him."

"Ramsden's man? Chauffeur, do you mean?" asked Beverley.

"Why, you can call him that, if you like fancy names. He's a fellow that attends to the garden at Mill House and does odd jobs, and drives Ramsden's car now and then. Sam Thorp – that's his name."

"Where's Sam live, then?" demanded Beverley. "Near the mill?"

"Two or three doors away – anybody'll tell you," said Outwin. "Just up the lane, his cottage is – close by."

"Very well. Now, mind what I've told you," said Beverley. "Keep things to yourselves."

He turned to the rest of us when the two men had gone away.

"It's very serious news, that," he went on. "What was Sugden Martenroyde doing here last night when it was supposed that he'd gone to London? And if what these two men say is true – and I should say it is – where's Sugden now? His mother's evidently under the impression that he's in London."

Mr. Eddison turned to me.

"I think Mr. Camberwell has something to tell us," he said. "Possibly it has some relation to what we've just heard."

I had been thinking matters over while Beverley was questioning the two men, and had come to the conclusion that there was nothing for it but to tell all I knew. And I proceeded to do so, setting forth all the facts, from my firm's receipt of James Martenroyde's letter – which I had with me and produced – to his leaving me in my room at the grange. Finally I handed Mr. Eddison the letter from William Heggus. This, after reading it, he passed over to Mr. Halstead and Beverley. Beverley's face assumed a new expression.

"Sugden's at the bottom of this!" he exclaimed. "I'd give a lot to know where he was going last night when those men saw him! Mr. Eddison – just talk this over with Camberwell, you and Mr. Halstead, while I go round to see Sam Thorp."

He hurried away, and the three of us left behind discussed matters. One fact that had come out in James Martenroyde's talk with me seemed to Mr. Eddison to be of significance and importance. James Martenroyde had told Sugden that he, James, would be in town very shortly and would take the opportunity of going through the books with him. Did Sugden know that the books wouldn't bear examination?

"We shall have to fetch William Heggus up here," said Mr. Eddison. "I know him – his brother lives across the river there; they're a Todmanhawe family, respectable, trustworthy. William wouldn't have written that letter to James Martenroyde unless he'd been seriously concerned about Sugden. I'm afraid that Beverley was right – Sugden Martenroyde's at the bottom of this."

Beverley came back just then, shaking his head as if puzzled.

"I've seen Sam Thorp," he said. "Found him up. They're all up in these cottages – I'm going back in a minute to make some more inquiries. Well, Sam Thorp – I pledged him to silence, of course – says that he did drive Sugden to Abbeyside station yesterday afternoon, to catch the 5.41. What's more, he saw him and his luggage into the train."

"That's a local train to Leeds," remarked Mr. Halstead. "He could leave it at two or three places."

"I shall have to go into that," said Beverley. "Anyway, he set off. What I want to know now is – is he anywhere about?"

We left the mill after that. Mr. Eddison said that he must go up to the grange and asked Mr. Halstead and myself to accompany him. We left Beverley and his men making a further examination of the riverbank, and, crossing the weir bridge, followed the path along which Orris and I had come, a few hours before, in search of the man who had now been carried back to his house dead. That was midnight; it was now approaching the first grey of the winter morning.

We let ourselves into the house and turned into the dining room. There was a roaring fire in the grate, and at a little table drawn up to it sat Mrs. John Martenroyde, calmly refreshing herself with tea and buttered toast. Her attitude was that of possession.

6

FAMILY AFFAIRS

A MERE GLANCE AT the faces of my two companions was sufficient to show me that neither approved Mrs. Martenroyde's assurance (to use no stronger expression) in thus taking possession of a dead man's hearth before he was even laid in his coffin. Mr. Halstead, whom I had set down as a very quiet, reserved man, gave a start of unfeigned surprise at what he saw; Mr. Eddison's upper lip stiffened and his manner became starchy and professional. But Mrs. John Martenroyde saw nothing of this; she was too much occupied with her present enjoyment and her own affairs. As if Todmanhawe Grange had belonged to her from the time of its building, she waved us forward to the fire.

"Come your ways in, gentlemen," she said, cheerfully. "I'm just having a cup of tea and I'm sure I needed it after all we've been through, me and Ramsden. But we've got all done now; I sent for Mrs. Catherall and Mrs. Spence from the village; they're experienced hands, and they've laid poor James out beautiful, as you'll see if you go to his chamber. But perhaps you'd take a cup of tea first? This tea has been made a bit, but if one of you'll ring yon bell, Sarah Haines'll make a fresh brew for you, and no doubt you could do with it after such a trying night as we've had."

She pointed to a bell-pull which hung down the wall on one side of the big fireplace. Mr. Eddison was now standing there facing Mrs. John and her teatable, but his hands remained in the pockets of his overcoat.

"Thank you; not at present," he said. "Where is your son Ramsden?"

There was a distinct iciness in his tone which anyone but a self-absorbed woman would have noticed; Mrs. John, at any rate, showed no sign of noticing it. She gulped down a mouthful of toast and tea.

"Ramsden," she replied, "has gone down to the post office. Of course, they aren't supposed to send any telegrams off before eight o'clock, but Ramsden thought that as this was a special occasion he could maybe persuade Watkinson to send one a bit earlier – you see, Mr. Eddison, we must have Sugden here as quick as possible. If Ramsden can get a wire off early this morning, Sugden will be able to catch the ten o'clock train from London – I forget which of them stations it is; I always get mixed up with London stations; but I know there is a train at ten o'clock which'll get him here by the middle of the afternoon. And of course we want Sugden here – now that Ramsden and him have come into their uncle's property there'll be a deal to see to, especially down at yon mill. I said to Ramsden just now, before he went out, 'Ramsden, my lad,' I said, 'now that you and Sugden are masters'—"

She paused suddenly, catching Mr. Eddison's eye and seeing something there which reduced her to instant silence. Mr. Eddison lifted a hand.

"Stop there!" he said. "Mrs. Martenroyde, you're under a very serious misapprehension. Your sons are not masters of the mill, nor have they come into their uncle's property. You'll know all the particulars in due time, but so that you mayn't cherish any false hopes, I may as well tell you that everything that your brother-in-law possessed – everything – has been left in trust.

And the two trustees are Mr. Halstead and myself. In plain words – words you'll understand – we are the masters!"

As Mr. Eddison went on speaking, the colour on Mrs. John's cheeks, naturally high, rose to a deep crimson. Slowly, as if fascinated by what the solicitor said, she rose to her feet. A plate on the edge of her tea-tray, caught by her action, slipped off the table and, crashing against the fender, shivered into small pieces. Mrs. John paid no attention to it. Planting her hands on her hips, she faced Mr. Eddison and spoke – sharply.

"Do you mean to tell me that James Martenroyde has left yon mill away from my sons?" she demanded. "That they're not—"

"You will hear all particulars later, Mrs. Martenroyde, at the proper time," replied the solicitor. "This is not the time—"

"And do you mean to say, too, that this house isn't ours?" she went on. "That he's left—"

"This house is certainly not yours, Mrs. Martenroyde," interrupted Mr. Eddison, who was showing signs of impatience. "That I can tell you at once."

"Then damn and blast James Martenroyde for a mean-hearted hound!" Mrs. John burst out. "I hope he's roasting in hell this minute! Not ours? Not my lads'? He'd no kith nor kin the world over but them. But I'll not take your word for it, Eddison – you lawyers are all liars and thieves. There's others than you, and cleverer than what you are, and we'll set them on your track. Leave Todmanhawe Mill and this house away from us—"

"My good lady!" said Mr. Halstead. "Mr. Eddison mentioned a trust. Calm yourself, now—"

"Damn you and your trusts!" cried Mrs. John. "You're in it with him – I trust you no more than what I trust him. Trust indeed! – where are my two lads going to be with you and your blasted trusts, I should like to know? It's nowt but another way of robbing us of what we've a right to. But—"

The door opened and Ramsden Martenroyde walked in, to stare at what he saw. His mother turned on him, still furious, still declamatory.

"Ramsden!" she shouted. "Ramsden! What do you think Eddison says? He says that nowt of what James has left comes to you and Sugden, neither mill nor house nor business nor owt – it's all left to him and Halstead there, a couple of blasted mischief-makers! They're the masters, it seems, and we're—"

"Ramsden," said Mr. Eddison, "your mother is wrong – she neither understands nor will understand. Your uncle has left his property in trust, and Mr. Halstead and myself are the trustees. You'll know everything when the will is produced – and you'll have no cause to complain. Take your mother away and get her to be sensible."

"Sensible!" exclaimed Mrs. John. "I'll let you see whether I'm sensible or no! You answer me in plain words, if such as you can use plain words. Is yon mill ours?"

"No!" replied Mr. Eddison.

"Is this here house and what's in it ours?" she demanded.

"No – certainly not," said Mr. Eddison. "Most certainly not."

For a moment Mrs. John glared at him almost maniacally. Then she suddenly caught sight of the tea-tray lying before her on the table. With a sharp sweep of her hand she dashed tray and table into the fireplace, and amidst the clatter of crashing crockery turned to her son.

"Come away, lad," she said. "We'll go and find lawyers of our own. I'll show you!" she went on, turning on the two men and shaking her fist. "You've led James Martenroyde to this, to feather your own nests! Trustees indeed! Thieves – bloody thieves!"

"Come away, Mother," said Ramsden. "It's no use—"

"Get her away, Ramsden," urged Mr. Eddison. "She's beyond herself – and she's no reason for it, as you'll find out before long. Get her to go home."

Mrs. John suddenly calmed down – and looked more vindictive than ever.

"I'm going," she said. "But you mark my words, Eddison. You try to rob my lads, and I'll hound you down till you'd be glad to find a corner in hell! And I hope James Martenroyde is there now – blast him!"

Ramsden pushed her towards the door and through it. I had been watching him since his entrance, wanting to know what sort of man he was. I took him now for a quiet, stolid, unimaginative sort – a man who would do anything for a quiet life. That he was not easily upset was proved the next minute by his putting his head into the room.

"I'll take her down home," he said, nodding at us. "She's got upset, one thing and another. You mustn't think owt of what she said, Mr. Eddison. She has a bit of a temper, you know, at any time."

"All right, Ramsden, my lad," replied Mr. Eddison. "But – have you managed to wire to your brother?"

"Watkinson'll send a wire off at eight o'clock sharp," answered Ramsden. "I've sent it to Sugden's lodgings, so he'll be able to catch the ten o'clock." He stood hesitating for a moment. "I'd best be off with her," he said, jerking his head towards the hall, where I heard Mrs. John's voice, still lifted up, though in quieter tones. "If you should want me, send down. There's women upstairs – looking after – you know."

He gave us another nod and withdrew, and Mr. Eddison looked down at the broken crockery and sighed.

"A dreadful woman!" he said. "Her father was like that at the last. We shall have more trouble with her, Halstead."

More indications of possible trouble arrived before Mr. Halstead could make any response. Mrs. Haines, obviously much disturbed and trembling with indignation, put her head into the room. Seeing it clear of Mrs. John Martenroyde, she came in altogether. But before she had advanced many steps she caught sight of the wreckage in the fireplace and let out a shocked exclamation.

"A slight accident, Mrs. Haines," said Mr. Eddison. "I hope the china is not very valuable."

Mrs. Haines threw up her hands.

"Our best, sir – she would have it," she answered. "Oh dear, oh dear – half of it in pieces, Mr. Eddison. I came in, sir, to ask you a question. Is Mrs. John Martenroyde become mistress of this house? She came in here, Mr. Eddison, when they brought my poor master in – her and Ramsden – and she's been ordering us all about – nay, I'll say no more! But if she's mistress here, then I'm going. And so will the two girls, and Orris. Mrs. John Martenroyde we will not stand – not for an hour – her that's old John Skad's daughter!"

"Be easy, Mrs. Haines," replied Mr. Eddison. "Mrs. John Martenroyde is not only not mistress here, but has no right to enter unless she's invited to do so. If she comes here giving you any annoyance, send for me, at once. If you want to know who's master here, I am – for the present. I put you in charge of the house for the time being, so you're mistress. Now, my good soul, have that mess cleared away, and don't distress yourself."

Mrs. Haines, mollified, went off. The parlour-maid came with brush and pan and cleaned up the hearth. When she had gone, Mr. Eddison turned to me.

"Mr. Camberwell," he said, "what are you going to do?"

I was wondering about that myself.

"I suppose my commission is ended," I replied. "My employer's dead. I'd better return to town."

"Nothing of the sort!" he answered. "You can't, either. You'll be wanted at the inquest – you found James Martenroyde's body. No – I want you to stop here. I'll commission you. I want you to see this thing through – I'm beginning to suspect a lot, and I can see that you and Beverley will have your hands full. No – when I asked what you were going to do, I meant where are you going? You can't stay in this house now; it wouldn't be comfortable for you. Come and stay with me – I'm an old bachelor, but I'll see that you're all right."

"He's a good host," said Mr. Halstead. "He'll look after you well."

"That's very kind of you, Mr. Eddison," I replied. "I'll come – on condition that you turn me out when you've had enough of me."

"I'll do that," he answered, smiling. "Now then, let that young fellow Orris pack your things and bring them down to my house. Halstead, come with us and we'll have an early breakfast and consider what's to be done. I'll just see those women again and give them some orders, and then we'll walk down."

I was relieved when we got out of that house. The morning had worn on to daylight as we took the road to the valley, and the storm of the previous night had died down to a calm. But there was no calm in the atmosphere of the village. People were at their doors or standing in groups about the bridge and near the mill, and the mill itself was silent – for the first time for many a long year, said somebody, the machinery had not been set to work that morning.

Near Mr. Eddison's house we met Beverley; Mr. Eddison asked him to breakfast with us. During breakfast we discussed matters. Beverley, since our leaving him at the mill, had been making inquiries of various sorts. Of one thing he had satisfied himself. Nowhere could he hear of any enmity against the dead man. According to the men and women who worked at the mill, James Martenroyde had been not merely popular, but held in high esteem. If there ever had been dissension between him and his workpeople, it had been on economic points which had needed little settlement. In all the history of the business there had never been a strike or a lock-out.

"In short," concluded Beverley, giving us an account of what he had learned, "I've heard nothing – except what Outwin and Guest told us. And, between ourselves, I'm going to know if Sugden Martenroyde, when these two men saw him last night, was on his way to the Mill House or to the mill – or to lay in wait for his uncle at the weir bridge. It's no use denying it – everything points to him! He'd some reason for silencing his uncle."

"Where is he? – that's the present question," remarked Mr. Eddison. "I'm convinced – with you, Beverley – that Outwin and Guest did see him last night. But where is he this morning?"

We were soon to have some information on that point. As we were still talking, after breakfast, a boy brought Mr. Eddison a telegram, stating that Mr. Ramsden had just received it and now sent it on for Mr. Eddison to read. And Mr. Eddison read it and passed it round. It was from Sugden Martenroyde, sent off from London at a quarter to nine o'clock. And it merely said that Sugden was returning home at once and would be at Todmanhawe early in the afternoon.

Mr. Halstead voiced what three, at any rate, of us were thinking.

"If Sugden was in London so early this morning," he said, "it's impossible that he should have been at Todmanhawe at ten o'clock last night – the time at which James was killed. Impossible!"

But Beverley shook his head.

"No, it isn't!" he exclaimed. "He could have caught the Scotch express at Shipton at 2.36."

7

DEAD MAN'S GOODS

BEVERLEY'S CONFIDENT ASSERTION MET with immediate assent from Mr. Eddison and Mr. Halstead: the local train arrangements, evidently, were well known to both.

"You're right, Superintendent," said Mr. Halstead. "Yes, if he took the Scotch express at Shipton at 2.36 this morning, he'd reach St. Pancras at eight o'clock. I've often gone up to town by that train myself."

"So have I – a score of times," added Mr. Eddison. "Sugden could have remained here at Todmanhawe till midnight, nearly two hours after James was killed, and then have caught the 2.36 at Shipton, even if he'd had to walk in; it isn't two hours' walk. Well, now, Superintendent, what are you going to do? Let us know where we are and what you're planning. You suspect Sugden?"

"Well," said Beverley, "I put it to you as a lawyer, Mr. Eddison – what else can I do, considering what we've heard from Mr. Camberwell, first of all, and then from Outwin and Guest? I do suspect him. If he's been playing hanky-panky with his uncle's business in London and got wrong on the financial side, and if he suspected that his uncle had found him out or that there was danger of his being found out when the books came to be examined, then, I say, there's a motive. I consider there's certainly a *prima facie* case against him."

"Very likely," agreed Mr. Eddison. "Well, he's coming – coming at once. Are you going to arrest him?"

"Not yet," replied Beverley. "I'll tell you what I propose. Let him come; at first I shall do nothing – direct, at any rate. The inquest on Mr. James Martenroyde will have to be opened tomorrow, and I shall get the Coroner to do no more than take the strictly necessary evidence about the finding of the body and the cause of death, and then to adjourn for, say, a fortnight – at my request, as they'll put it in the papers. That'll enable you to get the funeral over. And when that's out of the way – well, I shall then ask Mr. Sugden Martenroyde to account for his movements from the time he left Abbeyside station at 5.41 on Monday – yesterday – afternoon until the moment of his receipt of Ramsden's telegram in London this morning. On what he says, my next course of action will depend."

"You believe Outwin and Guest's story?" asked Mr. Eddison.

"Absolutely!" said Beverley. "They're both decent, honest fellows – they wouldn't say what they do if there was any doubt. I haven't the least doubt that they saw Sugden on the top road there, last night. I see no difficulty in the situation. Granted that Sugden did leave Abbeyside station yesterday afternoon at 5.41 – that's a slow train to Leeds, and he could have left it at Heathley or at one of two or three other stations and retraced his steps back to Todmanhawe. And as you said just now, Mr. Eddison, he could have remained hereabouts until midnight, and then have had plenty of time to catch the Scotch express at 2.36 at Shipton."

"What did he come back for when he'd once set off?" asked Mr. Halstead.

"Oh, that!" exclaimed Beverley, with a scornful laugh. "That was all part of the scheme, Mr. Halstead. Carefully worked out. However, we'll tackle him. He's got to say why he came back, where he went when he came back, what he was doing. There are my views, gentlemen – and I think Camberwell will agree with me."

I did agree with him, and said so, and presently he and I left Mr. Eddison and Mr. Halstead and went out to make some further inquiries. We spent the morning in the neighbourhood of the mill, talking to men and women living around its walls. And we learned nothing of any value, and certainly heard no more of Sugden: Outwin and Guest had kept their promise and refrained from telling what they knew to any of their fellows.

Events crowded on one another during the next forty-eight hours. I heard that Sugden Martenroyde had arrived, that afternoon. Early in the evening Colonel Houston and his daughter also arrived and took their old rooms at the Scarthdale Arms; Mr. Eddison and I went to see them. Colonel Houston was almost furiously indignant at the cowardly attack on his old friend, and impatient to hear news of what was being done; Mr. Eddison and I purposely refrained from telling him of our suspicions. Miss Houston was quietly resigned and patient. But getting me aside while Mr. Eddison talked to her father, she put a plain question to me.

"I have heard about you, Mr. Camberwell," she said. "Read of you in the papers, I mean. You have had a lot of experience. Tell me frankly – do you think Mr. Martenroyde was murdered?"

I hesitated before replying.

"Tell me – honestly," she said.

"I think he was killed, Miss Houston," I replied.

"Intentionally?" she asked.

"I can't say that," I answered. "There may have been an altercation."

She looked at me in silence for a time.

"His workmen were fond of him," she said quietly. "I can't suspect them – any of them."

"No," I agreed.

Again she was silent for a moment or two.

"Mr. Camberwell, I'll be frank with you," she said at last. "Mr. Martenroyde had relations who were not pleased that he was going to marry me. Am I – is that the cause of this?"

"Honestly, Miss Houston, I can't answer that question," I replied. "We shall know more before long. Inquiries—"

It was a lame reply to make to her, but I think she understood, and she said no more and went away. I knew quite well, however, that she had a definite opinion – and perhaps she saw that I shared it.

The inquest was opened next day. It was a merely formal affair – carefully arranged, no doubt, between the Coroner and the police. The only evidence taken was that which established identification, my own and Orris's as regarded the finding of the body (I said nothing in explanation of my presence at Todmanhawe except that I was a guest at the grange), and Dr. Ponsford's in respect of the cause of death. Then the Coroner adjourned the proceedings for three weeks, and the people who had crowded the village schoolroom and waited in groups outside dispersed, to vent theories and indulge in speculations. And next day James Martenroyde was buried in the little churchyard which lay on the banks of the river, not far away from the mill. An hour later his relations met in the dining room of the grange to hear Mr. Eddison read the will. There were only three of them – his sister-in-law and her two sons. But Mr. Eddison had asked me to be present, and with me were Colonel Houston and his daughter and Mr. Halstead.

I never set eyes on Sugden Martenroyde until I saw him at his uncle's funeral. He was of a different type from his brother Ramsden. Ramsden was a hefty, solid, stolid fellow, reserved in manner and slow and sparing of speech; Sugden, built in a smaller mould, was a pert, dapper person, foppishly attired, even in his suit of mourning, somewhat aggressive and forward in his way of comporting himself, and affecting a style of speech which he doubtless fancied to be in accordance with London mode, but which was really offensively Cockney and formed an

irritating and objectionable contrast to the unadulterated broad
Yorkshire accent of his mother and brother.

Mrs. John Martenroyde let us hear her Yorkshire accents, at
their broadest and most rasping, as soon as we had been marshalled into our places.

"Mr. Eddison," she said, as the solicitor and his clerk began
to produce their papers, "I've always understood that nobody
but relations are allowed to be present when a dead man's will
is read. There are those in this room who aren't related to James
Martenroyde, as far as I'm aware."

"There is no one in this room, Mrs. Martenroyde, who is not
present on my invitation," replied Mr. Eddison acidly.

"Well," persisted Mrs. Martenroyde, "happen Colonel
Houston and his daughter has some right to be here, considering everything. But that young man" – here she pointed a
black-gloved hand in my direction – "what call has he to be
present? A total stranger, as far as I'm aware. What's he got to
do with our affairs?"

"Mr. Camberwell is present by my wish, Mrs. Martenroyde,"
said Mr. Eddison. "I have the right to ask the attendance of
anyone I please. I have already told you of the position which
Mr. Halstead and myself occupy. Now I must ask you to let me
read the late Mr. James Martenroyde's will."

"Well, whatever you and Mr. Halstead may be, I think I've
my rights," retorted Mrs. Martenroyde. "I'm not going to be a
poor dumb—"

"Whisht, Mother, whisht!" said Ramsden, laying a hand on
Mrs. Martenroyde's arm. "Let Mr. Eddison go on. There's no
call to say owt – let him read."

Mr. Eddison took from his clerk what looked to be a formi-
dable document and cleared his throat.

"I wish you all to know," he said, "that this will was made
by the late James Martenroyde quite recently – you will hear
the date presently. I also wish you to know that, in accordance
with the Law of Property Act of 1925, it was expressly made in

contemplation of James Martenroyde's forthcoming marriage to Miss Mary Houston. Had that marriage been celebrated, all that would have been necessary to establish the validity of the will would have been a formal reacknowledgment by the testator. Now, if you please, give me your attention."

Mr. Eddison began to read – slowly, distinctly. He continued to read; he read for a long time; the will was a lengthy one. The legal phraseology was beyond me, but I contrived to make out the principal provisions. Boiled down into plain language, the will amounted to this: everything was left to Mr. Eddison and Mr. Halstead as joint trustees. But there were full and explicit instructions as to what they were to do with what was placed in their hands. Each of the domestic servants at the grange, from Mrs. Haines to Orris, got a nice little legacy. Every man, woman, boy, and girl employed at Todmanhawe Mill got a sum of money, varying in amount according to length of service. Certain local hospitals and charities were remembered; a sum of money was left to the funds of the parish church. Then came the first really important part of the will. Todmanhawe Grange – a freehold property – and all its contents of whatever nature were left to Mary Houston; to her also was left a sum of forty thousand pounds, which amount was to be raised by the sale or transfer of the testator's Government securities – all, Mr. Eddison mentioned incidentally, of the gilt-edged variety. I glanced at Mrs. Martenroyde when these particulars came out; Mrs. Martenroyde merely gave her son Ramsden a knowing look and turned again to Mr. Eddison. I knew what she was waiting for – there was still the mill to dispose of.

She was not kept waiting. Todmanhawe Mill – that is to say, the business carried on there – was left to the trustees as a going concern; they were to have full control of it as a business. Ramsden and Sugden Martenroyde were to continue in their present positions as managers – one at Todmanhawe, the other in London. From time to time their salaries might be increased at the discretion of the trustees. At the expiration of five years

from the date of the testator's death the trustees, if satisfied
with the way in which the business had been carried on, should
convey it and any accrued profits to Ramsden and Sugden in
equal shares. But if they were not so satisfied, then they were
to sell the business in open market, and the proceeds, when all
liabilities had been discharged, should be divided – one-third
going to Mary Houston, and the remaining two-thirds in equal
shares to the two brothers. There was a dead silence when Mr.
Eddison had finished reading.

Mrs. Martenroyde broke it.

"Then – we get nowt?" she said. "Me and my lads – we get
nowt?"

"Your sons get the whole business at the end of five years,
Mrs. Martenroyde," replied Mr. Eddison. "They've nothing to
do but carry it on properly."

"But they get nowt now?" persisted Mrs. Martenroyde. "And
other folks—"

"Come away, Mother," said Ramsden. "There's nowt to
growl at. It'll be ours—"

Mrs. Martenroyde shook off the hand which Ramsden laid
on her arm.

"And this house should have been ours!" she exclaimed.
"Flesh and blood? It's been little that James Martenroyde
thought of flesh and blood when he signed that there paper. Martenroyde money, Martenroyde property – to strangers!
Shameful!"

Then Ramsden got her out of the room and the house, and
her voice died away in the grounds outside.

8

HANNAH'S CASTLE

As Mrs. Martenroyde and her sons disappeared from the garden, Miss Houston turned to Mr. Eddison.

"Mr. Eddison," she said, "this – this generous bequest to me will cause trouble – I can see that it will. Don't you think—"

The old lawyer smiled, shaking his head.

"Now, my dear," he said, "don't you begin bothering yourself about your bequest, nor about anything else. The people who have just left us have no cause whatever for complaint. James Martenroyde has done more for them than anyone knows of – though I, as his solicitor, know. He took the full responsibility of the family on his shoulders years ago, when his brother died – every penny they have had since came out of his pocket. He educated the two lads, clothed them, fed the whole family, and gave Mrs. John the house they live in – it's her own freehold property. As to this will," he went on, looking round at the rest of us, "it was made with special design; that is, as regards the future of the business and the mill. James Martenroyde wanted to test the qualities of his nephews. Up to now they've had him at the back of them; he wanted to see – or to let Mr. Halstead and myself see – how they turned out when the full management of things came into their hands. If Ramsden and his brother behave themselves and do their duty by the business, that business in five years' time will be theirs – absolutely. And a fine legacy for two young men, starting out in life, that will be! All they've got to do is to stick to the business, do right by it, and we shall hand it over to them and end our trust. It depends entirely on them. And if the business is properly managed and trade goes on – well, even as it's going on now – Ramsden and his brother in five years' time will come into a property that'll be worth a good many thousands a year to each of them."

"You're forgetting something, Eddison," said Mr. Halstead. He had been standing near the window, watching Mrs. Martenroyde and her sons walk down the garden; now he came over to the table at which Mr. Eddison and his clerk were sitting with their papers. "Something that may come in between."

Mr. Eddison looked at his co-trustee. A glance passed between them.

"Ay," he said, "I know what you mean. Well, of course that's got to be settled. Perhaps we'd better tell Colonel and Miss Houston – now."

"It's got to come out," said Mr. Halstead. "Beverley is at work."

Mr. Eddison turned to the Colonel and his daughter.

"Halstead," he said, "is referring to a matter of which you're so far in ignorance. The fact is, there's the beginning of an ugly suspicion afoot, though confined to a few people. It concerns Sugden Martenroyde. Briefly, it's this: Sugden, who'd been having a fortnight's holiday here, at his mother's house, was supposed to return to London on the afternoon of the day in the evening of which his uncle came by his death. Now, we've been informed by two trustworthy witnesses that Sugden was here, at any rate close to Todmanhawe, two or three hours previous to the discovery of James Martenroyde's body. And, as Halstead has just remarked, Superintendent Beverley is making inquiries into this. They'll have to be faced – by Sugden."

Colonel Houston and his daughter exchanged glances. Miss Houston spoke.

"But – but surely, Mr. Eddison, Sugden isn't suspected of—" she began. "You don't mean – that?"

"It's somewhat early to say anything definite," replied Mr. Eddison, "but it's a very remarkable thing that Sugden should – as he certainly did – have left Abbeyside station at 5.41 that afternoon for London and yet have been seen about a mile from this house some two hours or so later. But now that we have got on to this subject, I want you to hear what Mr. Camberwell has to say. Camberwell," he went on, "tell your tale – and show Colonel and Miss Houston that letter from William Heggus."

Once more I had to tell the story of my coming to Todmanhawe Grange and of what its now dead owner told me. The Colonel and his daughter grew grave of face now and then – especially during the reading of William Heggus's letter – exchanging glances. At the end Colonel Houston put a question.

"But don't I understand – I heard something about it – don't I understand that Sugden Martenroyde was certainly in London very early on the morning after his uncle's death?" he asked. "There was a wire from him, I think. How could he be in London at half past eight on that morning if he'd been here at a late hour the night before?"

"Easily!" replied Mr. Eddison. "He could have been here – somewhere – at Todmanhawe at midnight and still have been in London by eight o'clock next morning. The Scotch express, due at St. Pancras at eight o'clock, stops at Shipton at 2.36. We have no doubt – considering the source of our information – that Sugden was here that Monday evening. We want to know where he was, what he was doing, in whose company he spent his time – Superintendent Beverley is at work already, making inquiries. It will have to be cleared up – this matter."

"Hasn't Sugden been asked for an explanation?" inquired Miss Houston.

"Not yet – but he will be," replied Mr. Eddison. "And it will have to be a very full one. There are rumours in the air – you know what these people are. And Mrs. John Martenroyde has already created ill feeling by making a foolish charge – hinting that some one or other of the workpeople was responsible for her brother-in-law's death. No – in view of what Mr. Camberwell here knows, and of that letter from William Heggus, there is a good deal of explanation due from Sugden."

"William Heggus," remarked Mr. Halstead, "will have to be fetched up here. We shall want to know if there is anything in what he says in that letter. If Sugden's been deceiving James Martenroyde about the business in London, there was a motive—"

"Now, now, Thomas," interrupted Mr. Eddison, "we won't say anything about motives just yet. Wait till we see Beverley again. If he's found out that Sugden did leave Shipton by the 2.36 that Tuesday morning, we can act. Beverley and Camberwell can then tackle Sugden with some positive knowledge and ask him to explain matters."

"And he'll say nothing," remarked Mr. Halstead. "He's a Martenroyde!"

"Is it a family characteristic, Mr. Halstead?" I asked, perhaps a little satirically. "His mother says a good deal! And I didn't find Mr. James Martenroyde at all uncommunicative."

"What Thomas Halstead means," observed Mr. Eddison, "is that Sugden will say nothing to incriminate himself."

"That's it," agreed Mr. Halstead. "You'll get nowt out of him that he doesn't want to say. Nor out of any of 'em. It is a characteristic."

"My daughter and I saw Sugden Martenroyde in London not long ago," remarked Colonel Houston suddenly. "We don't want to tell tales, but I should say Sugden was having what these modern young people call a good time – very!"

"Oh?" said Mr. Eddison. "Still, if you and Miss Mary were there, Colonel – eh? Perhaps you were having a similar time?"

"It was at the Grand Transatlantic Hotel," said Colonel Houston. "We had been invited to dinner there by some American friends who were staying there. Sugden came in with two young fellows, both of whom I feel sure I have seen when staying here to fish – their faces were familiar. These three, and three young ladies, had dinner at a table near ours. They drank a good deal of champagne and appeared to be in very high spirits. The young ladies were, I should say, of the actress class – very lively girls."

"Oh, well," said Mr. Eddison, "young people will be young people, and an occasional bit of enjoyment does no harm. But of course if we knew that Sugden was making a regular practice of that sort of thing we should know that he was living beyond his means. I know what his salary is, and always has been, and while it's been enough to enable him to live very comfortably indeed in London, it wouldn't justify him in frequenting fashionable hotels and giving expensive dinners. However, I shall know more when I've seen William Heggus and the Gresham Street books. And the next thing is to hear what Beverley says."

Beverley walked in on Mr. Eddison and myself next morning. From the expression of his face it was evident that he had something of consequence to tell us. Out it came, at once.

"I've settled that point!" he said, triumphantly. "Sugden Martenroyde did travel by the Scotch express from Shipton to London on the morning after his uncle's death."

"You've got proof of that?" asked Mr. Eddison.

"Quite sufficient," replied Beverley. "Of course, the Martenroydes, all of them, are well known at Shipton railway station. I've got the evidence of a booking-clerk who was on duty that Tuesday morning and who clearly remembers issuing a first-class ticket for St. Pancras to Sugden, by the 2.36 a.m., and I've found a porter who's known Sugden ever since he was a boy and who saw him enter the train. Sugden, as a matter of fact, was the only passenger who boarded the train at Shipton that morning. So that's settled."

"What's settled?" asked Mr. Eddison.

"Why, that Sugden was in this neighbourhood between the hours of 7.30 on Monday evening and 2.30 on Tuesday morning," replied Beverley, "during which time his uncle James Martenroyde was murdered."

"Well," said Mr. Eddison, "what do you do next?"

"I'm going to see Sugden – now," answered Beverley. "Just to ask him for an explanation. That'll do to begin with. Will you come with me, Camberwell? We'll go down to Mill House."

I set out with him. But as soon as we had left the grange I clapped a hand on his arm.

"Beverley," I said, "you're the boss here, and I'm – more of a spectator, I think, than anything, though it's quite true that Mr. Eddison has given me a sort of watching brief. But you're the official representative of the law, and I want to say a word to you. You're on the wrong tack, old chap!"

Beverley pulled himself up and stared at me.

"Eh?" he exclaimed. "Wrong tack? What d'ye mean, Camberwell?"

"You're on the wrong tack if you think Sugden murdered James Martenroyde," I replied. "If Sugden had done that, he'd never have openly boarded that Scotch express at Shipton station, where he was so well known."

"Why not?" he demanded. "It was the only way he could get to London so as to be there early in the morning."

"Oh, no, it wasn't!" I retorted. "I spent a few minutes studying Bradshaw yesterday. Sugden could have got that train at Leeds."

"Thirty miles away!" he exclaimed.

"He'd have managed that little matter," I said. "How did he get back to Todmanhawe from whatever station it was that he left that train at – the 5.41 from Abbeyside? Probably Sugden had a car, or a friend's car, somewhere about. But I repeat – Sugden, had he murdered his uncle, would not have gone openly to Shipton, where he was so well known that you'd no difficulty in finding two men who remembered all about it. So I repeat, Beverley – wrong tack!"

He responded to that with something like a growl of disappointment. Suddenly he turned on me.

"But he was here that evening!" he exclaimed. "I'll back those two men, Outwin and Guest – they're straight, downright chaps. He was here! What did he come back for? Who did he come to see? He'd set off – and he came back. Why?"

"Ah," I said, "that's more like it. Why did he leave that train – somewhere – and return to Todmanhawe for a few hours? That's what we want to know. I've a pretty good notion, myself, as to Sugden's reason for interrupting his journey."

"Well?" he asked, half-sullenly. "And what may it be?"

"James Martenroyde," I replied, "had told Sugden that he was going to be in town soon and would take the opportunity of going through the books at the Gresham Street office with him. Now, supposing Sugden knew he was wrong in his cash? He hadn't much time to put matters straight. I think Sugden turned back to Todmanhawe to borrow money!"

"Just as reasonable to think that, knowing he was in a mess, he got rid of the old chap before he was found out," muttered Beverley. "Money? Who is there about here that he could borrow of?"

"That I don't know," I answered. "And probably you don't. I believe these people – dalesfolk – have a good deal of money, though they make no show of it. But now tell me, frankly – do you think Sugden Martenroyde killed his uncle?"

"I think it damned likely!" he replied. "Perhaps not intentionally. They may have had a scrap and got to blows. As things are – yes, I think Sugden did it."

"Well, I don't," I said. "Not after hearing about the Scotch express."

"Who did, then?" he exclaimed. "Can you put a name to it?"

"No," I replied, "not yet."

"Come on, then," he said; "let's ask Sugden a few polite questions."

We walked down to that part of Todmanhawe which clustered about the mill, and, crossing the river by the bridge, approached the Mill House – a big, rambling old place of the grey stone of the district, having on a gable over its front door the date 1685. Save for a wisp of smoke curling out of one of the queer old chimney-stacks, there was not a sign of life about the place and when we had knocked on the door in the stone porch for several minutes, we were still without any response.

A labourer leading a horse and cart came along the lane which led to the front of the great mill, and seeing us still knocking, halted, smiling.

"Eh, you'll never make nobody hear there, mister," he said. "They never let on if they do hear. Nobody ever gets inside that house – didn't you know that? Not even police," he added, with a sly glance at Beverley's smart tunic and cap. "They wouldn't let the King himself in there!"

"What do you mean?" demanded Beverley.

"Just what I say, mister," replied the man. "Nobody's ever admitted, except their own selves. Don't you know what they call this house hereabouts? No? Why, they call it Hannah's Castle, because Mrs. Martenroyde – her name's Hannah – won't let anybody cross the threshold without her leave. Nay, you can knock as hard as you like, but nobody'll come. They let their selves in and out, but nobody else enters. All the same, if you went round by that corner to the back and knocked there, you might be so lucky as to get old Mally Brewster, their servant, to attend to you. You'll get no attention where you are."

He chirruped to his horse and went on, chuckling, and Beverley and I followed his advice and, keeping to a paved path which skirted this strange house, turned a corner and proceeded towards the back, where one found a paved yard set between high stone walls. A door gave upon it which looked as firmly closed as the one in front. But here we had better luck – after we had knocked loudly three times, a window above the door opened and an old woman looked out on us.

9

HEAR ALL: SAY NOWT

IT WAS A QUEER face that I saw framed in the casement of
the window – a face enclosed in an old-fashioned, tightly fit-
ting cap of white linen, the edges of which curled in little frills
about apple-tinted cheeks and a chin all the more prominent
because there was an apparently toothless mouth between it and
a dumpy nose. There were twinkling, close-set eyes, still bright
and blue above that nose, and the inspection of us that came
from them was a sharp, watchful one. Whoever this old thing
was, a mere glance at her intelligent face showed me that she had
all her wits about her and that they were of no common order.

"Hello, hello!" exclaimed Beverley. "Thought you were all
asleep here – we've been knocking ten minutes!"

The tightly compressed lips opened.

"What might you be wanting?" they inquired.

"Wanting? Why, we want to see Mr. Ramsden or Mr. Sugden
or both," replied Beverley. "Where are they?"

"Mr. Ramsden and Mr. Sugden's down at the mill, mister,
and the mistress is out in the village somewhere," answered the
old woman. "They'll be home to their dinners before long, I
expect."

"Well, can't we come inside and wait for them?" asked Beverley. "Why don't you open the door when callers come?"

The white-capped head shook itself with decision.

"Mrs. Martenroyde doesn't allow strangers in when she's out," the toothless mouth replied. "I can't let anybody in. You must go away, mister, and come back when they're in."

"Nonsense!" said Beverley. "Come down and open the door. We aren't going to steal anything."

The old woman wasted no further words on us. She shut down the window with a decisive bang, and we heard the catch snapped. Beverley looked at me.

"Queer doings!" he said. "What's it mean? Well, as they're coming home to their dinners, we'll wait for them. Come round to the front of the house again. And look here, Camberwell, I'm going to change my tactics. I said we'd ask Sugden a few polite questions. Now I won't. You don't know our good old Yorkshire motto, do you? 'Hear all: say nowt.' Well, we'll hear – whatever we can – and say nowt in return – at present. You listen, and I'll listen, and we may hear – something."

"I told you I was merely a spectator, Beverley," I said. "You're the boss – follow your own methods."

"Ay, well," he replied, "my method at this juncture is going to be what you'd call a diplomatic one. These Martenroydes are Yorkshire folk. Well, Camberwell, I'm of the same breed. So it's like this – I want to know what they know, and no doubt they want to know what I know. Conflict of wits, eh? So we'll drop the direct method for the time being and just indulge in a bit of general talk, do you see? Keep your ears open – and your eyes. Say nothing to excite suspicion that we're after Sugden."

"I'm not going to say anything, Beverley," I said. "I'll listen."

"Well, you'll no doubt pick something up even if you hold your tongue," he said. "They say that spectators see most of the game – you watch mine."

We had reached the front of the house again by that time. Looking down the lane leading to the mill, we saw Ramsden and Sugden coming towards us. At the same time Mrs. Martenroyde came out of a cottage on the opposite side and joined her sons. The three walked towards Mill House, and Beverley and I went into the lane to meet them. As we drew near each other, I saw that mother and sons were watching us narrowly, and though their lips remained immobile and their expressions steady, there was unmistakable suspicion in the eyes of all three.

"Good morning, Mrs. Martenroyde!" said Beverley, assuming a friendly manner which suited his always good-natured appearance. "Morning, gentlemen. We've been trying to get into your house, Mrs. Martenroyde, just to sit and wait till you came in, but that old girl of yours knows how to say no! Are you afraid of the silver being stolen – or what?"

"I don't allow anybody in my house when I'm out," answered Mrs. Martenroyde. "Mally Brewster has strict orders to admit nobody – neither parson nor squire, slave nor king, when I'm not there. What might you be wanting?"

Beverley laughed and seated himself on the low stone wall which fenced the courtyard of Mill House from the road.

"Exactly what Mally asked," he said. "Same inquiry. Well, not much, Mrs. Martenroyde. We just wanted to have a bit of talk with you, and with Mr. Ramsden and Mr. Sugden. You know," he went on, dropping his half-bantering tone and becoming serious, "we've got to clear up this matter of your brother-in-law's death. That can't be allowed to rest."

"Well, that's your job," retorted Mrs. Martenroyde. "We're not police folk. And if we had any ideas or suggestions, it's no use putting 'em to you – you'd never credit 'em."

"Oh, come, Mrs. Martenroyde, don't say that!" exclaimed Beverley. "I should give every attention to anything you said."

"There was no attention paid to what I said that night in the mill when you were all gathered round James's dead body and wondering who'd killed him," replied Mrs. Martenroyde. "I said then that I expected some of his men had been getting a bit of their own back, and because I said so I was miscalled. But I know what I think."

"But the late Mr. Martenroyde was always on such good terms with his workpeople, wasn't he?" said Beverley. "It's generally understood that he was, in the district."

Mrs. Martenroyde shook her head.

"Ay, well, them that's closer acquaintance knows better," she said. "Ramsden there can tell different."

Beverley turned to Ramsden. Ramsden, taciturn as ever, had stood by, watching us silently while his mother talked. Sugden, cigarette in his lips, and hands in the pockets of his plus-four knickerbockers, had seated himself on the wall near Beverley, to listen at his ease.

"There's been unpleasantness time and again," said Ramsden. "We've never had a strike nor a lock-out, but Uncle James has had rows with some of 'em, at odd times."

"Yes, but that isn't any proof that somebody wanted to murder him!" said Beverley. "If you knew of anybody that had a desire for revenge—"

"I suppose, as you're a Yorkshireman yourself, Mr. Beverley, that you've heard the old saying about a Yorkshireman? – that he'll carry a stone in his pocket ten years, and then turn it and carry it another ten, but he'll fling it at last," said Mrs. Martenroyde. "Do you think that among the two or three hundred men that works in this mill there isn't one that's kept a stone to throw? Don't tell me!"

"But – can you point to any particular individual?" asked Beverley. "I want something definite. If I knew of anybody who had a grudge against Mr. Martenroyde, anybody who'd an old score to pay off, I could get to work. But I can't do anything on vague generalities."

Ramsden looked at his mother. The look conveyed the impression that he had an idea in his mind and was not sure whether he should let it out or not. Mrs. Martenroyde making no reply to Beverley, Ramsden spoke, diffidently.

"There was that chap Marris, you know," he said, still looking at his mother. "That's about all I can call to mind."

"Who was Marris?" asked Beverley. "One of your men?"

"No – leastaways, not at the mill," replied Ramsden. "He was gardener, up at the grange. Uncle James found out that he was selling stuff out of the gardens and the greenhouses and putting a pound or two a week into his own pocket, so he chucked him out. And Marris – he was a foul-tempered chap. The sort," added Ramsden, "that would have his knife into anybody if he got a fair chance."

"He threatened Uncle James," remarked Sugden.

"When was all this?" asked Beverley.

"Happen eighteen months ago," replied Ramsden; "about that."

"I'd forgotten about Marris," said Mrs. Martenroyde. "He was a bad 'un – he cheated James right and left. Ramsden says a pound or two – I'll lay he made a small fortune out of that garden. James never took any heed of what the man was doing; it was pure accident that he found him out."

"Where's Marris live now?" asked Beverley.

"Other side of Todman Fell," replied Ramsden. "He came from there – Elthwaite, his village is – and he went back there."

Beverley made a note in his pocket-book and got off his seat on the wall.

"Well," he said, "we've got to get down to the bottom of it. It's a stiff problem, you know, Mrs. Martenroyde – but there's guilt somewhere. Somebody did it."

"Ay, and there'll not be wanting evil-disposed folk and wicked tongues in these parts to say that innocent folk did it!" exclaimed Mrs. Martenroyde. "I know 'em, Mr. Beverley. They'll be saying, before they've done, that me or my lads or all of us put an end to James before he could wed this fine young madam from London. But we're clear, anyhow. I was in my bed when James was coming across that bridge to meet his death, and Ramsden here was with his friends in Shipton, and Sugden there was in London."

"On the way to London, at any rate," said Sugden, with a laugh that sounded a little forced. "Not quite there, Mother – I didn't leave Leeds till pretty late."

"Well, you were in the train, anyway," retorted Mrs. Martenroyde. "You weren't anywhere about Todmanhawe. And, as I've said, neither was Ramsden, and I was in my bed – so there was none of us near what they call the scene. And if you ask me, Mr. Beverley, it'll take you all your time to find out who put an end of James Martenroyde, for it was neither thief nor robber – they'd taken nowt out of his pockets, so you've nowt to go by."

She made a move towards the door of her house, and as the two young men followed her, Beverley and I moved off. When we had turned the corner into the main road, Beverley laughed.

"Take me all my time, will it?" he said. "I think not, Mrs. Martenroyde! Well, Camberwell, we've settled one thing. That young Sugden is a damned liar! In the train between Leeds and London, was he, at the time James Martenroyde was killed, when I know that at half past two, a few hours later, he was booking his ticket at Shipton! There's a lie for you – Camberwell, Sugden's the man! Now listen – are you doing anything tomorrow morning?"

"I'm doing nothing any morning, Beverley," I replied, "unless Mr. Eddison gives me something to do. I'm staying here at his pleasure – in case I'm wanted. Why?"

"Tomorrow morning," he said, "we'll go in my car and trace Master Sugden's movements from the moment he left Abbeyside station at 5.41 that Monday afternoon to the time he was seen by Outwin and Guest on the top road at Todmanhawe – if we can. At any rate, I think we can find out where he left the train. For he did leave it, and he did come back here, and I want to know why he came and where he was until he turned up at Shipton for the Scotch express. Oh, I'll have Sugden in a trap yet – don't bother yourself. I believe he did kill his uncle. And now let's go and get Mr. Eddison to send straight off for William Heggus and the books from the London office. I want to establish motive, Camberwell. Motive! Let me get the motive, and then – ah!"

"Heggus will have to come here secretly," I said. "It won't do to let Sugden know he's coming, or has come."

"I'll suggest that to Mr. Eddison," said Beverley. "It can be managed. But we must have Heggus and these books at once."

We went back to Mr. Eddison and told him of all that had passed in front of the Mill House. He pooh-poohed the Marris idea and counselled Beverley to take no further trouble about it – Marris, he happened to know, had got another equally good job as gardener and was not likely to have risked his own neck for the sake of revenging himself on James Martenroyde for punishment which he richly deserved. And he agreed with Beverley that the evidence against Sugden was strong and must be thoroughly gone into. Therewith he wrote a long letter to William Heggus in London, explaining that the Martenroyde business was now under his and Mr. Halstead's control, and instructing him to come down to Todmanhawe at once and to bring the office books with him.

Next morning Beverley and I set out in his car to carry out his project of tracing Sugden Martenroyde's movements on the afternoon and evening of the murder. We left Todmanhawe exactly as Sugden left it – by a road which ran straight from the village to Abbeyside station, a little railway halt, insignificant in size, so called because of its contiguity to the ruins of a once famous religious house. And here, at the very beginning of our researches, we made a first discovery, small in itself, but certainly tending to show that when Sugden boarded the 5.41 train at that place he had a definite intention of leaving it at some other station along the line. The traffic from Abbeyside was so unimportant that the duties of booking-clerk and porter were combined in one man.

This functionary, discreetly questioned by Beverley, had a clear remembrance of Sugden's arrival at the station in Ramsden's car on that particular Monday evening; the news of the

murder at Todmanhawe, communicated all over the countryside next morning, had fixed it in his memory. Mr. Sugden, he
said, bought a first-class ticket to St. Pancras, London. Then,
having bought it, he said to the porter-clerk that he didn't want
to be bothered with his suitcase when he arrived in London;
he had to go down to the City as soon as his train got in (a
somewhat remarkable statement to make, seeing that if he had
gone straight on by the 5.41 and its connections from Leeds or
Bradford, he would have been in London in the small hours
of Tuesday morning, at which time the City is a desert!), and
couldn't lug the case down there. And, borrowing a label from
the man, he had written on it: "To be called for," had told him
to label the suitcase: "St. Pancras," and, leaving it to him to hand
to the guard, entered his compartment free and untrammelled.
So, apparently, his resolve to quit the train somewhere had been
formed even before he drove up to the station at Abbeyside.

But – where had he left that train? He could not have gone
far in it, for if the story told by Outwin and his fellow-workman,
Guest, was true, Sugden Martenroyde was in the immediate
neighbourhood of Todmanhawe about half past seven Monday
evening. He must have got off at some station not far along
the line, found some means of getting back to Todmanhawe,
and after spending some time there, somewhere, have made his
way to Shipton. Now, the 5.41 was a local train, stopping at
every station on its way to Bradford – if a passenger wished to
go to Leeds, he changed trains at Wiseley, some twelve miles
from Abbeyside. But Beverley's idea was that Sugden had left
the train almost at once – probably at Heathley, where he would
have no difficulty in finding a car to take him back to Todmanhawe. Heathley, four miles from Abbeyside, was a place
of some size, a health-resort, having a railway station at which
two or three lines met and where Sugden would not be likely to
be noticed; at that hour of the evening, just before six o'clock,
there would be a great deal of traffic in Heathley station, trains
arriving just about then filled with business men from Leeds

in one direction and Bradford in another. Clearly, Heathley was the place in which to make inquiries, and we re-entered Beverley's car and drove off down the valley in its direction.

"Looks to me as if he'd worked all this out pretty carefully, Camberwell," remarked Beverley. "He'd thought over that suitcase dodge before he left Abbeyside, I'll bet. I dare say he'd reckoned everything up, right on to getting the Scotch express at Shipton. Now if we can only find out how he got back to Todmanhawe, eh? He couldn't walk it in the time – somebody must have driven him. And there's no place but Heathley at which he could get a car."

But we had no luck at Heathley. We spent hours there, questioning, interviewing, without result. The car-drivers who plied for hire at the station knew nothing of Sugden. There were three garages in the little town at which a car might have been hired; we got no help at any of them. Eventually we went forward to Wiseley, the only other place in that part of the valley at which Sugden could have got any sort of conveyance. We had no better luck there. And since Wiseley was the last place from which Sugden could have got back to the neighbourhood of Todmanhawe by the hour at which Outwin and Guest saw him near there, we gave up that part of our quest. Beverley was beginning to agree to a theory which I ventured to suggest – that Sugden had slipped out of the local train while it was standing in one of the small stations (it would be quite dark soon after he left Abbeyside) and had made his way to some friend's house, where he had secured the means of retracing his steps.

"Anyway," said Beverley, still persistent, "we know exactly where Outwin and Guest saw him that night, and we'll follow the probable route to it. I've a good ordnance map here – let me show you."

We were then at Wiseley, our last place of call, and had spent a couple of hours there without profit. Beverley, spreading out his map, pointed out to me that whether Sugden had turned back from Wiseley or from Heathley or from any of the smaller stations in between those places, he would, in order to reach Todmanhawe at the point where the two men saw him, have had only one possible route that he could follow. This was the main road through the valley as far as Abbeyside. There the road forked. One branch went on to the bridge at Todmanhawe in a straight line; the other, to the left, went along the high ground on the north of the dale, passed through the village of Hartwick, and reached Todmanhawe at a point just above Todmanhawe Grange.

We took this road. We halted at Hartwick and made guarded inquiries. There were two inns there, one in the village, one at a crossroads. We heard nothing of Sugden, nor of any car or vehicle having been put up at either inn on the evening we were so anxious to get particulars of. Eventually we reached the spot at which Outwin and Guest had seen Sugden hurry past, going in the direction of Todmanhawe. A few minutes later, rounding a corner of the road, we came in sight of Todmanhawe itself, lying in the valley far beneath us. And there, on the right-hand side of the road, its windows commanding a wonderful view of the upper reaches of Scarthdale from Todmanhawe Mill to the mountain chain rising to the northward, stood an old house of grey stone. In its porch, on which the afternoon sun was throwing its last beams, sat, alone, a man, wrapped in heavy shawls.

10

WHO WAS IT?

AT THE SIGHT OF this man, obviously an invalid, sitting there, solitary, in the grey setting of the stone-walled porch, Beverley pulled up the car.

"That's poor Dakin Heggus," he said. "Brother of the Heggus – William – who's in Martenroyde's London office. Dakin's on his last legs, poor chap, though I don't think he knows it. Sad fate! He's well off, and comparatively young, and he's got a handsome wife, and – well, I've heard that the doctors can do nothing for him. Some mysterious wasting disease – he's been getting weaker and weaker for months. We'll just ask how he is and, Camberwell, we'll not say anything about what we're doing here. If he or his wife says anything, we'll listen – and we won't ask any questions. Direct questions are not the fashion in this part of the world."

We left the car on the roadside and walked up through a neatly arranged garden, destitute now of flower or leaf, save for its clumps of evergreen, to the porch. Its occupant sat in an easy chair, rugs about his legs and feet, shawls about his shoulders. He was a man of presumably fifty years of age, and, stripped of his many coverings, was probably thin and worn; his face, meagre and emaciated, was of the colour of old parchment; his hands, one of which he waved to us as we advanced, were little more than skin and bone. But his eyes, seen at a closer angle,

were keen and bright, and at sight of Beverley a new light came int
o them.

"Well, Dakin," said Beverley, as we reached the porch, "and
how's things with you? This is a friend of mine, Mr. Camberwell. We thought we must stop and pass the time of day with
you. How are you nowadays?"

The sick man smiled wanly, shaking his head.

"Why, I don't seem to make any great improvement, Superintendent," he answered. "Some days I'm a bit better, like, and
some days I'm a bit worse, and so it goes on. Your servant, sir,"
he continued, with an old-fashioned bow to me. "Take a seat,
sir. Sit you down, Superintendent – we keep a chair or two to
sit in, you see. The doctor, he makes me keep out in the open
air all day long – some folks would never stand it, but then, I've
been used to outdoor life ever since I can remember."

He motioned us to chairs which flanked the little table at
which he himself sat and on which, among other things, was
placed an object that had at once caught my attention and that
I knew – having seen similar things in other parts of the dale
country – to be a sheep-bell. This he took up and began to ring
vigorously.

"That's how I call Mira when I want owt," he said with a
smile. "They can hear that bell all over the house – I took it off
one of my best sheep when I gave up farming. It's an old bit, that
– I'll lay my great-great-grandfather had it once – and happen
his father before him."

He rang the bell again – twice. And at the last summons the
door of the house opened and a woman appeared, making a
little start of surprise as she saw her husband's visitors. Then she
smiled and came forward, giving her hand to Beverley.

"Nay!" she exclaimed. "I never thought to see you here, Mr.
Beverley – you haven't been to see us for I don't know how
long!"

"Haven't been your way – at least on this side of the river –
lately, Mrs. Heggus," replied Beverley. He waved his hand in my

direction. "Friend of mine, Mr. Camberwell," he added. "I've just been giving him a ride round, like, and seeing Dakin sitting here, I thought we'd say how do."

Mrs. Heggus gave me her hand – and a keen, if quick, glance; I felt sure that she knew quite well that I was the mysterious London gentleman who had suddenly appeared in this out-of-the-way Arcadia. On my part I looked at her – rather longer than she looked at me. I was sizing her up. In my estimate of her she was probably about twenty-eight years of age, rather over than under the medium height of women, with a remarkably good, well-developed figure and a trick of erectness that showed off her well-modelled shoulders and generous bosom. If not quite a beauty, she was an attractive woman to look at, having a mass of hair which was something between auburn and gold, a pair of eyes in which there was a prevailing tint of violet, and a mouth and chin which denoted a good deal of character. And, in contrast to the poor invalid, sitting wrapped up in his shawls and rugs, she looked what people call a picture of health and vigour.

"Mira," said Heggus, "these gentlemen'll do with a sup of something after their drive – it's a coldish day. Fetch the whisky, my lass."

Mrs. Heggus looked from one to the other of us.

"Why, hadn't you better come into the house?" she said. "It's cold work sitting out here, and besides it's about time you were coming in, Dakin: the sun's getting low. Come inside, Mr. Beverley, and I'll help Dakin in."

"Allow me," I said, going forward. "Take my arm, Mr. Heggus."

"Why, you're very kind, sir," he said. "I find it a bit difficult to move about nowadays. Mira, my lass," he went on, "take these here shawls and things – I look respectable in body, wrapped up in this fashion, but Lord bless you, Mr. Beverley, I'm losing weight so rapid that I shall be nowt but an atomy before long – all skin and bones!"

He was right there. The arm which he slipped into mine as
he rose from his chair felt like a small child's, and the weight he
leaned on me as I helped him into the house was far below what
even a sparely-built man's should have been. Clearly, Dakin
Heggus was on his last legs in more senses than one. But when
I had assisted him into a big, old-fashioned parlour where a big
fire of logs threw flashes of yellow light on the dark furniture
and oak-panelled walls, and had settled him in an easy chair
by the hearth, his hospitable instincts asserted themselves, and
once more he told his wife to bring out the whisky. When it had
been produced and Mrs. Heggus had helped all three of us to a
drink, he formally pledged us.

"You'll have been a bit busy, I reckon, with this James
Martenroyde matter?" he continued, turning to Beverley.
"Have you made owt out, like?"

"Not yet, Dakin," replied Beverley. "Trying to pick up what
we can, you know. Have you heard anything? Always glad of a
bit of information, if you have."

"Nay, we've heard nowt," replied Heggus. "At least, nowt
that's what you might call definite. We're out of the way here
to hear owt – I'm tied down, and Mira there, she doesn't oft go
to the village."

"And when I do, I pay no heed to what's said," observed Mrs.
Heggus. "Them that say anything don't know anything, and
them that know something say nowt, so there you are!"

"Do you think there's anybody who really does know something?" asked Beverley. "Real knowledge?"

"Why, you know what Todmanhawe folk are," she answered.
"Close as they can be, if you like. If there is anybody that knows,
they'll not tell you, Mr. Beverley."

"Ay, that's right," remarked Heggus. "You policemen are always the last to hear owt. Them blue coats of yours is sufficient
to shut their mouths, do you see, Mr. Beverley. I dare say there is
them round about that could tell you a good deal – but they'll
say nowt."

"You've got to ferret it out," said Mrs. Heggus. "Happen," she continued with a sly, half-roguish look that took Beverley and myself in its range, "happen you're doing it!"

"Not much progress made so far," said Beverley. "You're right when you say people hereabouts are close. Best hands at keeping things to themselves that ever I knew! Why does Mrs. John Martenroyde keep that old house of hers like a fortress? Evidently she won't let anybody cross the threshold."

Husband and wife looked at each other and smiled; it was evident to me that they had some secret knowledge about the fact to which Beverley had made allusion.

"Oh, well," said Mrs. Heggus, "Mrs. John always was like that – you'd have a job to get across her doorstep. It's a way of hers."

"Mrs. John seemed to think it was one of the workmen at the mill who killed her brother-in-law," said Beverley. "What do you think, Dakin?"

Heggus shook his head and spread his thin hands.

"Nay," he answered, "I think nowt. It might have been – and again, it mightn't. There's two or three hundred of 'em – there may be a man that's had a crow to pick with James. I never heard of one, all the same – taking it altogether, James got on very well with his workpeople. Poor wind-up for James, for all that. Now," he continued, with a whimsical smile, "there's an old lass who lives a bit farther up this road who knew it was going to happen that night! What do you think of that, now?"

"What do you mean?" asked Beverley. "Knew it was going to happen? Knew that James Martenroyde was going to be—"

"Well, I mean she knew something was going to happen," replied Heggus. "She saw the Todmanhawe ghost, or spirit, or whatever you might call it. And she says that wherever that's seen, something out of the way happens."

"He's talking about old Prissy Mallison," explained Mrs. Heggus. "She was coming home by the churchyard and the weir bridge and she saw the ghost – that very night, it was. And she told me next day what she'd seen, and she said that as soon as she'd seen it she knew something would happen before morning. She'd seen the same thing some years ago, and it was on the same night that the mill took fire."

"Who is this old party?" asked Beverley. "Where does she live? Prissy Mallison – what is she? What's she do?"

"She does nothing but live – she's a parish allowance," replied Mrs. Heggus. "And maybe she's a bit of money put away somewhere. I wonder you've never seen her, Mr. Beverley – she's a sight to see, when you do see her! Some folks say she's a witch – she looks like one, I'm sure."

"I should like to see her now," said Beverley. "Do you think she'd tell me and Mr. Camberwell about this ghost?"

"Nay, I can't say," answered Mrs. Heggus. "It all depends on which side she happens to be turned out – she's a queer old thing. If you happened to take her fancy—"

"Give her half a crown and she'd tell you all the tale from one end to the other," said Heggus. "And if she talks, she talks! – full measure."

Beverley drank off his whisky.

"Can you spare a few minutes, Mrs. Heggus?" he asked. "Take me and Mr. Camberwell along to see this old lady, then. I should like to hear about this ghost. You say it was the night James Martenroyde was killed?"

"Same night – and not so long before," replied Mrs. Heggus. "Yes, I'll go along with you – Dakin'll be all right till I come back."

We said goodbye to Heggus, and his wife, scorning wraps or head-gear, took us out and along the lane in the direction of Todmanhawe. Some fifty yards farther along, a small cottage stood in the corner of a plantation of Scotch firs; in one window appeared a feeble gleam of light.

"She's in," said Mrs. Heggus. "Take a peep at her through the window before I open the door, and see what you think of her. You'll not wonder some say she's a witch!"

Beverley and I tiptoed up to the little window and peered into the interior of the cottage. What light there was came from the stick fire burning in the hearth and from a small lamp set on a table in front of it. Between table and hearth sat an old woman smoking a short clay pipe; her face, framed in a once-white frilled cap, was fixed on the crackling sticks. She was indeed very witch-like in appearance, and she was very, very dirty, and very, very forbidding generally, and I was not at all surprised when Mrs. Heggus, with a whispered word to us, opened the door and ushered us into an atmosphere which seemed to be a compound of rank tobacco, onions, and foul air.

"She's got a cat!" whispered Beverley. "Witch, right enough!"

The cat – a big black Tom – saw us first and rose to its feet, spitting at our intrusion. Then the old woman looked up. She said nothing and made no sign. Mrs. Heggus went up to her and bent to her ear.

"Prissy," she said loudly, "here's two gentlemen come to see you. They want to hear about the ghost. Do you hear? The ghost." Then she bent still lower and spoke a few words which I could not catch, but which, apparently, were quite audible to the old woman – probably they referred to the douceur suggested by Heggus. "Tell 'em about it, Prissy," concluded Mrs. H eggus.

The old woman slowly lifted a pair of eyes, bright, cunning, and looked Beverley and myself over, carefully, watchfully. Her lips, wrinkled into a thousand tiny seams, relaxed and she smiled knowingly.

"Eh, ya're a couple o' proper lads!" she said in a cracked voice. "Sit yersens down."

"She'll talk to you," whispered Mrs. Heggus. "You've found favour. I'll go – I'm always afraid of Dakin falling out of his chair or into the fire if he's left alone."

She bade us goodnight; I opened the cottage door for her and with a half-shy, half-wondering glance of thanks at a small courtesy which she was evidently not accustomed to receive, she passed out into the night. I turned to the odd couple on the hearth – Beverley sitting straight in his chair, gazing, a little awestruck and frightened, at the old woman; the old woman, the queer smirk on her witch-like face, staring at him.

"Who told ye lads about t' ghost?" she demanded. "Heggus, happen, or happen his wife? And what do ye want to know about ghosts – young fellers like you? I'll lay owt you don't believe in such things. But I do – 'cause I see 'em. I seed this here Todmanhawe ghost – I've seen it more nor once. And it wor in the nature o' things that I should see it the night James Martenroyde were murdered. It wor a sign. Once before I seed it when it wor a sign. That wor when t' mill got on fire. Allus it appears just before summat's going to happen."

"Where did you see it this time, missis?" asked Beverley.

"Wheer? Well, you see, it wor the same night as James Martenroyde wor put an end to. A wild night that wor – t' river wor running up to its bank level. I'd been to Kelston, t'other side o' th' dale, and I were coming home when I seed t' Ghost; about half past nine to ten o'clock it 'ud be when I set eyes on it. Do you know these parts, ye two young fellers?"

"We know 'em, mother," replied Beverley.

"Not as well as me, you don't know 'em," said the old crone. "I'm ower ninety years old – I've buried three, or happen it's four, husbands i' my time, and wed or single, I've never been far away fro' Todmanhawe. Howsiver, do ye know t' lane that comes down fro' Kelston across t' moor and falls into Todmanhawe bottom road between Martenroyde's mill and t' church? Well, I come down that lane, and I'd just got to t' bottom on it and wor going to cross t' main road and take to t' mill weir bridge when I seed t' ghost. An' it wor t' same ghost 'at I'd seen years before – when t' mill gat on fire."

"Where did you see it this time?" asked Beverley.

"Same place, young feller – standing under t' lych-gate, at t'entrance to t' churchyard. Just where I seed it before – t'exact spot. I knew it!"

"But – wasn't it a very dark night?" said Beverley. "How could you see?"

"Theer are some cottages opposite, young feller," replied the old woman, "and they'd none gone to bed, and they'd their lamps burning, and t' leet shone full on t' figure o' t' ghost, bidin' there under t' lych-gate. Oh, I seed it – I knew it same as if it had been an owd friend. 'Tha'rt theer again, arta, mi lad?' I says to misen, as soon as I saw it. 'Then we shall hev trouble afore morning if thou's about. It wor a fire t' last time; let's hope it'll be nowt worse on this occasion.' And I made nearer to it, but of course it had gone then."

"Gone?" exclaimed Beverley. "Where?"

"Nay, it made off into t' churchyard – wheer else?" replied Prissy Mallison. "It had done its job then, d'ye see. It's bound to appear to somebody. When it's made its appearance I expect it's free to go back where it came from."

Beverley rubbed his chin, staring at the old woman as if wondering whether she believed all this.

"What's it like, this ghost?" he demanded suddenly. "Did it look this time just as it was when you saw it before?"

"Ay, it was just about th' same, young feller; I didn't see no difference. A tallish sort, covered fro' head to foot in a whitish garment – of course, I never was close enough to see much more nor that."

"Man or woman?" asked Beverley.

"Nay, lad, ghosts is neither men nor yet women!" retorted Prissy Mallison. "They're ghosts."

"What did you do when it went into the churchyard?" inquired Beverley.

"Do? Why, I made for t' mill weir bridge and come home. And I knew summat 'ud happen that night, and of course next day I heard about James Martenroyde. I reckon that there ghost is one o' t'owd Martenroydes, 'at comes out of its grave whenever owt serious is going to happen i' t' family."

"And you've seen it just twice?" asked Beverley. "Once before the fire, and once just before Mr. Martenroyde's death? Tall figure all in white, eh?"

"Whitish is what I said, young feller – some light stuff 'at would look white in t' lamplight. Grave-clothes, likely."

Beverley got up, putting his hand in his pocket; I followed his example. We each gave the old woman some loose silver; she spat lavishly on the coins before hiding them away in some cranny or crevice of her dilapidated garments. Then she gave us a sly look.

"Good lads!" she said. "A bit o' summat for tea and 'bacca's allus welcome. But it's a cowd night – will yer hav' a sup o' gin? This here young feller," she went on, pointing a skinny finger at Beverley's tunic, "is a p'lice-man, but they're same as all other men when they're stripped! And I've a drop o' gin put by 'at came straight fro' Holland and never paid no duty, neither. Will you put your lips to a drop?"

But we hastily declined Mrs. Prissy Mallison's hospitality and, bidding her farewell, got out of the cottage and its fetid atmosphere to draw long breaths of relief in the keen, frosty air of the little garden.

"Well, what do you think of that, Beverley?" I asked as we walked back to where we had left the car outside Heggus's gate. "An experience for me, anyhow!"

"I shall know what I think in a few minutes," he answered oracularly. "I'm damned glad I thought of calling here at Dakin Heggus' – it's giving me the very link I wanted. Jump in, Camberwell – I'm going to call at Outwin's cottage. He lives up in the top part of the village, and he'll be home from work now."

We drove on to that part of Todmanhawe which lay beyond the grange and the crossroads, and with a little difficulty found Outwin's cottage. Outwin had just come in from the mill and came out to the side of Beverley's car.

"Outwin," said Beverley, stooping over to him, "I want to ask you a question. Can you remember what sort of a mackintosh Sugden Martenroyde was wearing when you and Guest saw him on the Hartwick road that Monday night? Think, now – be careful."

But Outwin's answer came readily.

"Yes, Superintendent," he answered. "One o' these light things – nearly white. I'd seen him in it before, a time or two."

Beverley bade him keep quiet a bit longer and drove off. Then he turned to me.

"Camberwell," he said, "it's turning out tiptop! Sugden was the ghost – Sugden, hanging about, lying in wait for his uncle. I'll hang him yet! See if I don't."

11

MOTIVE

I MADE NO REPLY to this emphatic declaration, and Beverley, good friends as we were, was quick to notice my lack of enthusiasm.

"You think I'm on the wrong tack?" he said. "Clean out?"

"I don't say you're on the wrong tack, nor that you're clean out, Beverley," I replied. "I think there's no doubt that Sugden Martenroyde, after leaving for London that Monday afternoon, got out of his train before it had gone many miles, and came back to Todmanhawe. But if he came back with the distinct purpose of murdering his uncle and did murder him, then he's the clumsiest murderer I've ever had any experience of!"

"You mean because he went off from Shipton by the 2.36?" he asked.

"That's exactly what I do mean!" I answered. "Went off from a station where he'd be sure to be well known and, as you've already found out, where he was seen – by two reputable witnesses."

"He'd never think of that," muttered Beverley. "They all of 'em make some slight mistake. We should never catch some of 'em if they didn't. It would never occur to him."

"Then he's a fool," I said. "That was a fatal mistake."

"We profit by it," said Beverley. "If he didn't come back to murder James Martenroyde, what was his object in coming back?"

"That," I replied, "is just what I should like to know. And – perhaps – I shall find out."

"Um!" said Beverley. "Stiff job, Camberwell. Well, I like sailing on a straight course. I think I'm on one now. I feel convinced that Sugden did for his uncle, and I shall follow it up."

"Will you let me give you a bit of advice?" I asked.

"A thousand bits!" he answered readily. "What is it?"

"Don't do anything – he'll not run away, for he's no suspicion that he's suspected – until you've seen and heard William Heggus," I said. "What you want is to find out what motive Sugden had. William Heggus may be able to supply evidence that will show what that motive was – if there was one."

"Your evidence – and that letter from Heggus – and the intimation that James Martenroyde gave to Sugden about examination of the London accounts go a long way to suggesting a motive," replied Beverley. "Sugden wanted to silence his uncle before James could find out – something. But of course I'll wait for William Heggus. When will he be down here?"

"He should be here now," I said. "Eddison, when he wrote to him last night, told him to leave at once, bringing everything with him. You'd better come back with me to Eddison's and see if Heggus has got here."

We were in Todmanhawe by that time, and Beverley drove to Eddison's house. William Heggus had arrived and was with Eddison in the dining room; Halstead was with them. Eddison had taken the utmost precaution to make William Heggus's visit a secret one. So that no one in the neighbourhood should see him, William had been met by Orris and the car at Seddlesfield, a junction lying some miles to the north of Shipton, and driven to Eddison's house by a road which avoided the village of Todmanhawe. Eddison's servants had been admonished to say nothing of his presence. Eddison's intention was to send him back to London in the same secret way as soon as we had heard all he had to say and had gone through the books and papers with him. This examination Eddison proposed to make at once, and he suggested to Beverley that he should stay there and dine with the rest of us and after dinner take part in the investigation. Beverley, keen enough to do anything that would establish motive on Sugden Martenroyde's part, readily fell in with the suggestion and housed his car in Eddison's garage. Presently the five of us dined together – avoiding all mention of the purpose of our meeting – and when dinner was over, adjourned to Eddison's library to begin our work. And there William Heggus, a quiet, reserved little man who had taken small part in our talk at dinner and seemed to be much oppressed by his mission, opened a suitcase which he had lugged into the room, and from it took and laid out on a table the books and papers which he had brought from the London office.

But before we turned to these, Eddison wanted to question William Heggus on the contents of the letter which William had written to James Martenroyde and had been handed by James to me. That letter was now in Eddison's possession, and he produced it, explaining to William what he wanted to know.

"You'd got uneasy about things at Gresham Street, I suppose, William?" he began. "That was what made you write to Mr. Martenroyde?"

"I'd been getting uneasy for some time, sir," replied William. "It had been on my mind to write long before I did."

"You thought things were going wrong?"

"I knew Mr. Sugden wasn't attending to things as he should have done, sir. You see, he'd too much power. Mr. Martenroyde very rarely came up to town. When he did he'd only just look in at our office. He scarcely ever looked at the books – he'd take Mr. Sugden's word for anything. If he ever asked me a question he paid next to no attention to whatever answer I made him. I'm bound to say, Mr. Eddison, that Mr. Martenroyde was careless."

"Well, you say Sugden didn't attend to the business as he should have done. Do you mean he wasn't regular in attendance at the office?"

"What I mean is this, sir: He spent half his time away from the office. He'd look in of a morning, do a few things, and go away. Sometimes for a day or two at a time he'd never come near. And I know that he used to go to the races. I can't, of course, say for certain, but I've an idea that he bet a good deal. There were some what I should call questionable characters used to call on him now and then – racing men, by their look. They'd drop in and he'd go out with them, and when he did, the office saw no more of him that day."

"You say he'd full power there – too much power. Who kept the books?"

"He was supposed to keep them. He did keep them – in a way. They're there, Mr. Eddison – you can examine them for yourself. I doubt if they're posted up. He did what he liked with them. He'd full control over all the books, and the banking account, too."

"Didn't Mr. Martenroyde control that?"

"Well, of course I didn't know what precise arrangement they had. All I know is that all banking transactions in London were done by Sugden."

"What did you do?" inquired Halstead. "What was your job?"

"To look after the stockroom, sir. Nothing else. It was through that that I began to get uneasy."

"Why, exactly?"

"Because I felt certain that Sugden now and then sold stock and never accounted for it. Of course, all I'd to do was to carry out his orders and deliver stuff on his instructions."

"That'll take a bit of looking into," said Eddison. "Well, now, your letter to Mr. Martenroyde seems to suggest that you didn't think Sugden's life in London was all that it should have been.

Before we get on to these books, is there any particular fact or matter you want to tell us about?"

William Heggus hesitated.

"We want to know all we can, you know," continued Eddison, "and this is all in strict confidence. Don't be afraid to speak."

"Well, there is a matter that I know of that's perhaps nowt to do with the business," replied William, slowly. "A private affair, but it may have something to do with Sugden's goings-on. I don't know if you, Mr. Eddison, and you, Mr. Halstead, remember a young woman named Louie Sparks, who was employed as a clerk in the office here at Martenroyde's mill and who disappeared suddenly about eighteen months ago? There was some talk about it at the time, I remember, when I came down here for a holiday, summer before last. A very pretty girl – came from Leeds way."

"I remember her," said Halstead. "Case of French leave. She was a typist in James Martenroyde's office at the mill. She went off without giving any notice – I remember James's talking to me about it. A smart lass! – she'd been a sort of favourite of his, and he'd given her very good wages."

"What about her, William?" asked Eddison.

William Heggus gave us a sort of shy look.

"Well, I don't want to say anything that would seem to reflect on a young woman's character," he said diffidently, "but the fact is, I've seen Louie Sparks with Mr. Sugden – twice. They seemed very thick, too."

"Where did you see 'em?" asked Eddison.

"Once was one Sunday morning, in Hyde Park. They didn't see me, but I was as close to 'em as I am to you. Sugden – he's always been a swell, since he got up there to London, and he was dressed up proper. And the girl – well, I shouldn't care to have to pay for what she'd got on!"

"Expensively dressed, eh?" suggested Halstead.

"Height of fashion, sir," replied Heggus. "Carried it off well, too."

"You said you saw them together twice?" said Eddison.

"Yes. The other time was at the theatre – the Shaftesbury. I'd been to another, near by, and I was coming past the Shaftesbury as the audience came out, and I saw Sugden and this Louie Sparks. They were in evening dress that time – regular nobs. I'd a close look at 'em as they were getting into a taxicab."

"You're sure you aren't mistaken?" asked Eddison.

"Nay!" replied Heggus promptly. "I've known him ever since he was a lad at Shipton Grammar School, and I saw her a good many times when she was in Mr. Martenroyde's office here. No mistake."

There was a brief silence after this. Then Halstead spoke.

"Happen Sugden's wed her?" he said. "If he has, he'd hear his mother's voice about it – I mean if he wedded this lass on the sly."

Nobody offered any comment on that, and Eddison turned once more to William Heggus.

"Where does Sugden live in London?" he asked. "Lodge, I mean."

"I know where he did lodge," replied Heggus, "and I know that he doesn't lodge there now. When I got the news about what had happened to Mr. Martenroyde I went up to his old lodgings, thinking to catch him there before he set off for home, but the woman that keeps them, she said he'd left her some time before, and she didn't know where he'd gone. So I know nowt about his present private address in London."

"Ramsden must have known it," observed Beverley. "Ramsden got in immediate touch with him as early as he could the morning after their uncle's death."

Eddison turned to me.

"If we could get that address," he said, "your people in London could make an inquiry or two there, Camberwell. We ought to know if this young lady is there, and if she's Mrs. Sugden

Martenroyde. She may be. Anyway, according to William here, somebody's buying her fine clothes. Well, now, William, is there anything more of what you'd call the private side? Any more revelations – or suspicions?"

"Nay," replied Heggus, "I don't know that there is, Mr. Eddison. I've not cared about retelling all that you've heard. I felt it a duty to write to Mr. Martenroyde, believing as I did—"

"Quite right, William, quite right," said Eddison. "Well, now, then, let's get to work on these books. Pull your chairs round that table and we'll make a thorough job of it. William, you'll have to explain everything. Keep, to begin with, to the main points, the really important points."

We drew up our chairs, and William Heggus began his task. It was then approaching nine o'clock. Two hours later we were still at it, and, indeed, only just getting fairly into it. Eddison interrupted matters then to ring for his housekeeper and order some refreshments. Midnight came and we were still following Heggus from one transaction to another, still laboriously tracing entries in ledgers and cash-books and stock-books and – only too often! – seeking for entries which were not to be found. Not until five o'clock in the morning did the end come. But when it came, it was decisive. There was no doubt whatever that for some little time Sugden Martenroyde had been helping himself to stock and cash, and that had James Martenroyde lived he would have made some very unpleasant discoveries.

Eddison's servants, roused at this unearthly hour, made us some coffee, and over it we discussed our next proceedings. Beverley was now quite sure he had got what he wanted. James Martenroyde had signed his own death-warrant when he told Sugden that he should be in London shortly and would then examine the books at Gresham Street. Anyway, Beverley should now put all the facts he knew before his superiors; it would be for them to decide on the next step. He suggested that William Heggus should be sent back to London as secretly as he had been brought down, and that nothing should be done there or at Todmanhawe to arouse any suspicion in Sugden that he was being watched or suspected. He asked further if Eddison and Halstead, as trustees of the business, could not contrive to keep Sugden at Todmanhawe for a while, until the police authorities came to a decision about their procedure. Eventually Eddison decided on a plan of action. We all snatched a couple of hours sleep and woke to find breakfast ready for us. That over, William Heggus was packed off to London in the same secret way by which he had been brought down to Todmanhawe. The books and papers, however, Eddison retained for examination by a firm of accountants. Beverley, armed with his newly acquired knowledge, went off to lay it before his superiors – and I was left to do I scarcely knew what. And what I did was to sit down alone and review the situation as I saw it.

It was useless to deny that I saw things in a very different light from that in which Beverley was seeing them. He had got it firmly fixed in his head that Sugden Martenroyde was the murderer of his uncle. Sugden, knowing himself guilty of various defalcations and misappropriations at the London office and that the examination of the books threatened by James Martenroyde would reveal his guilt, had sneaked back to Todmanhawe that Monday evening, lain in wait for his uncle at the mill weir, and silenced him – in very brutal fashion. It was an obvious conclusion – in Beverley's opinion. But it was not mine. From the little I had seen of Sugden, I had formed the opinion that he was sly, crafty, capable of shifts and evasions, and no fool. Would anybody but a fool have done what we knew Sugden had done – gone, at half past two in the morning, to a station where he was well known and would be sure to be recognised? He would have known that somebody would recognise him and that the first inevitable result of the recognition would be an inquiry as to his movements between 5.41 on the Monday evening and 2.36 on the Tuesday morning. I could not conceive it possible that any man of even average common sense could – with the guilty knowledge of murder in his heart – so render himself liable to what would be almost certain detection.

Yet – believing the evidence of the two workmen, Outwin and Guest, to be reliable – there was no doubt whatever that Sugden Martenroyde, after boarding a local train at Abbeyside station at 5.41 on that Monday afternoon, left it at some other station almost at once and made his way back to the immediate neighbourhood of Todmanhawe. Why? What was his object? Where was he going when Outwin and Guest saw him hurrying along the Hartwick-Todmanhawe road? Somewhere, of course. Was it to his mother's house? He could have gained that very easily and unobserved from where the two men saw him. At a point not far from there, near Dakin Heggus's house, a footpath turned away from the road and led down to the weir bridge. At the end of the bridge – the mill end – he could have turned along the riverbank to where the garden of the Mill House stretched down to the river. Was the Mill House the object of his return? Had he forgotten something? Did he – having reflected on James Martenroyde's statement about James's forthcoming visit to London and what he knew would be a consequence of it – want to see his mother and Ramsden on that matter? Or was there anybody in or near Todmanhawe that he wished to see? Was it a case, for instance, of his wanting to borrow money from some friend or acquaintance wherewith to put his accounts straight? That was a possibility which had occurred to me from the first. But I did not know sufficient of the neighbourhood or of its people to know of anyone to whom Sugden could turn for financial help, and Beverley, on this point, had no suggestions to make.

I was faced with certain facts – facts which were indisputable. One: James Martenroyde was murdered that night. Two: Sugden Martenroyde was somewhere in the neighbourhood. Sugden, in view of what we had discovered, had a motive for ridding himself of his uncle. But the more I thought things over, the more I felt convinced that of any actual murder Sugden was innocent. So – who was guilty? Who was it that lay in wait for James Martenroyde at the end of that bridge and struck him down in the darkness?

Here I began to think a great deal about a certain piece of information at which Beverley had smiled – the story told us by the old woman, Priscilla Mallison. I had watched her carefully as she told her tale, and I was convinced that she had seen somebody lurking near the lych-gate at Todmanhawe churchyard. A ghost, in her opinion – in mine, a thing of flesh and blood. Who was it? In all probability, the actual murderer. Then – who was he?

The more I thought over all these things, the more I was convinced that there was a mystery behind them at which, so far, none of us had even guessed. More than once I wondered if the slight sounds which I had heard in the conservatory of the grange during my talk with James Martenroyde – put down by him to the straying of one of his cats – had any significance. Had there been someone in that conservatory listening to our conversation? Was it Sugden? But how was I to find that out? I found it difficult to find out anything. I got nothing from the people to whom I talked. I was a stranger, a foreigner, to them, and to me they would say nothing and tell nothing.

During the next few days things remained as they were; I certainly made no progress. Then, just a week after our interview with William Heggus, Beverley, accompanied by two of his detectives, walked in on Eddison and me one morning and told us that a warrant for Sugden Martenroyde's arrest was in his pocket.

12

WHAT OF TOMORROW?

I WAS NOT PRESENT at the arrest of Sugden Martenroyde. I had no official status in that matter; moreover, as I have already explained, I was by no means assured that Beverley and his superiors were not making a mistake. Mr. Eddison, I think, shared my opinion, however puzzled he might be by the facts already known to us.

"I suppose you know what you're doing," he remarked when Beverley told us what he was going to do.

"I've no option," replied Beverley. "It's been fully gone into at headquarters, and my duty is to execute this warrant."

"Well—" said Eddison. He hesitated as if about to make some comment, but made none. "There's no more to be said, then. You'll bring him before the magistrates – when?"

"Ten thirty tomorrow morning," replied Beverley. "Just a formal affair – but you'll both be there, of course."

"We'll be there," agreed Eddison. Then, as Beverley went off, he added: "Get him away as quietly as you can, Beverley – we don't want any scenes. And his mother will probably make one if she's about."

We watched Beverley and his two men drive off; from the windows of Eddison's dining room we saw the car go down the hill and turn into the lane leading to Mill House. In what seemed a very short time we saw it come out of the lane again and turn in the direction of Shipton. And in a few minutes more, still watching from the window, we saw Mrs. Martenroyde and Ramsden turn the corner of the lane and come in our direction.

"I expected that," said Eddison. "They're coming to see me. Well, I'd better see them." He rang the bell and gave his parlour-maid an instruction. "Stay here, Camberwell," he added when the girl had gone. "You'd better hear what they have to say. I knew they'd come here!"

A minute or two later mother and son were shown into the room. They had evidently come straight from whatever they were doing. Ramsden wore the linen overalls in which he went about the mill; Mrs. Martenroyde was in her workaday gown with its sleeves rolled up; it seemed to me, from a deposit of flour on her muscular arms, that she had been interrupted in the act of baking bread. I looked at her closely as she entered; one look showed me that this was not the virago who had smashed the dead man's china and wished ill to his departed soul. She was in a chastened mood, and I saw fear in her eyes.

"Mr. Eddison," she said, speaking as soon as she got into the room, "Mr. Eddison, Beverley's taken our Sugden off to Shipton and says he'll be charged with the murder of his uncle! Of course, it's impossible, Mr. Eddison! I cannot think what Beverley means by such a course. But do you know owt about it, Mr. Eddison?"

"No more than that Beverley considers he's cause to make the arrest, Mrs. Martenroyde," replied Eddison.

"But it's an impossible charge, Mr. Eddison," she said. "We all know that at the time James Martenroyde came to his end, Sugden was on his way to London! He couldn't have done owt to his uncle. He was miles and miles away!"

Eddison made no reply. Instead, he looked at Ramsden. In Ramsden he saw what I had already seen – an expression of blank surprise. And Ramsden, catching the interrogative look, spoke.

"Went off by the 5.41 that afternoon," he said. "I know he did."

Still Eddison hesitated. And Mrs. Martenroyde spoke again.

"Mr. Eddison – I'm his mother," she said. "If you know owt—"

Eddison looked at me as if to seek advice. Getting no response – for I was more interested in his visitors than in him – he took a turn or two about the room.

"Mrs. Martenroyde," he said, coming to a sudden stop, "I may as well tell you and Ramsden, for you'll hear it all before long: Sugden was not on his way to London that evening on which his uncle was murdered. He was here in Todmanhawe."

Watching Mrs. Martenroyde closely, I saw at once that this news came to her as an absolute revelation, and that whatever Sugden's movements had been that Monday evening, he had given no particulars of them to his mother. She stared at Eddison – and at Ramsden – and at me: a stare of amazement. Then she shook her head.

"He went—" she began.

"My man saw him off!" exclaimed Ramsden. "He did go! He couldn't have been at Todmanhawe that night. It's damned nonsense! He was in London at half past eight next morning, I do know. He got that telegram from me, in London, at that time."

"Who says he was here?" demanded Mrs. Martenroyde. "Whoever does is a liar!"

Eddison waved his hand as if to dismiss further discussion.

"It's no use going into it now," he said. "It'll all be gone into before the magistrates. But I may as well tell you that Sugden was seen here that evening, and that he was also seen to leave Shipton a few hours later, by the 2.36 express. That," he added, "would get him to St. Pancras at eight o'clock. He'd get your telegram, Ramsden, just as he reached his lodgings."

"But who saw him here?" persisted Mrs. Martenroyde. "I've a right to know. I'm his mother. And a charge like that – murder!"

"You'll hear all about it in due course," said Eddison. "Now, as you've come to me, tell me – what did Sugden say when Beverley came to him just now?"

"Say?" exclaimed Mrs. Martenroyde. "He was too much taken aback to say owt!"

"He said nowt," replied Ramsden. "I told him to say nowt. I knew there was some mistake. I told him to go with 'em, quiet, and to hold his tongue till we'd seen you. Mr. Eddison – what's to be done?"

"There's only one thing to be done, my lad," replied Eddison. "He'll have to face the charge and answer it. If he can clear himself, all the better. Now, have you got a solicitor in Shipton?"

Ramsden shook his head.

"Never had no occasion for owt of that sort," he answered.

"I know Mr. Sharpley," said Mrs. Martenroyde. "I once went to him when I'd some linen stolen."

"Sharpley's an old man," remarked Eddison. "Now, you do what I tell you, Ramsden. Get your car and drive your mother into Shipton. Go to young Pybus – tell him I've sent you. Take him straight off to see Sugden. Make Sugden tell him his side of the story. The plain, absolute truth, mind you! – no lies and no keeping anything back. Then Pybus will see to his defence, and to his witnesses if he has any. And go at once."

"Will they let us or Pybus see him?" asked Mrs. Martenroyde.

"Beverley will let you all see him," replied Eddison. "Go straight to Pybus – he'll see to everything for you. Now be off! And, Ramsden, mind you impress on Sugden that he's to tell Pybus everything – everything, do you hear?"

"I'll see to it," answered Ramsden, with a grim look. "He'll have to. But it licks me, Mr. Eddison. Sugden did go away on the 5.41."

"Be off with you both and get your car," said Eddison. "The sooner Pybus and you see Sugden, the better. Have it out with him."

Mother and son went away without further speech. Watching them go side by side down the garden, I noticed their quietness and silence and commented on it to my host.

"Ramsden Martenroyde never was a man of many words," said Eddison, "and his mother has had the shock of her life. I'm wondering if she will be able to get Sugden to say anything. If she can't, and Pybus can't, then nobody can. Pybus is a smart fellow – a bit brusque and bullying, but that's what's wanted in this case. If Sugden was here, in the neighbourhood, that Monday evening, Sugden's got a good deal to explain. You'll not be surprised, I suppose, if he does give an explanation?"

"No," I replied, "I shan't."

"An explanation that will upset Beverley?" he added.

"I shan't be surprised at that either," I assented.

"You still think Beverley may be on the wrong tack?" he asked, with a sly smile. "Not the tack you'd have taken?"

"I think Beverley has been a little precipitate," I said. "I should have made more exhaustive inquiry."

"Oh, well, Beverley's a policeman," he said indulgently. "Policemen love a straight line, and Beverley thinks he's on one, with nothing to do but follow it to the end. We'll see how he works things out. If Sugden has a good case and confides in Pybus, Beverley will find his theories upset. We may get a revelation tomorrow – I know Pybus and his methods. He'll fight."

Some few hours after that, as Eddison and I were down in the lower part of the village, returning from a call on Colonel Houston and his daughter, who were still staying at the Scarthdale Arms, Ramsden and his mother came along in their car, evidently home again from their excursion to Shipton. With no more than a mere acknowledgment of our presence, they were passing us, but Eddison hailed them loudly, and Ramsden, with obvious unwillingness, pulled up.

"Well?" said Eddison, going up to the side of the car. "You've seen Pybus?"

Mrs. Martenroyde opened what until then had been tightly shut lips.

"We've seen Mr. Pybus," she replied, "and Mr. Pybus has seen our Sugden."

"Well?" inquired Eddison, expectantly. "And—"

"We haven't anything more to say – at present," answered Mrs. Martenroyde, acidly. "You can go on, Ramsden."

"Here, stop a bit!" exclaimed Eddison. "Come, now! I sent you to Pybus. Did Pybus—"

"We've no call to say more just now," said Mrs. Martenroyde firmly. "There's a time for speech, Mr. Eddison, and there's a time for silence. And we can hold our tongues as well as anybody. Now, Ramsden, drive on."

Ramsden drove on; the car moved off in the direction of Mill House, and Eddison turned to me.

"Not very promising for Beverley's case, that, Camberwell!" he said. "That woman's in quite a different mood now from what she was before I sent her to see Pybus. Pybus has got something out of Sugden! I shouldn't wonder if you're right – and Beverley's all wrong."

Beverley himself turned up at Eddison's late in the day. He looked worried and puzzled.

"Have you seen those Martenroydes since they came back from Shipton?" he asked. "Yes? Did they tell you anything? No? Um! – Well, Pybus has been to see me. A rather high-handed sort of chap, Mr. Eddison! He lays down the law!"

"What's he been to see you about?" asked Eddison.

"Just to tell me that when Sugden's put before the magistrates tomorrow morning, he'll oppose any application for a remand," replied Beverley. "He as good as said that I was a fool and that he'd upset any evidence we could bring as soon as it was brought. He knows something. He'd a long talk with Sugden, and when he left him I saw Pybus and Mrs. Martenroyde and Ramsden go across to the bank. They were there some time. Pybus – however, it's no good bothering about it now. I say there is a case against Sugden. What do you suppose Pybus's defence will be?"

But Eddison smiled and shook his head.

"You'll hear it in the morning, Beverley," he said. "I can make a good guess at it. If it's what I think, the magistrates won't give you a remand, so you'd better be prepared with your case and witnesses. Has Sugden made any statement to you?"

"No," replied Beverley; "not one word!"

13

THE PERFECT ALIBI

SUGDEN MARTENROYDE, IN THE presence of a crowded court, was duly placed before the local magistrates next morning, charged with the murder of his uncle, James Martenroyde, and after some discussion between the Chairman, Mr. Cordukes, appearing for the police, and Mr. Pybus, representing the accused, it was agreed, all the necessary witnesses being present, that the case should be gone into at once. Thereupon Mr. Cordukes opened for the prosecution, whose theory, summarised, was that Sugden, having reason to fear James Martenroyde's threatened examination of the books and accounts at Gresham Street, had secretly returned to Todmanhawe immediately after his departure for London and, lying in wait for his uncle near the weir bridge, had killed him by a blow from some heavy weapon. The evidence brought forward in support of this theory was, of course, fully familiar to me, but in pursuance of my usual plan I made a summary of it in my notebook, as follows:

Orris, chauffeur to the late James Martenroyde, examined by Mr. Cordukes, said that on the night of Monday, January 25th, Mr. Martenroyde, following his invariable practice, left Todmanhawe Grange at ten o'clock to walk round his mill. The witness and Mrs. Haines, housekeeper, sat up for him, as usual. At 12.15 he had not returned. Usually he returned by half past ten. Mrs. Haines, feeling sure that something had happened, went up with witness to rouse Mr. Camberwell, a visitor who had arrived that evening from London. After matters had been explained to Mr. Camberwell, he and witness set out to look for Mr. Martenroyde. Witness knew exactly which way Mr. Martenroyde went every night, and took Mr. Camberwell that way. They found Mr. Martenroyde's dead body on the river-bank near the end of the footbridge which crossed the river near the mill weir.

Dr. Ponsford, practising at Todmanhawe, said that he was fetched to the riverbank near Todmanhawe Mill about half an hour after midnight on Tuesday morning, January 26th. He found several people grouped about the dead body of Mr. James Martenroyde. He made a preliminary examination there and then and a more definite one later. He had no hesitation in saying that Mr. Martenroyde's death was caused by violent blows on the head – precise particulars of which he gave. There had been two blows, and either was of sufficient violence to cause death. Death would be practically instantaneous and, in witness's opinion, took place some two and a half hours, or thereabouts, before his examination of the body.

Ronald Camberwell, a partner in the firm of Chaney and Chippendale, private inquiry agents, of Jermyn Street, London, said that he arrived at Todmanhawe Grange on Monday, January 25th, as a result of a request from Mr. James Martenroyde that a member of the firm should visit him at once. He gave a detailed account of Mr. Martenroyde's conversation with him on the subject of a letter from William Heggus, an employee at the Gresham Street warehouse, and produced the letter spoken of. He could not say that Mr. Martenroyde was definitely suspicious about his nephew Sugden's conduct of the London business, but he was certain that Mr. Martenroyde intended to satisfy himself about the somewhat vague charges brought by William Heggus, and he also knew that Mr. Martenroyde had told Sugden that he himself during his approaching visit to London would take the opportunity of going through the books and accounts with him. Witness then corroborated the evidence of the chauffeur Orris as regards the search for Mr. Martenroyde and the discovery of his dead body.

Stephen Eddison, solicitor, now retired from practice, said that as one of the trustees of the will of the late James Martenroyde, and in consequence of information supplied to him by the last witness immediately after Mr. Martenroyde's death, he sent to London for the books and papers of the Gresham Street office and, in company with his co-trustee, Mr. Halstead, Mr. Camberwell, and Superintendent Beverley, made a thorough examination of them. The accounts were in great confusion and none of them satisfactory. The account at the London bank was overdrawn. In his opinion, Mr. Martenroyde, had he lived to make the examination himself, would have found everything not merely irregular but culpable. Mr. Sugden Martenroyde appeared to have had unusual licence accorded to him by his uncle, and, in witness's opinion, he had abused it. Witness, knowing James Martenroyde as he did, felt sure that had he lived to make the proposed examination of books and accounts, Sugden would have come under his heavy displeasure.

Up to this point Mr. Pybus, representing the accused, had not asked a single question of any of the witnesses for the prosecution. But when Mr. Cordukes had done with Eddison, Pybus rose.

"I want to ask you a very simple question, Mr. Eddison," he said. "Was there anything in these books, accounts, and papers which Mr. Sugden Martenroyde, who was responsible for them, could not have put straight?"

Eddison was somewhat taken aback by this question.

"Well," he replied, after a slight hesitation, "I suppose there wasn't."

"The bank account, for instance. You have just said it was overdrawn. Couldn't Mr. Sugden Martenroyde have put that straight?"

"He could, of course – by paying in sufficient funds," replied Eddison.

"Supposing Mr. Sugden to be faced by two alternatives," asked Pybus; "one: to put the bank account straight; the other, to kill his uncle before his uncle could find out that the bank account wasn't straight – which do you think he'd be likely to adopt?"

"I think that's an absurd question," retorted Eddison. "I—"

"No more absurd than to ask their worships to believe that my client murdered his uncle and employer because the bank account was a bit on the wrong side!" said Pybus. He turned to the bench. "Your worships," he went on, "the bank account in London is straight. There was never any question of its being straight. If Mr. James Martenroyde had lived to make his proposed examination of the Gresham Street office bank accounts, he would have found it strictly in order."

"It was not in order when I examined the pass-book!" declared Eddison.

"It is in order – perfect order – now, anyway," said Pybus quietly, "and could have been put in order at any moment. I have no more to ask this witness."

(Eddison and I subsequently discovered that the previous afternoon Pybus, Mrs. Martenroyde, and Ramsden Martenroyde, after interviewing Sugden in the police station, had visited the local bank at Shipton, and thence sent considerable funds to the bank in London at which the Gresham Street account was kept, thereby putting it in credit.)

Nor – a matter of surprise, I think, to those of us who had known what evidence they would give and what its importance was – had Pybus any question to put to the next two witnesses, the workmen Outwin and Guest. He accepted this evidence quietly, indifferently, making no sign. Yet it was positive evidence, proving beyond doubt that Sugden Martenroyde certainly returned to Todmanhawe that Monday evening – returned after openly departing for London. Those two witnesses were of the sort whose testimony is invariably believed by magistrates or by juries – plain, unimaginary men who tell a straight tale, devoid of all trimmings. That Outwin and Guest saw Sugden on the road between Hartwick and Todmanhawe on the evening of James Martenroyde's death no one could doubt after hearing their evidence.

But Pybus did a little questioning of the old woman, Prissy Mallison, who, in answer to Mr. Cordukes, repeated the story which she had told to Beverley and me. Cordukes humoured her about her belief that the figure she saw was the Todmanhawe ghost; his theory, of course, was that what the witness actually saw was Sugden, lying in wait for his victim. Pybus humoured her, too; his questions were directed to fixing the exact time at which she saw the ghost. He did this to his own evident satisfaction; Prissy, old as she was, was in full possession of her faculties and of an unimpaired memory, and Pybus had no difficulty in establishing the fact that what she saw, ghost, goblin, or human being, at the lych-gate of Todmanhawe churchyard was seen between nine thirty and ten o'clock.

There remained only two witnesses for the prosecution when Prissy Mallison had stumped out of the box, still chattering about the ghost. One was the booking-clerk who had been on duty at Shipton station in the early morning of Tuesday, January 26th; the other was a porter also on duty at that time. Both these men professed an intimate knowledge of Mr. Sugden Martenroyde's appearance; both testified that he left Shipton for London by the Scotch express, leaving Shipton at 2.36 and arriving at St. Pancras at eight o'clock.

With this evidence the case for the prosecution came to an end, and Pybus rose to address the magistrates. He said little, beyond making some caustic remarks as to the theory of the prosecution with regard to motive. Their worships, he said, were asked to believe that his client had got the affairs of the Gresham Street office into such a mess that, hearing of his uncle's intention of looking into them, he had no way of escape but by murdering that uncle! However, he was not going to waste the time of the court over discussion of that matter – the real question before their worships was one of his client's guilt or innocence. That James Martenroyde died as the result of a savage attack upon him, there was no doubt; there was no doubt, either, that his death took place – never mind the exact moment – between the hours of ten o'clock on the Monday night and twelve thirty on the ensuing midnight. And he would now show that during the space of time covered by those hours Sugden Martenroyde was not in nor indeed near Todmanhawe.

The Chairman: "Your defence, then, Mr. Pybus, is an alibi?"

Mr. Pybus: "Precisely, your worship. When your worships have heard it, I think you will admit it to be the perfect alibi. Call Mr. Mawson Calvert."

Mawson Calvert, a smart, well-dressed young fellow of probably twenty-five years of age, stepped into the box with something like a show of eagerness. I had noticed him when I first entered the court, sitting in company with another young man of similar appearance, who sat by a pretty girl, evidently his wife or his sister or, perhaps, his fiancée. Examined by Pybus his evidence was thus summarised in my book:

Witness said he was a junior partner in the firm of Samuel Calvert, Limited, manufacturers, of Wiseley. He knew the accused, Sugden Martenroyde, well – they were old schoolmates. On Monday, January 25th, Sugden came to him at the mill office at Wiseley, about ten minutes past six in the evening, just as he himself was leaving business for the day. Sugden said he wanted him to do something for him. Sugden had set off for London and had remembered when in the train that there was something he had left undone at Todmanhawe, so he had left the train on its arrival at Wiseley station. He wanted witness to drive him back to near Todmanhawe, and then, after he had done what he wanted to do, to Shipton, where, Sugden said, he could get a train to London early in the morning. Witness consented to do this and, his car being in the mill yard, he and

Sugden got into it and went in the direction of Todmanhawe. On the way Sugden told him that what he wanted to do – the thing he had forgotten to do – was of a secret and confidential nature, and he didn't want anybody to know anything about it. He asked witness to pull up his car at a certain place near Hartwick village and to wait there for him an hour, and witness agreed to this. They arrived at this place – a crossroads – a little before half past seven and agreed to meet there again at half past eight. Sugden set off along the road to Todmanhawe. Witness, not wanting to spend an hour by himself on a wind-swept hillside, ran his car down the valley to Abbeyside and had a drink at the inn there. At half past eight he was back at the appointed meeting-place. Sugden came along the road from Todmanhawe a few minutes later, and they drove away towards Shipton. On the way witness asked Sugden what he would do with himself while waiting for the train Sugden had spoken of. Sugden replied that he would wait at one of the hotels in Shipton. Witness suggested that instead of doing that they should call on a friend and old schoolfellow of both, Mr. Charles Pollard, who lived in Shipton. Sugden agreed, and they drove to Mr. Pollard's, arriving at his house soon after nine o'clock. They had supper at Mr. Pollard's, and afterwards Mr. Pollard, his sister, Sugden, and witness played bridge until nearly two o'clock in the morning. At two o'clock Sugden left Mr. Pollard's house to catch the Scotch express. Witness drove home to Wiseley. In answer to a final question from Pybus, witness said that from eight thirty o'clock on Monday evening, January 25th, until two o'clock on Tuesday morning, January 26th, Sugden Martenroyde was never out of his sight.

Questioned by Mr. Cordukes, witness said that he had no knowledge whatever as to Sugden's movements between half past seven and half past eight on the Monday evening. Sugden did not tell him where he was going when he left the car at the crossroads near Hartwick, nor mention the names of any persons he wanted to see. All Sugden ever said to him on those points was that he'd forgotten to do something very particular before leaving Todmanhawe and wanted to go back there for a few minutes. After rejoining him at half past eight, Sugden made no further reference to the matter.

Pybus now called Mr. Charles Pollard, but the Chairman intervened before Mr. Pollard could enter the witness-box.

"After the evidence we have just had, Mr. Pybus," he said, "we consider that there is no necessity to hear further evidence. Mr. Pollard, I suppose, would corroborate Mr. Calvert as regards the accused's movements and whereabouts from nine o'clock on the Monday evening?"

"Not only Mr. Pollard, your worship, but also Miss Maisie Pollard," replied Pybus. "I propose to call both."

"There is no need," said the Chairman. "The bench is satisfied. Mr. Sugden Martenroyde is discharged."

Pybus: "I ask for costs, your worship – on the ground that this is a prosecution which should never have been brought."

Cordukes: "I submit, your worships, that my friend is not justified in making that assertion. This prosecution was started in the same way as any important prosecution is. It was not started by the Superintendent nor by his immediate superiors; it was started after due consideration by police headquarters and further consideration by their legal advisers. It would be a lamentable thing if the authorities, after such consideration, were ordered to pay the accused's costs."

The Chairman: "There will be no order as to costs."

Eddison and I left the court on that. There was a great crowd outside the court-house, largely composed of Todmanhawe folk, and the result of the magisterial sitting was already known. It seemed to me a strange thing that the crowd was utterly silent; it just melted away, whispering. As for myself, I was wondering – wondering why Sugden Martenroyde got his friend to drive him back to Todmanhawe.

14

PLAN OF CAMPAIGN

BEVERLEY, BRIEFLY INTERVIEWED BY Eddison and myself after the court proceedings were over, was plainly in high dudgeon. He had worked himself up into a state of firm belief in Sugden Martenroyde's guilt, and to see his carefully built castle knocked to pieces by one discharge of matter-of-fact evidence from Mawson Calvert had given him a surprise from which he was slow to recover. To doubt Mawson Calvert's word was – so Eddison said, knowing everybody in the district – absolutely impossible. Mawson belonged to a well-known trading family, of high repute thereabouts; so, too, did the brother and sister whose evidence the magistrates had not even troubled themselves to hear. All that had resulted from Beverley's gathering of witnesses had been the establishment of Sugden's innocence.

"Came a cropper there!" said Beverley, with a rueful grimace. "Got to begin all over again."

Eddison and I went back to his house at Todmanhawe to talk things over. Somebody was responsible for James Martenroyde's murder, and Eddison was not the man to let the thing figure as a nine days' mystery and then to relapse into the category of problems which remain unsolved. And once more he commissioned me to go still further into the matter.

"Just tell me, frankly, how things strike you now, Camberwell," he said. "Now, I mean, that Sugden's cleared."

"That's a very difficult question to answer," I replied. "I'm in this position – a stranger like myself has little or no chance of getting information from your Todmanhawe people. I've already seen that they won't talk to me – an outsider. Probably you have here more than one person who could tell something, perhaps a good deal, but he or she or they won't tell it to me. If I had any means of getting into their confidence—"

"For that matter, though I've lived here half my life, they wouldn't tell me anything," he interrupted. "Clan feeling. These folk can be as close as limpets if they think that one of the clan's in danger. Yet there may be a way of hearing something."

"Yes? What way?" I asked.

"Well, I've wondered if it would be of any use to offer a reward, a substantial reward – nothing less would do – for information," he replied. "What do you think?"

"A very good idea," I answered. "But – would anyone in possession of real information sell it if he or she knew that possibly a neighbour, even a friend, was going to be put in peril? What about the feeling you've just referred to?"

"They would – if they knew that what they told was to be told in absolute secrecy and confidence," he replied. "Yes!"

"Then a reward is an excellent thing to offer," I said. "If I could only get the merest clue—"

"You've no idea that you're keeping to yourself?" he asked.

"I've a lot of ideas," I said. "Perhaps not so much ideas as speculations – questions that I put to myself! Lots of 'em! Was there anybody in Martenroyde's conservatory that night, listening to his talk to me about Sugden? He said it was a cat – it sounded to me like human footsteps, stepping softly – I even fancied I heard a door close. Then, why did Sugden Martenroyde turn in his tracks and get Mawson Calvert to drive him back to Todmanhawe? And whose was the figure that the old woman, Prissy Mallison, saw lurking about the churchyard gate? There are other questions."

"Do you – from what you've heard and seen – actually suspect anyone?" he asked. "Say, if you do."

But I was not going to answer that – at that time. I had a growing suspicion that Mrs. Martenroyde might turn out to be the murderer of her brother-in-law, but it was not sufficiently formed to warrant me in mentioning her name.

"I've scarcely got to that," I replied. "I don't know enough. I wish I had some assistance. If this were a case in, say, London, I could make use of two assistants, our junior partner, Chippendale, and our chief woman assistant, Fanny Pratt. But here, among these people, they'd be of no more use than the man in the moon. Your folk wouldn't say a word to a couple of Cockneys!"

"What sort of assistance do you want?" he asked.

"What I want," I answered, "is to find somebody, man or woman, who is in intimate touch with the Todmanhawe people – the villagers, mill-workers, and so on – somebody who can tell me what they are saying, thinking – possibly what they know. If we were elsewhere – London, for instance – my first step would be either to get hold of some such person or to introduce one of our own assistants into the concern with instructions to keep his or her eyes and ears open. But I can't do that here – I've already seen enough of your people to realise that I'm a foreigner among them. They won't give themselves away to outsiders."

He smiled at that and for a minute or two sat silent, thinking.

"There may be means," he said after a pause. "Do you happen to have noticed a red-headed damsel about this house, now?"

"A red-headed damsel?" I exclaimed. "No."

"Oh, well, she doesn't come into this part of the house much," he said, "but she's here, all the same. A niece of my housekeeper's – her father and mother died about the same time a few years ago, and I told my housekeeper she could bring the lass here – she'd no other relations. She works at Martenroyde's mill, and her name's Avis Riley."

"Yes?" I said.

"I think," he went on, giving me a sly smile, "I think Avis might suit your purposes very well. She'll know all that's being said among the people."

"Yes, but will she talk?" I asked.

"I think she might – if we talk to her," he answered, again smiling. "We can try her, at any rate. I'll go round to the house-keeper's room and see if Avis is there. She's a smart lass," he went on as he rose and made for the door, "no fool – and if she warmed to the job, you'd find her invaluable. And she'd keep whatever we say to her to herself."

He went off, to return a few minutes later, ushering in a young woman of apparently twenty years of age, whom I had certainly not seen before, for if I had I should not have forgotten her. To say that she was a red-headed damsel was to give a mild description of a mass of auburn hair clustered round a homely but highly intelligent face in which the prominent features were a pair of honest grey eyes, a decidedly snub, wide-nostrilled nose, and a mouth somewhat capacious and indicative, by the curve of the lips, of a certain amount of sly humour. Neatly gowned in a dull green which made a worthy setting to her general high colouring, this specimen of dale womanhood had brought her knitting with her, and when Eddison bade her be seated, she took a chair between him and myself and proceeded to click her needles as steadily as if he and I were mere pieces of furniture.

"Now, Avis," said Eddison, "Mr. Camberwell and I want to have a bit of confidential talk with you. Mr. Camberwell's here to help me in trying to find out the secret about Mr. Marten-royde's death – murder, to be plain. Mr. Camberwell's a famous detective, you see, and—"

"That's what some of 'em are saying down at the mill, Mr. Eddison," interrupted the girl. "They sized Mr. Camberwell up pretty quick."

"Oh, they did, did they?" said Eddison, with a glance at me. "They've labelled him already?"

"Well, you see, Mr. Eddison, Mr. Camberwell went about with the Superintendent," replied Avis, "so they made it up that he was a plain-clothes policeman from London. They knew he wasn't a business gentleman."

"There you are, Camberwell!" said Eddison. "They've seen through you – trust 'em for that! Well—"

"Besides, Mr. Eddison," interrupted Avis, "there was what Mr. Camberwell said in Shipton police court this morning – it was all over the mill before the afternoon was over."

"Ay – to be sure it would be," assented Eddison. "I'd forgotten that. Well, now, my lass, Mr. Camberwell wants a bit of help. So do I. We must find out who killed James Martenroyde. And as you work down there and hear a lot of talk, we want you to tell us what's being said and what has been said since James Martenroyde's death."

The girl knitted steadily and silently for a minute or two. When she spoke, it was without lifting her eyes from the rapidly moving needles.

"It's between ourselves, Mr. Eddison," she said quietly. "I don't want anything that I say to get back to them folks down there. They'd have the skin off my back if they knew I told owt."

"Oh, you can be sure of that, my lass," replied Eddison. "Absolutely private and confidential – anything you say."

But Avis turned to me, giving me a straight, steady, searching look.

"I would like to hear Mr. Camberwell say that, too," she said. "Us Yorkshire folk like to know who we're talking to."

"It's my job to respect confidence," I said. "Anything that you tell me will be as if I'd never heard it – so far as repeating it goes."

"Well, I think you look a straight 'un," she answered frankly. "And no doubt Mr. Eddison'll go bail for you. Of course I do hear a good deal, and have heard a good deal – they do nowt but talk about it down yonder."

"And they say – what?" asked Eddison.

"All sorts of things, Mr. Eddison," replied Avis. "One says one thing, and one another."

"Such as – what?" said Eddison. "Tell us some of these things."

"Well, there's one thing they're all agreed on, Mr. Eddison," replied Avis. "They all say that the Mill House folk are at the bottom of it, all because Mr. Martenroyde was going to be married to Miss Houston. The Mill House lot were going to have their noses put out, so Mr. Martenroyde had to be shifted before he could pull it off. But as to how it was done, and who did it, they differ. One lot says that the truth hasn't come out and never will, because Mrs. Martenroyde's too clever – that lot say she worked it all. And there's another lot says that evidence that was given at the police court today was all cleverly got up, and that young Calvert said what he did to shield Sugden. They've all got ideas of their own, you see. But it all comes to what I said – that the Mill House folk know more than they'll ever tell. There are some of 'em," concluded Avis, with a click of her needles, "what I call whisperers, that say that Mrs. Martenroyde did it. They think she'd a row with Mr. Martenroyde that night and struck him."

"You've picked all this up?" asked Eddison. "They don't talk of it openly?"

"Why, Mr. Eddison, you know well enough how folk talk," replied Avis. "They talk amongst themselves, in holes and corners. If you were to talk to them, they'd say nowt – at least, nowt much. They're always afraid, as you know, that if they said owt that you'd call straightforward, they'd be made to prove it. Between themselves it's different."

"The general impression, then, is that the Mill House people were concerned – is that it?" said Eddison. "They're suspected?"

"Why, who else could there be?" asked Avis. "Somebody killed Mr. Martenroyde. And what they say is that you couldn't find man or woman amongst us mill-folk that would have lifted a hand against Mr. Martenroyde – no, nor anybody in this neighbourhood. He was liked, was Mr. Martenroyde. And you know, Mr. Eddison, they've all of 'em got their knives into Mrs. Martenroyde – they'd be glad enough if it was fastened on her!"

"Why?" asked Eddison.

"Because of what she said when Mr. Martenroyde was found," replied Avis. "She said – so it was reported – that some of the mill-folk had done it. And they'll never forgive her for that. She did for herself when she said a thing like that – they've stored it up against her."

Eddison and I exchanged glances. We both remembered the incident to which Avis referred, and the protest made, at once, by one of the workmen.

"You know what our folks are, Mr. Eddison," continued Avis. "They won't stand for what they consider an injustice. There isn't a man or woman in that mill that'll ever forgive Mrs. Martenroyde for what she said that night, because they felt it was accusing one and all. And if they could pin it down on her they would, I can tell you!"

"But you've never heard anything, any little rumour, that would help to pin it down on her?" asked Eddison. "Any mere incident that would show she'd something to do with it?"

But Avis shook her vividly coloured head.

"Nay," she answered, "I've never heard owt of that sort. If anybody knew anything, it would come out."

Eddison turned to me.

"Now, Camberwell," he said, "can you suggest any way in which this young lady can help?"

"Yes," I replied promptly. "Can she find out for me why Mrs. Martenroyde keeps that house of hers like a castle – refusing entrance to anybody unless she herself happens to be at home?"

"Some say it's because of Mrs. Martenroyde's teapot," said the girl.

"Teapot?" exclaimed Eddison. "What about that?"

"Eh, Mr. Eddison, I should have thought you'd have known about that!" replied Avis. "Why, Mrs. Martenroyde had a grand solid silver teapot, with a sugar bowl and cream jug to match, worth no end of money, she said – I'll lay she'd picked 'em up cheap at some auction or other, but she made out that they were worth a deal, and happen they were – and they used to stand on the mahogany sideboard in their living room, all for show. And one day when Mrs. Martenroyde was out and old Mally Brewster was busy washing in their back premises, somebody nipped into the house and made off with the lot. Mrs. Martenroyde blamed some of the neighbours for that, and since then she's never allowed a soul to cross the threshold unless she's about. Old Mally has to keep every door locked when the missus isn't there. But some folks say there's another reason than that," added Avis with a shake of her head. "They say that she kept everything very close before the silver went."

"Well, what reason?" asked Eddison.

"Why, they say she went queer when her sister died over in Lancashire; came so she wouldn't even believe it, like, and said to lots o' folks that Mill House should never be opened to outsiders till Miss Deborah came home, she being always the bright one and the hostess. Anyway, it's a fact that nobody's allowed in if she isn't there. That old Mally Brewster, they say, has never been out of the Mill House for many and many a year."

Avis and her knitting departed soon after that, with an understanding between her and me that if she heard anything said at the mill or in the village which seemed to throw any light on the mystery of James Martenroyde's death, she was to acquaint me at once. When she had gone, I remembered a question which I had meant to put to my host for some days and had up to then omitted to ask.

"The old woman who lives near Dakin Heggus, Prissy Mallison," I said, "told Beverley and me that when she saw what she calls the Todmanhawe ghost for the first time, its appearance heralded an outbreak of fire at the mill. Was there such an outbreak?"

"A slight outbreak, two or three years ago," replied Eddison, "and it looked very much like the work of an incendiary. There was a wooden shed at the rear of the mill premises, filled with waste stuff, and one night it was found on fire. The outbreak might have been serious, for the shed joined on to an old part of the mill which was entirely built of wood, and if the fire had spread, the whole place might have gone. Fortunately, it was discovered in time. That again," he added, "was on a wild winter night – I remember how the flames lit up the valley and the river."

"Did they ever find out how the fire originated?" I asked.

"No, never," replied Eddison. "James Martenroyde always believed that some workman, leaving the shed, had flung away the end of a cigarette. I don't think he ever had the idea that the fire was set going on purpose. But other people had. It looked, as I said, like an incendiary's work, and just about that time, James certainly was having a bit of bother with some of his men. But he never could be brought, at any time, to suspect any of his workfolk – he'd too much belief in them."

"Odd – that the ghost (probably a very substantial one) should appear just before the fire and then again just before Mr. Martenroyde's death," I said. "I should like to know more about that ghost. However, there's another matter – what about the reward we were talking about? Do you intend to offer one?"

We settled that there and then, and presently I drafted the copy for an advertisement to be inserted in the local paper and for a small poster to be exhibited and circulated in the Todman-hawe district. It promised a hundred pounds to anyone who could give any information which bore on the supposed murder, and asked any person capable of giving such information to communicate in strict confidence with Eddison himself. Next morning we had the posters printed, and before evening they were all over the neighbourhood.

A few days passed and nothing happened. Then, late one night, as Eddison and I sat in his dining room, smoking a final pipe before retiring, a faint tap, tap, tap sounded on the panes of a French window which communicated with the garden. We started in our chairs – and the tap, tap, tap was repeated.

15

THE CONSERVATORY DOOR

As the second series of gentle tappings ceased, Eddison sprang from his easy chair by the hearth and turned towards the window in a listening attitude. A moment of silence passed and then the tapping came again. He twisted sharply towards me.

"Camberwell," he exclaimed, "that's an answer to the advertisement! Somebody's there who wants secrecy. Some villager, evidently, who knows this house. Whoever it is won't talk before you. Slip behind that curtain – there – and when I've let in whoever it is, keep quiet and listen."

He pointed to a heavy curtain which overhung a deep-set doorway communicating with an inner room, and as he finished speaking I slipped behind it. There was plenty of room in this retreat, and the curtain being a heavy affair of silk plush, divided in the middle, I was able to so arrange its folds that I could see as well as hear. That there was something to see as well as to hear I knew a moment later. Eddison, going over to the window, drew the curtain aside and opened the sash. A keen breath of the night air blew into the room, and with it came the figure of a woman – a tall, spare figure, closely shrouded in one of those capacious shawls which the women mill-workers affected and wore draped over their heads and shoulders. This woman slightly drew back the shawl from her head as she stepped into the room, revealing a sharp-featured, dark-skinned face and a pair of watchful, sombre eyes, which as she came into the light took in the whole scene at a quick glance.

"Oh," said Eddison, "Ann Kitteridge!"

Ann Kitteridge drew the shawl further back, and I saw then that she was a woman whom I had more than once noticed about the village – a woman of something more than middle age and noticeable for her alert looks and upright, vigorous movements and figure.

"Ay, it's me, Mr. Eddison," she answered. "You're by yourself?"

Eddison waved his hand round the room.

"Sit you down," he said as he closed the window and pulled the curtains back in their place. "You want to see me?"

Ann Kitteridge took a chair by the hearth and nodded.

"That's what I come for, Mr. Eddison," she answered. "There's none of your folk'll come in, is there?"

"Gone to bed by this time," replied Eddison. "You're safe."

Ann Kitteridge let the shawl slip further from her head and shoulders and smoothed down the apron which covered her gown.

"You know me, Mr. Eddison," she said. "You know I'm a straight woman, as wouldn't tell you owt that wasn't true. I've got something to tell. You've offered money, a hundred pound, for information. I have some – but I'm not going to tell unless I'm sure what I tell will be kept secret."

"That's a condition," replied Eddison. "You know me, my lass. Say what it is without fear. If it's the sort of information I want, the money's all right. Now, it's about – somebody, eh? Who, now?"

Ann Kitteridge hesitated a moment, leaned forward, whispered.

"Hannah Martenroyde," she said.

There was a pause, during which the old lawyer, keen-eyed, always observant, and the woman, sharply alert, watched each other.

"Go on," said Eddison at last. "What about her?"

"Well, it's this, Mr. Eddison," replied Ann Kitteridge. "I've kept it to myself till now – not one word of it have I breathed to mortal soul. And should have kept it – but a hundred pound is a hundred pound and I could do with it, and I see no reason why I shouldn't tell."

"Tell!" said Eddison.

"Well, you remember that night when Martenroyde was put an end to, Mr. Eddison?" continued Ann Kitteridge. "A Monday night. I do a bit of washing for Mrs. Clough that lives the other side of the river, near the church. That night I'd taken the washing home, and as I wanted to get back to our house quick, I took the short cut, over the weir bridge, and came up the bank and through Martenroyde's grounds – it cuts off going round by the big bridge if you come that way, and though Martenroyde wasn't aware of it, lots of us as lives in the top here at Todmanhawe made use of his grounds and garden at night. Well, I come up that way – it was a wild night, you'll remember – and I'd got into his garden and was walking along the carriage drive in front of the grange when I heard the door of his conservatory open and saw somebody coming out. I thought it might be Martenroyde himself, and as I didn't want him to see me trespassing, like, I slipped behind a holly bunch. But it wasn't Martenroyde, nor yet a man. It was a woman – and the woman was Hannah Martenroyde."

"You're sure of that?" asked Eddison.

"Sure? Ay, certain, Mr. Eddison," replied Ann Kitteridge. "She passed as close to me as what I am to you now."

"Going which way?" inquired Eddison.

"Why, towards the path that leads from Martenroyde's garden to the weir bridge," said Ann Kitteridge – "the way I'd come up."

"That was a dark night," remarked Eddison, "a wild night, as you say. How did you manage to be sure it was Mrs. Martenroyde?"

"There was a deal of light from the house, Mr. Eddison. Several of the windows were lighted up, and the light fell full on her as she came past me," replied Ann Kitteridge. "And she's good to tell – a big woman like that. Oh, I knew her well enough. Passed close by me – talking to herself."

"Talking to herself, eh?" said Eddison. "What was she saying?"

"Nay, I couldn't tell that," answered Ann Kitteridge. "The wind was a strong 'un that night. Muttering, like, as if she was in a temper."

Eddison remained silent for a few minutes, the woman watching him. Then he rose, went over to the bureau, unlocked a drawer, took something from it, and, returning to the hearth, slipped that something into his visitor's hand.

"There's a bit to be going on with," he said. "If what you've told me proves useful you'll get the rest. Now then, go away and keep your tongue still – and if you've more to tell me, come again, at this time, the same way."

A moment later Ann Kitteridge, her shawl drawn closely about her, had gone as she came, and Eddison, closing the window upon her retreating figure, turned to the curtains behind which I had remained hidden, listening.

16

THE SILENT HOUSE

I HAD BEEN DOING some rapid thinking while hidden behind that curtain, listening to Ann Kitteridge's revelations. There was no doubt that the woman was telling Eddison a bit of plain truth. On the night of James Martenroyde's death, some little time before that had taken place, she had seen Mrs. Martenroyde of the Mill House leave the conservatory at the grange and go away towards the weir bridge, at the mill end of which James Martenroyde's dead body was found a few hours later. Nor was there any doubt that the sound which I had heard coming from the conservatory and to which I had drawn my host's attention, and which he had pooh-poohed as of no importance, was due to some movement of Mrs. Martenroyde's. And from this, knowing all that I knew by that time, it was not difficult to build up a theory which pointed to Mrs. Martenroyde's guilt in the matter of her brother-in-law's murder.

I argued things out this way: To begin with, Mrs. Martenroyde was just the sort of woman who, meeting me as she did on our ride together in James Martenroyde's car from Shipton to Todmanhawe, on the night of my arrival, would be suspicious as to the reason of my visit to the grange. It might be that she was not altogether easy in her mind as to her son Sugden's doings at the London office; Sugden, perhaps, had been raising money from her or Ramsden or both, for the purpose of putting his accounts straight. Intimately acquainted with the domestic arrangements of the grange, she had stolen up there and into the conservatory in the hope of overhearing some conversation between her brother-in-law and his guest. Remembering all that James Martenroyde had said to me during our conversation that first night of my visit, there could be no doubt that Mrs. Martenroyde, if she overheard what was said, would know that her son was in almost immediate danger: James was going up to London; James would examine the books at Gresham Street; and if James found that things were what they ought not to be, James would be merciless. Reckoning all this up, I considered it by no means impossible, and certainly not an unreasonable theory, that Mrs. Martenroyde, after stealing away from the conservatory, and knowing her brother-in-law's nightly habit of walking round his mill at a certain fixed time, waylaid him at the end of the weir bridge. What happened there, previous to the climax of the meeting, was a matter on which no one but herself could give a precisely true account. Probably all she wished was to have it out with the mill owner – to demand his intentions about Sugden, to ask why he was setting a private detective on her son's track. Probably she and her brother-in-law came to high words; probably, as he turned away from her, she lost all command of herself and struck him. She was a big, powerfully built, muscular woman, and a blow from the stick which she probably carried would be sufficient – had been sufficient – to clear James Martenroyde out of the way. And if she had done this thing of deliberate intention, who would suspect her? Sugden had left for London; Ramsden was away for the night at Shipton; the old servant at the Mill House, Mally Brewster, following the habits of the folk about there, was probably in bed – who would know or suspect that Mrs. Martenroyde's hand had cut short her brother-in-law's life? It was, at any rate, a theory; and if it was a true one, the figure which old Prissy, the so-called witch, had seen hanging about the lych-gate of the churchyard was, of course, Mrs. Martenroyde, waiting until

James came down the path from his house and across the bridge at the brawling weir.

I said all this, and more, to Eddison when Ann Kitteridge had vanished into the night and he and I had sat down again to discuss her information. And Eddison listened and in the end shook his head – not, I thought, in objection to my arguments, but in doubt.

"It wouldn't surprise me to find that Hannah Martenroyde killed James," he said. "Not deliberately, perhaps, but as the result of a row between them – I know that when she went about she always carried a heavy stick. Yes, and her fiendish temper's quite a byword in Todmanhawe, and beyond it. And I know, too, that she'd cherished a perfect hatred of James ever since he announced his forthcoming marriage to Miss Houston – she considered he was robbing her two lads of their just due. But if she did kill James, I see no chance of proving it. What direct evidence could you or I or anyone bring? The mere fact that Ann Kitteridge saw her in the grounds of the grange that night isn't enough, though important and significant. What other evidence is there? There's nobody who could say what time she returned to Mill House. Ramsden was away, at Shipton; Sugden was with his friends. And there's evidently no one in the village who saw her about; if there had been, we should have heard, before now."

"There's the evidence of the old woman, Prissy Mallison," I said. "It may have been Mrs. Martenroyde that she saw hanging about the churchyard."

"She couldn't swear it was," replied Eddison. "And nobody would convict Hannah Martenroyde on Prissy's evidence."

"There's the other old woman – Mrs. Martenroyde's servant," I continued. "She could probably say if her mistress went out that night, and when, and what time she returned. As a resident in the Mill House she must know something."

But Eddison shook his head at that.

"If I know anything," he answered, "you might as well try to get butter out of a dog's throat as get any evidence against her mistress from old Mally Brewster! Mally Brewster, Camberwell, has been in Hannah Martenroyde's service for, I believe, over thirty years, and whatever she knows about Hannah she'll keep to herself. You've no idea – being what we consider a foreigner – of the extraordinary fidelity of these dale folk to those whose bread they've eaten. Mally Brewster, whatever she knows, will say – nothing! And, in my opinion, she knows – would know – nothing at all of her mistress's movements that night. Mally, by eight o'clock that night, would be in bed. Folk who get up, as I know she does, at four and five o'clock every morning, go to bed very early – hereabouts, anyway. No, I see no prospect of getting any evidence against Hannah Martenroyde. Suspicion – yes; I've had ideas of that sort myself, all along. But if she did kill James, it's her secret – and it'll be kept."

I made no answer to that, for I didn't agree with him. Presently he spoke again.

"I've wished, more than once, that I'd never agreed to act as trustee to James Martenroyde's estate," he said, sighing. "It's turning out a very unpleasant business; Halstead and I have a heavy responsibility. Here's this matter of Sugden and the Gresham Street office, for instance; we shan't allow Sugden to go back there – to London. We've found out that Mrs. Martenroyde and Ramsden, acting on Pybus's advice, put the bank account in London quite straight the day after Sugden was arrested, and I've no doubt that Sugden could explain and smooth over those discrepancies in the stock-books of which William Heggus told us. But there had been a good deal wrong – James would have found that out if he'd lived – and we shan't give Sugden the chance of going wrong again. We shall keep Sugden here, at the mill, under Ramsden's thumb – and ours – and make William Heggus manager in London; I'm going to send for William presently to give him orders. And tomorrow night (I'd better tell you of it, so that you can keep out of the way if you like) Halstead and I, as trustees, are going to have a business meeting with the Mill House folk, at which we shall tell them of our proposed new arrangements. Mrs. Martenroyde and the two young men are coming here, and Halstead and I intend to lay down the law to them. Sugden won't like our orders – but he'll have to conform. And his mother will be on our side – she never liked his being in London."

This announcement gave me an idea, which I kept to myself and proceeded to think over. Ever since I had first visited it, in company with Beverley, I had wondered about the apparent mystery that surrounded the Mill House, and had wished that I could somehow or other get inside it. And now I saw a chance. As Mrs. Martenroyde and her two sons were to be at Eddison's the next evening and would probably be kept there, talking business, for at any rate a couple of hours, there was a fine chance for me to effect an entrance to the house they had left locked up. True, the old servant would be in it, but I did not count her as an obstacle, especially in view of the fact that – as Eddison had just said – she probably retired at a very early hour. Before I slept that night I had made up my mind – next evening, the Martenroydes, mother and sons, being clear of it, I would find a way, somehow, into the old place which Hannah Martenroyde kept so jealously guarded. I might have some little difficulty in doing so, but I was not afraid of encountering it. In the course of my professional experience as a partner with Chaney, himself an old Scotland Yard man, I had acquired a considerable store of what one might call unholy knowledge of the tricks and methods of professional criminals and had more than once been glad to adopt some of them – always, of course, in a legitimate manner and for some desirable end. And I had some further aid in the shape of equipment. Chaney had once made me a curious present, knowing of a certain penchant of mine for collecting odd things. This was a burglar's pocket outfit – a neat little affair of stout, well-polished leather, easily slipped into a hip-pocket and not very much bigger than a lady's scissor-case, but containing certain cunning and beautifully made steel tools which were uncommonly useful when it came to a question of opening doors, forcing window-latches, and dealing with locks. I had used the tools in this case more than once, and it was now ready to hand – in my suitcase at Eddison's. In it there was one particular bit of steel, artfully designed, which would turn an already turned key in any door at the Mill House.

With this useful aid to investigation in one pocket, and an excellent flashlight in another, and without saying anything to my host with regard to my intention, I made my way to the lower part of the village about half past seven on the following evening, in time, according to my reckoning of things, to witness the setting-out of Mrs. Martenroyde and her sons to the conference of which Eddison had told me. Ever since Beverley and I had first visited Mill House and had found no admittance to it, I had kept my eye on it, often walking round there of an evening, when all was dark and quiet, and noting whatever I could about it. From this cultivation of acquaintance I had ascertained two or three facts – one: that its inhabitants never used the lower rooms at the front of the house; another: that they seemed to spend their time in a room at the back, whose windows, three in number, looked out on the river; a third: that, except for this room, there was no vestige of light in any part of the place after dusk had fallen. I had also, one night, risking detection – and after assuring myself that Mrs. Martenroyde did not keep a dog – found out, by investigation, that exactly opposite the back door – the only entrance commonly used, for the front door seemed to be hermetically sealed – there was a range of outhouses from which anyone, there hidden, could see any entrance or exit of inhabitants or callers. And by a quarter to eight I was safely posted in a doorway of these buildings, watching.

I had not long to wait. Suddenly the light in the big room, or kitchen, or whatever it was, that fronted the river, went out. A moment later the back door, which was set in a deep stone porch, was opened and three figures became visible in the grey light. I heard the door closed, a key turned, the sound of steps on the cobbled paving of the courtyard which lay between me and the house. Then I heard Mrs. Martenroyde's voice as the three figures turned towards the road.

"Got that key safe, Ramsden?" she asked.

"All right," replied Ramsden. "In my pocket."

"Give yon front door a try as we pass it," said Mrs. Martenroyde. "I expect the latch is on, but it's as well to be certain."

I heard their footsteps on the flagged walks in the front garden, the click of the garden gate as they passed out on the road. Finally they died away in the direction of the big bridge over the river, and, the coast being clear, I came out of my hiding-place and stole across the courtyard to the stone porch. Within a couple of minutes, and probably before Mrs. Martenroyde had set foot on Todmanhawe Bridge, I was safely inside the house which she so jealously guarded from intrusion.

Everything was very quiet, utterly silent, in Mill House, but I did not enter on the darkness which I had expected to find. On opening the door with my master-key and stepping into an inner porch, I found myself in the full glare of a bright fire which shone through the open door of what I took to be the living room; evidently Mrs. Martenroyde had had that fire made up before going out. Its glow illuminated the living room and the inner porch and a good part of a stone-walled passage which led towards the front part of the house. In front of it was curled up, in the middle of the hearthrug, a large tabby cat; it stirred at the slight sound which I made in closing the outer door and presently rose, arched its back, stretched its limbs, and came purring towards me. I was thankful that it was not a dog – had it been, I should have made haste to get away. But the cat was the only live thing there; there was no sign of the old woman, Mally Brewster. Nevertheless I went into that living room in very gingerly fashion, remaining on its threshold for some minutes and listening for possible footsteps approaching from some other part of the house. No such sound came, and I advanced farther into the room, the cat, rubbing itself against my ankles, seeming to invite entrance. But as I stood in the centre, looking around, I wondered what good I was doing there and what I had expected to find or to see. Certainly there was a good deal there that was interesting. The old-fashioned fire-range, with a jack of bright brass dependent from the beam above; the langsettle on the right-hand side of the hearth; the old oak presses set in alcoves; the equally old chairs, chests, pictures, bits of glass, pottery, silver – at any other time I should have been glad to linger amid these things, for there was nothing at all there that one could call modern. But I was after something that had to do with life, and I saw nothing of that sort except the cat purring about my toes. Yet I noticed one – no, two signs of recent human presence. On a little table set in front of the langsettle lay, just where it had been dropped, a grey stocking, in process of knitting, the needles sticking upright in it, and close by, also thrown aside, a copy of the day's newspaper.

I stood there in the middle of that living room, a homely, comfortable place, some few minutes, listening for any sound that might come from any other part of the house. But I heard nothing beyond the crackling of the fire, on which one or other of the Martenroydes had piled two great logs of wood before going out, the purring of the cat, still anxious to ingratiate itself, and the steady ticking of a fine old clock which stood in one corner. And realising that I was doing no good there, I went out into the lobby again. In the light of my flashlight I saw that directly opposite the living room door an oak-balustered stair rose to the upper regions; leaving this for the moment, I turned along the passage and gave my attention to the front rooms, of which there were two, taking care as I entered each to make sure that their windows were so covered that no light from within could be seen in the road outside. On that point I was quietly reassured; the windows in each room were securely and heavily shuttered; the shutters had stout bars across them.

The room on the left-hand side appeared to be a dining room, from the character of its furnishings, but I doubted if it was ever used – the furniture was all set in formal order and the sofa and chairs were draped in covers of brown holland. There was nothing to see there, but on either side of the fireplace were two vilely painted portraits, in oil, in one of which I recognised Mrs. Martenroyde, as she had been some years previously; the other was of a man in whom I fancied I could trace some resemblance to her dead brother-in-law and who was probably her deceased husband.

The other room, facing this, was a sort of parlour; here again the furniture was all set out in formal fashion and showed no sign of use. There were a few pictures on the walls, a few books, in showy bindings, on a centre table, and on the mantelpiece an imposing-looking clock, flanked by ornaments of an equally heavy nature. Nothing to reward me there – but as I looked round I caught sight of an object which lay on a sidetable and reflected from its heavily gilded sides the flash of my torch. It was the most conspicuous thing in the room, and as soon as I saw it I knew what it was – a great folio family Bible. Out of sheer curiosity I lifted the heavy, morocco-bound lid. There were blank pages at the beginning, and, as I had expected, there was writing on them. Throwing the ray of the torch on the first of these written pages, I proceeded to read what some previous owner of this huge volume had there put down in a formal, precise, and old-fashioned script:

> *John Stead His Book*
> *God give him Grace therein to Look*
> *And what he Reads to Understand*
> *For Learning is Better than House or Land.*

Underneath this began particulars of John Stead's marital and parental career.

1871 – March 29th. John Stead, of Hollinshaw, married to Mary Sugden, of the same parish, at Hollinshaw Church by the Reverend Mr. Simpson, Vicar.

1872 – August 4th. William, son of John and Mary Stead, born. September 9th William died.

1874 – Thomas, son of John and Mary Stead, born dead. October 8th.

1875 – Hannah and Deborah, twin daughters of John and Mary Stead, born December 12th.

Then, but in a different handwriting, came two further entries, to fill the page:

September 13, 1891. Mary, wife of John Stead, departed this life, and was buried in Hollinshaw Churchyard, September 17th.

December 4, 1893. John Stead died, and was buried at Hollinshaw, December 7th.

So there was the record of John Stead of Hollinshaw and his family up to the time of his death. But on the next page of the ponderous folio were more entries in the same handwriting as that which recorded John Stead's death.

This book was given to me, Hannah Stead, by my father, John Stead, during his last illness.

I had by this time concluded that Hannah Stead was the maiden name of the present Mrs. John Martenroyde, and I looked at the succeeding entries with increasing interest.

May 19, 1897. Hannah Stead, daughter of John and Mary Stead, was married to John Martenroyde at Hollinshaw Church by the Reverend Mr. Lowthwaite, Vicar.

June 12, 1898. Ramsden Thomas, son of Mr. and Mrs. John Martenroyde, born.

October 5, 1901. Sugden Reginald, son of Mr. and Mrs. John Martenroyde, born.

January 3, 1905. Died, after a short illness, Mr. John Martenroyde, husband of the above Hannah Martenroyde, and was buried at Hollinshaw on January 9th, same year.

And finally I read this:

September 5, 1905, died, away from home at Chorlton in Lancashire, Deborah Stead, and was buried at Chorlton.

But the last entry, which had obviously also been made by Mrs. Martenroyde, had been crossed out, not heavily, but surely, with criss-cross strokes of the pen.

The death and then the disbelief in the death; it all fitted in.

Interesting, no doubt, but as I had not made illegal entry into Mill House to learn the past history of the Martenroydes, I presently closed the big Bible and, retracing my steps to the stairs, cautiously went up them to the higher regions. There was a long passage or gallery there, very much filled up by old oak presses, chests, and similar furniture. Making my way through these things and past several closed doors, I came, by the light of my torch, to a place where the gallery terminated at a short flight of stairs. And as I stood there, hesitating, there suddenly sounded, from somewhere close at hand, a groan or moan, deep, startling.

17

THE LONELY MOOR

IT IS DIFFICULT TO decide the exact nature of the sound which thus broke in on the dead silence which reigned over that upper part of the house – it was something between a deep, protracted groan, as of some person in pain, and a shuddering cry such as people let out who are struggling with a fearsome nightmare. In the silence which followed I stood listening, expecting the sound to recur. But there was no recurrence. And presently, feeling sure that the cry or groan or moan had come from the room at the head of the short staircase by the foot of which I stood, I crept gently up to it and tried the handle of the door, taking care to make no noise. The handle turned easily, but the door was securely locked.

For a minute or two I was half-minded to open this door as I had opened the door of the porch. But reflecting that if I did thus enter the room I should be obliged to use my flashlight if I wanted to see anything, and that the occupant was probably already awake or would be awakened by my entrance, I refrained from any further action and presently retreated. The occupant of that room was doubtless the old woman, Mally Brewster, retired to rest before the family had quitted the house, and, in pursuance of her mistress's mysterious policy, locked in and made safe during Mrs. Martenroyde's absence. After lingering in the corridor at the foot of the stairs for a minute or two, listening, but hearing no further sound, I went down to the living room again and soon afterwards let myself out of the house and went away, wondering what good I had done or what information I had secured by my adventure.

I did not see Eddison again that night. On returning to his house I found that the conference between him, Halstead, and the Martenroydes was still in session, so I went up to my own room and, after reading awhile, retired to bed. Next morning, at breakfast, he told me the result of the previous evening's talk. According to him, Mrs. Martenroyde had given no trouble, and Ramsden had approved the suggestions put forward by the trustees. Sugden, however, had shown some restiveness; he wanted to go back to London and denied that he had mismanaged things at the Gresham Street warehouse. But, in Eddison's opinion, Sugden's mother was anxious to keep Sugden at home, under her own wing, and, Ramsden being of the same mind, Sugden had been obliged to fall in with the trustees' wishes. The conference, accordingly, had ended with the understanding that Sugden was to remain at Todmanhawe as assistant manager to Ramsden, and that William Heggus was to be summoned from London and given instructions as to his future superintendence of the agency in Gresham Street.

"So it passed off quite peaceably," concluded Eddison. "And of course there wasn't a word about James's death. I said nothing – they said nothing. But we're not going to let that rest, Camberwell. What were you after last night? I heard you'd gone out."

I told him then what I had been doing. He seemed to be amused rather than surprised.

"Hannah Martenroyde would have the skin off your back for that!" he remarked, laughing. "I wish she could have caught you – there would have been a rumpus! To enter her sanctum – she'd be furious if she knew it. Lucky for you the old woman was in bed."

"In a locked room!" I said. "Why does Mrs. Martenroyde lock her up?"

"Oh, well, there's nothing very surprising in that," he answered, "to me, at any rate, knowing these folks as I do. Mally Brewster's a very old woman – Mrs. Martenroyde's probably afraid that, if left alone, she might set fire to something or let somebody into the house. Besides, I've known mistresses who always locked up their maidservants at night – and not old women servants, either. In those cases it was to prevent them from gadding about."

"Queer idea – and queer people," I remarked.

"We are queer people in these dales," he replied, laughing. "You can't judge us by ordinary standards. Well – you got nothing much out of your venture, then?"

"Only a bit of Martenroyde family history," I answered, and went on to tell him of what I had read in the big Bible. "I suppose you know all that already?"

"Ought to," he said. "I'm a Hollinshaw man myself, where both Martenroydes and Steads came from. Oh, yes, I know all that – every bit of it."

"Mrs. Martenroyde had a twin sister," I remarked.

He rose from the breakfast table and, going over to the hearth, picked up a cigarette-box.

"Ah, Deborah, now," he answered. "Debbie, as we called her, she died it's maybe twenty-five years ago. Debbie had a bit of history. I remember Hannah and Debbie well enough as young women – fine, handsome, strapping lasses they were. And Debbie was the best-looking. It was always thought – in those days – that James Martenroyde was going to marry Debbie."

"James?" I said.

"James," he answered. "John, his brother, as you know, married Hannah. And everybody in Hollinshaw believed that when John married Hannah, James would marry Deborah. But – James didn't."

"Did the family expect James to marry Deborah?" I asked.

"That was a common impression," he replied. "Whether there was any ground for it I can't say, after all these years. But I believed Hannah always cherished a grudge against James because he didn't marry Deborah. You see, just about the time that he might have married Deborah – the time at which Hannah married his brother John – James was in the first stages of building up his business here – he'd got Todmanhawe Mill going, and he'd no time for marrying."

"In other words, James jilted Deborah, then?" I suggested.

"About that," he assented. "There's no doubt he'd been expected to marry her. I know little about it – James never spoke to me on the subject."

"And Deborah died in Lancashire?" I asked.

Eddison nodded.

"Then why should Mrs. Martenroyde, after entering her death in the family Bible, have crossed the entry out?"

"I wouldn't know of that. But I can very well understand it. Hannah's never spoken of that vagary of hers to me, but you remember what Avis told you? Soon after the news of Deborah's death came, she began not to credit it, said her sister would be coming back some time. Ay, that crossing out of the entry's rather sad. Oh, well, that's all something of the past. We're concerned with the present. I'm wondering, every day, what's going to happen next – and if anything will happen. Or is the mystery of James Martenroyde's death going to be one of the unsolved order?"

What did happen next happened next day. At noon Avis Riley, coming home to her dinner from her morning's work at the mill, asked to see Eddison and me, and as soon as she saw us blurted out her news in brusque fashion.

"Mally Brewster's off," she announced.

"What do you mean – 'off'?" asked Eddison, startled out of his usual equanimity. "Off where?"

"Left Mill House," replied Avis. "Run away – at least, it looks like it. You know where Becca Thorp lives, Mr. Eddison? – that little cottage near the Scarthdale Arms. Well, Becca was up very early this morning, as usual, getting them lads of hers off to the mill, and Mally Brewster walked in on her and asked for a cup of tea. And she told Becca she was going – she said she couldn't bide at Mill House any longer."

"Who told you all that?" demanded Eddison.

"Becca herself," said Avis. "I chanced to meet her as I was passing that way."

"Did Mally tell Becca why she couldn't bide any longer at Mill House?" asked Eddison.

"Nay, I don't know that," replied Avis. "That was all Becca told me – and I didn't ask any questions. But I thought you and Mr. Camberwell would like to know." Eddison turned to me.

"We'll go down and see Becca Thorp," he said. "I'll get the car out."

I glanced at him in surprise. It was scarcely a stone's throw to Becca Thorp's cottage – why take the car? Then I guessed at his intention.

"You mean to follow the old woman?" I asked. "Mally?"

"Probably," he answered. "It depends on what we hear. Anyway, we've got to know what's made her leave Mill House."

Ten minutes later we were at the door of Becca Thorp's cottage. Becca herself opened it – a big, shrewd-eyed woman who, at sight of Eddison, held the door still wider.

"Morning, Becca," said Eddison. "Can we have a word with you?"

"Come your ways in, Mr. Eddison," replied Becca. "There's nobody here but our two lads, having their dinners, and you'll make no difference to them while they're on at that job – they're always as hungry as hunters when they come in from their work."

We followed her into the living room of the cottage, where at a table beneath the little flower-pots of the window-ledge two hefty young fellows in the linen overalls which the millhands wore were steadily at work with knives and forks on plates piled high with meat and vegetables. Each looked up and gave my companion a stolid nod; each went on with his eating as if nothing else in the world mattered. Eddison turned to Becca, who was already busy with something that was cooking on the oven top.

"You've had Mally Brewster here this morning?" he asked. "Avis Riley has just told us. What's it all about?"

"Nay, nowt but that she's off, Mr. Eddison," replied Becca. "She come in here first thing this morning, just as these here lads were starting for their work, and begged a cup of tea, and of course I saw there was something amiss and I made her sit down and have some breakfast. And she told me that she couldn't bide a minute longer at Mill House yonder, and she'd got up early, before any of 'em were stirring, and had made shift to get out of a chamber window and – well, there it was! She was going."

"But why couldn't she bide there any longer?" asked Eddison. "What had happened? She'd been there long enough to get used to anything, I should think."

Becca Thorp gave us a queer look.

"Why, I'll tell you, Mr. Eddison," she answered. "I didn't tell yon lass Avis, but I've just told them lads, and I'll tell you. She said she couldn't bide an hour longer at Mill House, for she was seeing James Martenroyde's ghost every night, regular!"

"Seeing James Martenroyde's ghost!" exclaimed Eddison.

"That's what she said," replied Becca. "James Martenroyde's ghost!"

"Where did she see it?" asked Eddison.

"Nay, she didn't say," answered Becca. "I reckon it didn't matter where she saw it. But I could tell that she believed she did see it – and I could see, too, that the poor old thing was fair frightened and upset. Anyway, she's gone – she went off as soon as she'd drunk a cup of tea and eaten a morsel of bread."

"Where has she gone?" asked Eddison.

"Why, she said she should go to her own place," replied Becca, "and I know where that is. She came from Shawes, the other side of Todmanhawe Fell, and she said there'd be them that knew her and would take her in. But I said to her, 'Why,' I said, 'it's many and many a long year since you were ever in them parts' – I said so, d'ye see, Mr. Eddison, because I knew old Mally had never set foot outside of Mill House for I don't know when – 'and,' I said, 'all your folks'll be dead and gone.' But she wouldn't have it – there'd be somebody as remembered her, she said, and she'd go where she came from. And away she went."

"Have any of the Mill House people been here to inquire about her?" asked Eddison.

"Nay, they haven't," replied Becca. "But I'll lay Hannah Martenroyde wouldn't be over-well suited when she found she'd flown. No – they haven't been here."

"How was she going to get to Shawes?" asked Eddison. "Why, it must be twelve miles across the fell – and in winter, too!"

"More like sixteen, sir," said one of the lads. "There'll be snow up on the top, and all."

"Well, she aimed at walking," said Becca. "She'd nowt with her but a little bundle. Oh, she'd walk sixteen miles – a strong woman, is old Mally. Were you for going after her, Mr. Eddison?"

"I am going after her," replied Eddison, buttoning up his overcoat. "And at once. But you needn't tell anybody – you lads keep your mouths shut when you get back to the mill."

Amid assurances of secrecy from Becca and her lads we left the cottage and went out to the car. Eddison turned it in the direction of the road which led to the upper reaches of the dale.

"Couldn't bide because she was seeing James Martenroyde's ghost every day!" he muttered as the car moved off. "Now, what on earth's the meaning of that? Anyhow, we've got to find out – if we can."

One o'clock struck from the church tower as we left Todmanhawe behind. Eddison accelerated the pace.

"She's had about seven hours' start of us," he remarked. "Still, it's a rough and a steep road, once you come to the fellside, and she's an old woman – we shall catch her before she's near Shawes. And even if we do—" He paused at that and drove on some little distance before finishing his sentence – "even if we do catch her, Camberwell, I'm doubtful if we shall get anything out of her – I know these dale folks! Still, you may take my word for it, the truth about Martenroyde's death is known to Mally Brewster!"

"You feel sure of that?" I said.

"I am sure – now," he answered. "And I'm surprised that Mrs. Martenroyde isn't away after the old woman. For that matter, she may be. We shall see – I'm going on, anyway, till I've run Mally to earth. It'll not take us long to cross the fell to Shawes. You've not been to Shawes, I think, but it's not far – lies in the next dale."

I had never been up Scarthdale, the way we were going, at all, having had no opportunity and not caring particularly to go exploring it in winter. This was a typical winter day: a grey, monotonous sky overhead, wreaths of mist circling about the tops of the fells and among the plantations of larch and pine on the hillsides, and a general feeling that snow was somewhere above and would fall before the day was out. For all that, it was impossible not to realise the wonderful beauty of the valley, with its winding river, now full and rushing along between its rocky banks, its old-world, grey-walled villages, its chasm of wood, crag, hill – I determined to return and explore it fully when summer came round. I was being hurried through it now; the road, if winding, was good, and we met scarcely any traffic; Eddison drove his car along at high speed. But at the end of the ninth or tenth mile the road and the scenery changed; the dale narrowed to a dark and gloomy defile, and the road became little more than a cart-track, along which it was necessary to slow down. A mile farther on we came to a little hamlet – an old church standing on the riverbank, a farmstead or two, a few cottages, and a quaint roadside inn. Eddison pulled up.

"Last inhabited place in the dale," he remarked. "nowt but solitude and eeriness beyond this. We've missed our lunch at home, Camberwell – get out and we'll have a bite and a drink. And we'll ask if old Mally's been seen."

We went into the little inn. Its landlady cut us some sandwiches and drew us some ale; we ate and drank in front of a roaring fire of logs. The landlady stared inquisitively at my companion.

"Not oft that we see you up in these parts, Mr. Eddison," she remarked. "You are a stranger!"

"Ay," assented Eddison, "and I shouldn't be here now, on a cold day like this, missis, if I hadn't had some business." Then, with an air that suggested confidence, he told her what we were after. "You haven't heard of or seen her?" he concluded. "If she's making for Shawes, she'd have to pass here."

"Nay, I haven't, Mr. Eddison," replied the landlady. "But then, of course, if she didn't call in, I shouldn't see her. Shawes do you say she'll make for? Eh, why, she'll have to cross Todmanhawe Fell, and the moor above there's thick with snow! You'll have a job to get your car up there."

"We'll try, anyhow," said Eddison; "and whether we do it or not, we'll drop in on you coming back, for a cup of tea, so keep your kettle boiling."

"Nay, it's always on the boil, is our kettle, Mr. Eddison," laughed the landlady. "I'll be ready for you. But eh, dear me, the idea of that poor old woman crossing yon moor – I hope you'll find her."

"We'll try, missis," said Eddison, with a grim smile, "and I dare say we shall – if somebody else hasn't found her already." He motioned me to follow him outside the inn, and we got into the car and went off again. "Last trace of civilisation, that, Camberwell," he said as we left the little hamlet behind. "We're for the wild now – and the hill-tops. You'll think you've come to the world's end."

The character of the dale had changed. It had now narrowed to a defile; the river was become a stream running over rocks and boulders; the road, which followed the windings of the river, afforded just sufficient room for the car. And from this point onward there was not a house or cottage to be seen – we were alone with the dark fells and the darkening sky.

We came at last, a mile or two farther on, to a point where the track turned abruptly to the right, revealing itself as a zigzag which ran steeply up the fellside. Eddison said this was the foot of the pass, and that we should have reached an altitude of over two thousand feet when we came to the moor above. His was a powerful car, and we were soon on the height; I found myself gazing with something like awe at a vast tableland of ling and heath, high above the world, yet flanked on every side by the great hills of the Pennine Range. Not a human habitation was in sight, and the mountain sheep were few. This, I felt, was solitude. But when we were halfway across the moor, Eddison let out a sharp exclamation and, looking ahead, I realised that our quest was not in vain.

18

LOYALTY

THE QUEER, DUMPY FIGURE in front of us was moving steadily along, slowly, but with a firm, regular gait which showed that it was good for more miles yet of that dreary moorland road. It carried a little bundle in one hand; the other grasped a stout umbrella, making use of it as a walking-stick – in every movement of foot and hand I saw determination. Mally Brewster had a goal ahead and was making for it before night fell.

"We musn't let her know we're after her," said Eddison as we drew near. "We shall get nowt out of her if we do. Surprise is the ticket."

He slowed down as we came up to the old woman – who, hearing us approaching, had moved a little aside, but without turning her head – passed her for a yard or two, and then abruptly pulled up.

"Why, that's Mally – Mally Brewster!" he exclaimed, with well-simulated wonder. "Bless me, Mally, what ever are you doing here, so far from home, and on a cold day like this?"

The old woman, checked in her walk, stared doubtfully at us. For a moment she made as if to slip past the car, which Eddison had steered a little across her side of the narrow track, but after another glance at her questioner she stopped and looked at him steadily.

"I'm going home, master," she answered. "I come from Shawes."

"Shawes, eh?" said Eddison. "Ay, well, you're none so far off it now, to be sure. But – you haven't left Mrs. Martenroyde, have you? I thought you were a fixture at Mill House."

The old woman shook her head.

"Nay, master," she answered, "it's time I went home. I want rest."

"I dare say you do," said Eddison sympathetically. "But couldn't Ramsden have driven you to Shawes? It's a long way for an old lass like you, across these fells."

"I'm none tired, master," answered Mally. "I've taken my time. It's none rest of that sort I want," she went on, suddenly showing signs of confidence. "I'm strong enough in body. Master! I couldn't bide in yon house any longer – I couldn't!"

"Nay!" exclaimed Eddison, still affecting surprise. "Why – weren't they good to you – and you such an old servant to 'em?"

But Mally shook her head again.

"It wasn't that, master – there was nowt to complain of that way – I was one of 'em, as you might say," she replied. "But I couldn't bide – I couldn't bide!"

"What for?" asked Eddison. "Come, now – you can tell me. You know me. What's the trouble?"

The old woman hesitated, looking from one to the other of us. Suddenly her queer old face grew dark with memory.

"It was James Martenroyde, master," she said in a low voice. "I ha' been seeing his ghost, day in, day out, ever since he was put away!"

"James Martenroyde's ghost!" exclaimed Eddison. "Nay! But where, my lass, where? And when?"

"I ha' seen it every day, master, but most at nights – it was night when he was killed," replied Mally. "There he was when I laid down in my chamber, and wouldn't go from my sight. And as long as I stopped in that house, I knew I should see him. And I came away – and now I must go home, master, I must go where I came from."

She made as if to pass us, but Eddison checked her.

"Stop a bit, my lass," he said. "Mally, you know me – and you know something else. Something about James Martenroyde's death. What is it, now?"

The old woman started, looking at him with a sudden fear. Again she made as if to go on.

"I ha' said overmuch," she muttered. "You must let me go, master."

"You needn't be afraid, my lass," said Eddison. "But come now, you do know something, don't you? Something about the Martenroydes, eh? Tell me – you know I'm a lawyer."

Mally paused, giving Eddison a long, steady look. Then she shook her head – and I knew Eddison would get nothing from her.

"Nay, master," she answered, "I cannot say anything about Martenroydes. I ha' eaten their bread and sheltered under their roof for more than thirty years, and I cannot say a word. You must let me go, master. The dark's coming."

I realised now how well Eddison knew his fellow dales-folk. He asked no further questions – on that subject, at any rate.

"Ay, the dark's coming," he repeated. "Get into the car, my lass, and I'll take you where you want to go."

But Mally made no sign of accepting this invitation.

"Nay, thanking you, master," she answered. "We're on the edge of the moor now, and it's nowt but a bit of a fell down yonder to Shawes, and there's a house on the way that I want to call at – I'd rather walk, master."

"As you like," said Eddison. "Have you relations at Shawes?"

"Ay, master – in the churchyard," replied Mally. "All dead and gone is my folk. But there's them i' the place that knows me and'll take me in. And I've money."

"Well, take care of yourself," said Eddison. Without further word he began to turn the car. "You know where to find me if you want a bit of help," he added as it came round. "Do you hear, now?"

"Ay, master," the old woman answered, "I know."

We turned in our seats to watch her. She went steadily forward again along the moorland track, never turning her head. Not far off rose one of the grey stone walls which ran in regular lines across the heather, pierced here and there by narrow gateways; through one of these she disappeared, and Eddison's car moved off again – by the way we had come.

" 'Eaten their bread and sheltered under their roof – and I cannot say a word,' " repeated Eddison. "There's loyalty for you, Camberwell. I knew it was useless to ask her anything after that. But – she knows something!"

"What do you think she meant when she spoke of seeing James Martenroyde's ghost?" I asked. "Did she mean it literally?"

"No," he answered. "I thought you'd not understand that. She meant she was always dreaming of it, seeing it – *something* – in her mind's eye. I tell you, my lad, that old lass knows! But, Lord save us, what is it she knows? Something that happened that night is known to her and has made a lasting impression on her. And she'll probably carry her knowledge to her grave – unrevealed."

"She must have been dreaming when I heard her call out, in Mill House, the other night," I remarked. "It was a startled cry, now I think of it."

"Very like," he assented. "Well, you may say we've had our journey for nowt, but we haven't. We know now that Mally Brewster has some certain knowledge; and if we never get to know anything from her, we may get at the secret from some other angle."

"What I'm wondering," I said, "is: does Mrs. Martenroyde know that Mally knows something? If so, I'm surprised that she isn't in pursuit of her."

"She may be, for all we know," he answered. "There's another road to Shawes, lower down the valley. Mally may find Hannah Martenroyde waiting for her – Hannah would know where the old woman would make for."

We went back by the way we had come. By the time we reached the roadside the gloom of the winter afternoon had deepened into the darkness of a winter's evening – I thought of the lonely old woman plodding her way down the fellside to the village where all her own folk lay in the churchyard. Sentimentalism, no doubt – but I half made up my mind as Eddison and I sat in the glow of the inn fire, drinking our hot and welcome tea, that I would go to Shawes next day and find out how Mally Brewster had fared.

But that was not to be. Next morning as Eddison and I were about to sit down to breakfast, Becca Thorp was shown in, and Becca was obviously full of news.

"Mr. Eddison!" she exclaimed. "I thought you'd like to know. Old Mally's back at Mill House! Our Reuben was coming past there late last night, and he saw Ramsden and his mother drive up in their car. And Mally was with them. They'd fetched her!"

19

DR. PONSFORD
CALLED IN

EDDISON POURED OUT COFFEE before making any remark on this piece of news, and Becca Thorp, having discharged it at him, stood open-mouthed, agog to hear what he had to say about it.

"Did your lad actually see Mally Brewster?" he asked at last.

"Oh, ay, he saw her, right enough, Mr. Eddison," replied Becca Thorp. "Of course, he was close to 'em."

"Did he hear anything said?" inquired Eddison. "Did she seem to be going back willingly?"

"I reckon she'd have no choice, once them two had laid hands on her," said Becca. "You know what Hannah Martenroyde is, Mr. Eddison. I knew they'd fetch the poor old thing back. It wouldn't suit Hannah Martenroyde to have old Mally out of her custody."

"Why wouldn't it?" asked Eddison.

"Nay, I reckon the old woman knows too much about what goes on, and has gone on, in that house," replied Becca. "And once away from it, she might be letting things out."

"Have you ever known of her letting owt out?" said Eddison.

"Nay, I haven't, but then, you see, Mr. Eddison, Mally Brewster's never been out of Mill House for I don't know when," answered Becca. "It's well known that she's been kept prisoner in there, same as if she was in jail. There is folks – me for one – that's had a word or two with her now and then, through the windows. But she's never been allowed out – never, for many a year."

Eddison devoted himself to his eggs and bacon for a minute or two. Then he suddenly turned on the woman with a challenging look.

"I reckon you know all the village talk, missis," he said. "Now, what do folk say about that – about Mally's being kept from going out, and nobody allowed inside – what's the opinion about it?"

Becca Thorp smiled and shook her head.

"Why, Mr. Eddison, it's just a fad of Hannah Martenroyde's, and has been since Miss Deborah died."

Eddison turned to me when the woman had gone. "I felt sure they'd fetch her back," he continued. "They must have gone after her, to Shawes, by the other road. And, as they've got her back, I don't see what we can do, Camberwell."

"I don't see what I can do," I answered. "It seems to me we're at a stage where my services are of no use to you. I've no direct clue, and, whatever suspicion I may have, I've nothing of real value to support it. Probably the old servant could give evidence which would solve the problem, but, from what I've seen of her, she won't. I dislike giving up any commission, but—"

"Now then, now then, go easy, my lad!" he interrupted. "I'm not going to let you give up any commission – my commission, anyway. Wait a bit! There'll be something turn up that'll start us out on a new trail, you'll see. You've no particular call to go back to London, have you? Very well, then, have a bit of patience. Bide quiet – keep your eyes and ears open. All we want is just that bit of something which'll give us an idea."

"How to get that is the problem," I remarked.

"I say: keep your eyes and ears open," he repeated. "Now, there's a chance this morning. Ramsden Martenroyde's coming up after breakfast with some papers relating to the business. When I've done with them, I'll have a word with him about this affair of the old woman. You listen, and hear what he says."

Ramsden came up, a bundle of correspondence in his hand, about ten o'clock that morning; he and Eddison transacted their business in my presence. When it was finished and Ramsden had gathered the papers together and was about to go, Eddison stopped him.

"Ramsden, my lad," he said, "I want a word or two with you. There's talk going on in the village about that old lass of your mother's, Mally Brewster. She ran away from Mill House early yesterday morning, telling a neighbour that she couldn't bide there any longer and must go. And now I hear that you and your mother fetched her back last night. What's it all about?"

Ramsden's face had darkened as Eddison spoke, growing gradually sullen, resentful, obstinate.

"The old woman's getting to her dotage," he muttered. "There's nobody to look after her but us – and her folks are dead. We found her wandering about there at Shawes last night, seeking a lodging, and we brought her home. That's all there is to it – I reckon it's nobody's business but ours. She's nobody to look to but my mother."

Eddison hesitated a moment, watching Ramsden. Ramsden, getting no further remark, made for the door. Then Eddison stopped him again.

"Wait a bit," he said. "Look here, my lad, I'll be plain with you. I went after the old woman. She told me she couldn't bide longer at Mill House because she was always seeing James Martenroyde's ghost. What's that mean?"

"I said she's getting near her dotage," replied Ramsden, sullenly. "She fancies things. If there'd been any of her own folk left at Shawes, we should have let her stop there, but there wasn't, so we brought her back."

"It's a pity people are talking about it," remarked Eddison.

Ramsden showed increasing sullenness.

"They've nowt to do with it," he muttered. "I reckon we've a right to manage our own affairs in our own way. The old woman's safe there – if she'd been left up yonder at Shawes, she'd only have wandered about and come to harm."

With that he made a sudden move for the door and went off, and Eddison shook his head and gave me a knowing look.

"Old Mally's not so far gone as all that," he said. "She was sensible enough when we saw her yesterday afternoon. Well, we shall have to pluck out the heart of her mystery somehow, Camberwell."

I failed to see how we were going to do it. And I was beginning to chafe under the forced inactivity of all this; it seemed to me that I was doing no good in staying at Todmanhawe. Certainly Eddison was a considerate and most attentive host, but it irked me to feel that I was accomplishing nothing and got no more results than an occasional scrap of gossip, usually worth little, from the village folk. Once again, after Ramsden had left us that morning, I suggested to Eddison that I might as well be allowed to give up my commission; once again he begged me to wait awhile. Finally I consented to stay with him another week. During that week Colonel Houston and his daughter, who had lived at Scarthdale Arms since James Martenroyde's funeral and had busied themselves in making arrangements for taking over the grange, left for London. A day or two later William Heggus came down to get his new orders and took up his residence at his brother's. Beyond these unimportant events nothing happened – and as the week drew to an end I became finally resolved to throw up my commission and go away, leaving the local police to pursue their inquiries, if – which I doubted – they were still making any.

Then – and, as it always happens, suddenly – something came to stir us all up. One morning, about eleven o'clock, as I sat reading the newspapers in Eddison's dining room, I heard him at the telephone in the hall. A moment later he came in.

"Camberwell," he said, "Ponsford wants to see us – at once. At his house. Something appears to have happened."

"Didn't he say?" I asked.

"No – only that he wants us – you, particularly – at once," he answered. "Come on, it's only a few minutes' walk."

We put on our hats and hurried down the road. Ponsford's house stood near the big bridge; his surgery projected into the garden. As we reached the gate of the carriage drive, Beverley came racing along in his car from the direction of Shipton; a constable in uniform sat on the front seat with him; another, in plain clothes, occupied the back seat.

"What's this?" muttered Eddison. "Is he coming here?"

That question was quickly answered. Beverley pulled up at Ponsford's gate, gave some instructions to the policeman, and, jumping out, hastened to join us.

"Has the doctor sent for you?" he demanded. "He phoned me to come here at once. What's the matter? Something happened?"

"We know no more than you do," replied Eddison. "Let's go in."

A parlour-maid showed us into Ponsford's dining room, saying that the doctor would be with us in a few minutes. But she had scarcely left us when Ponsford came bustling in. I had seen a good deal of him since my arrival at Todmanhawe; Eddison and I had dined with him occasionally, and he with Eddison; now and then, idling my time away, I had dropped in on him at his surgery hours to chat. I thought him just the sort of medico that these dale people needed – a big, bluff, bearded man of rough and ready manners, brusque in his address and a bit offhanded in his procedure, but sympathetic and understanding in his treatment of the folk with whom he had to deal. He was direct and plain-spoken enough now. Closing the door behind him as he entered the room, he turned to us with an ominous shake of the head.

"Glad you're all here together," he said. "Now then, listen – there's something just happened that you've got to hear about. Just an hour ago—"

He paused at the sound of voices in the hall without, then moved across to the door.

"That'll be Reeves-Norton, from Shipton," he said. "I phoned him to come along when I phoned you others. Come in!" he went on as the door opened and the parlour-maid ushered in an elderly, spectacled man of the true surgeon type. "You know these other fellows, Reeves-Norton, so I needn't introduce you. And now that you're all here, just sit down, all of you, and hear what I've got to say, and pay attention, for, by George, it's serious! Now listen. About an hour ago I was sent for by Mrs. Martenroyde, of the Mill House – she asked that I should go at once. I went, there and then. As soon as I was in the house – which I'd never entered before – she told me that her old servant, Mally Brewster, had fallen downstairs, hit the heavy oak baluster at the bottom, and injured her head. She – Mrs. Martenroyde – had sent for her sons from the mill and they'd carried the old woman to her room. She was unconscious, and they'd sent for me. Of course, I went up to see Mally at once. I saw her – and that's why I've sent for you!"

For the moment none of us spoke, but we looked questioningly at him and Ponsford went on.

"Sent for you – all of you. Because I know that Mally Brewster didn't fall downstairs, nor anywhere else!" he said with emphasis. "She'd been struck down by a heavy blow from a heavy stick – just as James Martenroyde was! That's – certain."

Reeves-Norton broke the silence which followed with one word.

"Sure?" he asked.

"Beyond doubt," declared Ponsford. "Listen—" and he went into low-voiced details which I for one was unable to catch. "But I want you to come down and see for yourself. If you aren't of my opinion, why, then, I've wasted my time ever since

I entered Bart's! And you others must come – if my theory's correct there's work ahead for you police chaps."

He turned to open the door, but Eddison laid a hand on his arm.

"Let's be clear about this, Ponsford," he said. "What you say amounts to this: Mally Brewster is suffering from an injury to her head. Mrs. Martenroyde says Mally fell downstairs. You say Mally has had a blow. And you want Dr. Reeves-Norton to see Mally so that you may know if your opinion is correct?"

"I know my opinion is correct!" exclaimed Ponsford. "I'll stake my reputation on it. Come on with you – we're going into that house. Listen – the old woman is done for!"

"Dead?" exclaimed Eddison.

"No – but she will be before tomorrow morning," replied Ponsford in his brusquest manner. "She'll never regain consciousness. Come on!"

He marshalled us out and led the way towards Mill House, himself and Reeves-Norton walking in front in deep consultation, while Eddison, Beverley, and I followed. Eddison, as soon as we were out of Ponsford's garden, began to tell Beverley of Mally Brewster's recent escape from the Martenroydes' service and of her speedy recapture. Beverley began to look grave and suspicious.

"Don't fancy its appearance, Mr. Eddison," he said. "Runs away – brought back – probably against her will – and is now dying, according to the doctor, from a blow. Ugly look, all that!"

"I quite agree," said Eddison. "The fact is, if the old woman's injury is really due to a blow, we're coming to something. What do you say, Camberwell?"

"I think so," I replied. "Ponsford, at any rate seems very certain of his assertion."

Ponsford turned back to us as we came in sight of Mill House.

"You three had better wait outside while Reeves-Norton and I go in," he said. "If he agrees with me – that the injury is due to a blow – I shall fetch you in, and you, Beverley, can then question

Mrs. Martenroyde. According to what she told me, she and the old woman were alone in the house when what she called the accident happened, so no one can give any account of it but herself."

We paused in the road and waited, near the corner of the garden, while the two doctors disappeared into the house. Ten, fifteen, twenty minutes passed. Then we heard Ponsford calling to us and presently found him standing near the back door, which stood open behind him.

"She's gone," he said quietly, as we approached him. "Died ten minutes ago. Never recovered consciousness. I knew she wouldn't. Come in, they're all here. Beverley, don't you forget that there'll have to be an inquest."

Unchecked, we all walked into the living room, in which, unknown to anyone, I had stood only a few nights before. As Ponsford had said, the mother and two sons were all there. Ramsden, wondering and upset, stood near the fireplace; Sugden, scowling and angry, lounged on the langsettle, his hands thrust into his pockets. Neither spoke on our entrance. But Mrs. Martenroyde, turning from some cooking operation at the hearth, gave voice at once, protestingly if not angrily.

"I don't know what call all of you men have to come into my house in that fashion!" she said. "There's no occasion for it. I don't see what right you have here, Mr. Eddison, for all you're trustee, nor what that man from London's here for, nor what police folk are doing here. I've told you, Dr. Ponsford, how it happened, and I can't see that there's owt to be done but for you to give a certificate and let's get the poor old thing quietly buried. What's the use of all this to-do?"

"I can't give a certificate, Mrs. Martenroyde," said Ponsford. "I'm not satisfied, and if Dr. Reeves-Norton agrees with me, there'll have to be an inquest."

Then he motioned us to follow him upstairs, and we turned to the gloomy old hall, leaving mother and sons silently staring at each other.

20

FAMILY EVIDENCE

THE FIVE OF US who had stood that morning round the dead body of Mally Brewster kept silence as to our conclusions and subsequently left the Martenroydes under the impression that the necessary inquest would be a formal affair; certainly nothing was said to give Mrs. Martenroyde the idea that she was an object of suspicion. And this conviction of security had been achieved in spite of the fact that Beverley, after hearing the first main conclusions of the two doctors, had withdrawn from the bedroom with Eddison for at least ten minutes and had, as I afterwards learned, prevailed upon the latter to keep the Martenroydes occupied in conversation while he himself made an unobtrusive examination of the ground floor of Mill House.

When, however, the diminutive Coroner began his inquiry at the village schoolroom next day, I saw that Mrs. Martenroyde had taken care to guard her own interests – Pybus, the Shipton solicitor who had defended Sugden, was there, in close consultation with her and her two sons. There, too, representing the police, was Cordukes, who had prosecuted Sugden in the magistrate's court. And Cordukes, of course, knew what evidence the two doctors would give. As far as I was aware, he, Eddison, Beverley, and I were the only people who had any idea of what that evidence would be. Between the time at which the news of the old woman's sudden death had spread through the

village and the hour at which the opening of the inquest had
been fixed, no rumour of foul play had been spread; according
to what we heard from Avis Riley and Becca Thorp, our two
principal sources of information, the people had accepted Mrs.
Martenroyde's story as to how Mally came by her death. Mally
was an old woman, not so spry and ready on her feet as she
had been; she had missed her footing on the dark stairway at
Mill House, fallen from top to bottom – and there you were. It
was a thing that might happen to anybody, and all this inquest
business was nowt but lawyers' fuss, to put money into their
pockets. Nevertheless, the villagers crowded to the schoolroom
to swallow all that was available, and Eddison and I, getting
there a few minutes late, had some difficulty in squeezing
ourselves into the centre of this improvised court.

There was some little delay at the outset of the proceedings –
the small Coroner, who had already made some investigations
himself, sent the jury to inspect the stairs down which Mally
Brewster was said to have fallen. Here there was a difficulty
which those of us who knew Mrs. Martenroyde's peculiar idea
about her house might have foreseen. The house, as usual, was
locked up, and Mrs. Martenroyde had the key. Eventually thi
s difficulty was got over by her giving the key to Ramsden, who
accompanied the jury, showed them what the Coroner desired
them to see, and shepherded them back. I noticed that when
they returned, Mrs. Martenroyde at once repossessed herself of
the key and stowed it safely away in her handbag.

Ramsden Martenroyde was the first witness called. In answer
to the Coroner, he said that on the previous morning, somewhere, as near as he could recollect, about half past nine o'clock,
a boy came to the mill saying that Mrs. Martenroyde wanted
him and his brother Sugden to go to Mill House at once. He
sent for Sugden from another part of the mill and they went
home. On arriving there and entering by the back door, they
found Mrs. Martenroyde in the back hall, standing near the foot
of the staircase, where their old servant, Mally Brewster (whose

dead body had been formally identified before the evidence began), lay, half in, half out of the doorway which opened on the living room. At first glance he thought she was dead, but Mrs. Martenroyde said she was still breathing, though unconscious. He noticed a big bruise on her forehead, but did not make any particular examination of it. There was a tray and some broken crockery lying about. Mrs. Martenroyde said that Mally had been upstairs to fetch these things and had evidently tripped on the stairs in coming down and had fallen to the foot; she herself had heard the crash from another part of the house and had hastened to the staircase, to find Mally lying there, as they saw her. She had endeavoured to restore her to consciousness, but, failing to do so, had gone out into the road and, seeing a boy passing, had sent him for Ramsden and Sugden. After their arrival Mrs. Martenroyde again tried certain things with the object of restoring consciousness, but none of them was any good. At her direction he and his brother carried the old woman upstairs and laid her on a bed in the first bedroom they came to. Mrs. Martenroyde again tried some remedy, but it was no good. In his opinion, Mally was near dying, and he told his mother they must send for Dr. Ponsford. Eventually Sugden went out to find a messenger, and the doctor was sent for and came. After being there some little time, Dr. Ponsford went away, and returned later with Dr. Reeves-Norton. Mally Brewster was still alive when the two doctors came together, and he understood that she died just after they went up to see her.

Ramsden gave all this evidence in plain, straightforward fashion, and it looked as if there was no reason to question him on any point arising out of it. But when the Coroner had done with Ramsden, Mr. Cordukes rose and addressed himself to the witness-box.

"Mally Brewster had been in the service of your family a long time, I believe, Mr. Ramsden?" he began.

"Ay – a long time," assented Ramsden laconically.

"How long, now?"

"Why, I can't say, exactly. She'd been there ever since I can remember owt, anyway."

"Thirty years, perhaps?" suggested Mr. Cordukes.

"I'm about that myself," replied Ramsden.

"And she was there – in your mother's service – when you first began to take notice?"

"Ay, she was there," said Ramsden.

"A very trusted servant, then – who became, one might say, as one of the family?"

"She was always treated as one, anyhow," Ramsden replied.

"Was she the only servant your mother kept?"

"There was no other."

"Since when?" asked Mr. Cordukes.

"Since ever I can remember owt at all," replied Ramsden. "We've had no other."

"She'd become, I suppose, quite a fixture?"

Ramsden looked at his questioner as if he considered this question as foolish as it was, in his opinion, superfluous.

"Haven't I just told you she'd been there thirty years or so?" he asked.

"You have – so I want to ask you something else," said Mr. Cordukes. "The police have been informed that a few nights ago – to be precise, very early one morning – Mally Brewster got out of your house and went away. Is that true?"

"Ay, that's true," answered Ramsden.

"Do you know of any reason for her doing that?"

"I know of nowt but that the old woman was getting near her dotage," replied Ramsden. "She was getting fanciful, too."

"The police have been informed that she said – to neighbours – after her escape that she couldn't bide any longer at Mill House because she was continually seeing the ghost of your uncle, the late Mr. James Martenroyde. Do you know anything about that?"

Ramsden shrugged his broad shoulders.

"nowt!" he answered, derisively. "Except that it's all a peck o' moonshine. I told you – she was getting fanciful."

"Did she ever complain to any of you about Mr. James Martenroyde's ghost?" asked Mr. Cordukes.

"Not to me, I can tell you! I shouldn't have listened to her."

"Well, there is the fact that she left your house. It is a fact, isn't it?"

"Oh, it's a fact, right enough, is that," admitted Ramsden. "Nobody denies it."

"Is it a fact, too, that you and your mother fetched her back from the village, Shawes, to which she made her way?"

"Ay, that's a fact, and all," said Ramsden impatiently. "Best thing for her, too. All her relations were dead, and she'd nobody to return to at Shawes. We went after her, and we found her traipsing about in Shawes, trying to find a lodging, and we put her in our car and brought her home. Who's owt to say against it ?"

"Nobody, I should think – if she came willingly," said Mr. Cordukes. "Did she?"

"She came back willingly enough, as far as I'm aware," replied Ramsden. "I'd nowt to do with it, beyond driving our car. When me and my mother got to Shawes, we started making inquiries, and we heard the old woman was in some cottage, up a fold there – trying to get a bed. My mother went after her and she brought her back to the car and I drove 'em home. That's all there was to it. What else could we do – an old woman like y on?"

"No coercion, then – she wasn't forced to return?" asked Mr. Cordukes.

"No!" snapped Ramsden. "Nowt of the sort!"

"Came home quietly with you and settled down again, eh?"

"Ay, as far as I know," said Ramsden. "I never saw no different."

"Just another question," said Mr. Cordukes. "When this accident occurred yesterday morning, there was no other person in the house with your mother but Mally Brewster?"

Ramsden frowned. He stared at the solicitor as if suspecting that he was somehow or other being played with.

"I've told you already we'd no other servant," he answered testily. "Me and Sugden had gone to the mill two hours before that."

Mrs. Martenroyde followed Ramsden in the witness-box. Invited by the Coroner to give her version of what had happened, she told her story in plain, straightforward fashion and – for her – without any lavish use of words. She said that about half-past nine the previous morning she and Mally Brewster were in the kitchen of Mill House, engaged in washing up the breakfast crockery. She remembered that she had forgotten to bring down the tray on which earlier in the morning Mally had taken her up some tea and bread and butter. She sent Mally upstairs to fetch it. A few minutes later she heard a cry, which was something between a scream and a groan, followed by a crash and the sound of smashed china. She hurried from the kitchen through the living room to the foot of the stairs, and found Mally lying across the hall, her head and shoulders within the living room door. The china on the tray was lying about, broken. As far as she knew, the old woman was already unconscious. She was moaning, very slightly. Mrs. Martenroyde fetched a bottle of smelling-salts and tried to restore consciousness. That failing, she tried some other simple remedies. Nothing being of any use, and being alone in the house and unable to move the old woman, she went out into the road, found a boy who was passing, and sent him to the mill with a message for her sons. They came and at once carried Mally up to her room. She again tried to restore consciousness, but without effect, and Ramsden insisted on sending for the doctor. Sugden went out to find a messenger, and Dr. Ponsford came. And that was all she could tell.

I am under the impression that if the matter had been left to the Coroner and his jury and if the medical evidence had supported the theory of a fall, the inquest would have terminated very quickly with a verdict of accidental death. But within a few minutes of the termination of Mrs. Martenroyde's evidence in chief, a new element came into the case. Mr. Cordukes, on being asked by the Coroner if he had any questions to put, rose and confronted the witness with the evident intention of putting a good many.

"How long had Mally Brewster been in your service, Mrs. Martenroyde?" he inquired blandly. "A long time, I believe?"

"Well, it would be a good thirty years," replied Mrs. Martenroyde.

"Continuously?" asked Mr. Cordukes.

"She never left me, if that's what you mean," retorted Mrs. Martenroyde. "She knew she'd a good place."

"How old was she when she came to you?" inquired Mr. Cordukes.

"Why, she'd happen to be about eight-and-twenty," replied Mrs. Martenroyde. "I couldn't say for certain, but thereabouts."

"Then she'd be about sixty years of age at the time of her death?" said Mr. Cordukes. "And one-half of her life had been spent in your service. She'd become quite a fixture in the household, eh?"

"She'd been there all that time, anyhow," said Mrs. Martenroyde, regarding her questioner suspiciously.

"Was she content with her lot?" asked Mr. Cordukes.

"She was an ungrateful old thing if she wasn't," said Mrs. Martenroyde. "She was treated same as one of oursens and wanted nowt."

"Why did she take French leave of you the other day, then?" demanded Mr. Cordukes. "We've heard from your son that she ran away – without notice. Why?"

Mrs. Martenroyde scowled.

"She was getting fancies into her head," she answered. "She never was what you'd call over-bright."

"One of her fancies was that she was seeing the ghost of your late brother-in-law, Mr. James Martenroyde, wasn't it?"

"Ay, something of that sort – I paid no heed to her. Such rubbish!"

"Anyhow, she did run away. Broke out of your house, didn't she?"

"I don't know what you mean by broke out – there was no occasion to break out. She went out by a window in a room on the ground floor – a window that opens to the ground – one of them French windows. There was no breaking out."

"But she went – at five o'clock of a winter's morning – didn't she?"

"Ay, she went."

"And later that day you went in pursuit and found her at Shawes and brought her back to your house? Why were you so anxious to bring her back?"

"Because she wasn't fit to look after herself," said Mrs. Martenroyde readily. "All her folk at Shawes were dead and gone, and there was nobody there as knew her, unless it was some very old people that couldn't do owt for her. Of course we had to fetch her back."

"Why didn't you go after her at once, as soon as you found that she'd gone?"

"Well, there were two reasons. One was that Ramsden was too busy at the mill that morning to take me out in the car, and the other was that I knew where to lay hands on her. I knew she'd make for Shawes – it was where she came from when she first came to us."

"Did she return willingly?"

"She made no bother about it."

"And she settled down again to her former relations, eh?"

"She went on as usual," said Mrs. Martenroyde.

"Made no more complaints about ghosts?"

"She never did make no complaints about ghosts – to me. She knew better than to talk such soft stuff as that in my presence. It was to folk outside as she talked that tomfoolery."

"I see. Then we're to understand that at the time this fatal accident occurred, you and she were on quite friendly and satisfactory terms?"

"We were just as we always had been," replied Mrs. Martenroyde. "There was nowt different."

Mr. Cordukes paused – to look for and find a sheet of paper, which he extracted from some other documents before him on the table. With this in his hand, he turned to the Coroner.

"This, sir," he said, "is a letter, an anonymous letter, which was received this morning by the Superintendent of Police, Mr. Beverley, who has placed it in my hands. In the ordinary run of things I should have handed it back to the Superintendent and advised him to throw it in the fire, and I only mention – and produce – it to you because, anonymous as it is, it bears the Todmanhawe postmark and contains a charge against Mrs. Martenroyde in respect of her treatment of the dead woman with which, in justice to her, Mrs. Martenroyde should be made acquainted. If you would read it—"

The Coroner was already reading the letter. It was apparently a very short one, for he handed it back almost at once.

"If it had not been for what you have said about it, I should have refused to take any notice of that communication," he said, turning to Mr. Cordukes, "but as you have given some indication of what the letter is about, it is only fair to Mrs. Martenroyde to question her upon the subject raised. Do you wish to put any question?"

"Merely one or two, sir," replied Mr. Cordukes. He turned to the witness-box. "Mrs. Martenroyde," he continued, "this letter signed 'One Who Knows,' makes a charge against you of ill-treatment of Mally Brewster. Is there any truth in that charge?"

"Truth?" exclaimed Mrs. Martenroyde. "I should think there isn't any truth! Ill-treatment? I would like to find any servant, wench or woman, anywhere in these parts who was as well treated! Ill treated, indeed! – I should think not."

"We may as well have the charge disposed of," remarked Mr. Cordukes, glancing at the letter. "Were you in the habit of beating Mally Brewster?"

"Habit?" replied Mrs. Martenroyde. "No, I wasn't in the habit! The idea!"

"Did you ever beat her?" asked Mr. Cordukes. "Ever, now?"

Mrs. Martenroyde hesitated.

"Well," she said, with a sudden burst of frankness, "I may have taken a stick to her back now and then – she wanted managing at times. But that was when she was younger."

"You haven't beaten her lately?"

"No – nowt of the sort!"

"Or struck her?"

"I may have given her a good slap time and again," admitted Mrs. Martenroyde. "She needed it – sometimes."

There was a suppressed ripple of laughter at this reply, and I saw one or two jurymen exchange knowing glances with each other. Mr. Cordukes appeared to be satisfied and sat down, but before Mrs. Martenroyde could leave the witness-box, Mr. Pybus jumped up, motioning her to stay where she was. She paused, faced him wonderingly.

"Mrs. Martenroyde, on your oath, did you beat, strike, or in any way lay hands on Mally Brewster yesterday morning?" he demanded. "Stop – I'll add to that. Did you beat her or strike her or lay hands upon her in such a way as to cause her to fall down those stairs?"

Mrs. Martenroyde's eyes and expression became mildly incredulous.

"Me?" she replied. "I never set a finger on her!"

Mr. Pybus sat down again. Mrs. Martenroyde was motioned to leave the witness-box. The Coroner looked up from his notes and across the court to where the two medical men were sitting together.

"We'd better have Dr. Ponsford's evidence now," he remarked. "Call him."

21

A CERTAIN SENTENCE

UNLESS THE CORONER HIMSELF had been given some idea of what was going to be said, I don't think anybody in that schoolroom anticipated the revelation which was presently made. Up to the moment at which Ponsford uttered a certain sentence, everybody, I think, among the spectators and the jury considered the affair one of mere accident. But as soon as that sentence had been spoken, suspicion, sinister enough, sprang to life, and every eye in the place was turned, as with a common instinct, on Mrs. Martenroyde.

Ponsford, questioned by the Coroner, said that he was summoned to Mill House the previous morning about nine thirty and went there at once. He found Mrs. Martenroyde and her two sons in Mally Brewster's room. Mally lay on the bed, fully dressed and unconscious. Mrs. Martenroyde told him that Mally had fallen downstairs from top to bottom. He had seen the broken crockery at the foot of the stairs as he entered the house. He made a superficial examination of the injury which Mrs. Martenroyde said had been caused by the fall, and at once came to a certain conclusion. In consequence of that he left Mrs. Martenroyde to look after the old woman and, returning to his surgery, telephoned to Dr. Reeves-Norton at Shipton and to the Superintendent of Police there, asking both to come to Todmanhawe at once.

"Why did you ask for the Superintendent?" inquired the Coroner.

"Because," replied Ponsford, very slowly and distinctly, "I knew that there had been foul play!"

"Foul play?" exclaimed the Coroner. "You did not think the injury which you have just mentioned had been caused in the way described by Mrs. Martenroyde?"

"No, I did not," replied Ponsford.

"Didn't you think there had been a fall downstairs?"

"No. There had been no fall downstairs."

"How, then, had the injury been caused?"

Ponsford's reply, deliberate, grave, was given in the midst of a dead silence.

"By a violent blow on the head from some heavy, blunt weapon."

The silence lasted for a full minute. As I have already said, every eye in the room turned on Mrs. Martenroyde. Her face flushed angrily, and I thought she was about to speak. But the Coroner spoke.

"You felt convinced of that?" he asked.

"Absolutely convinced," said Ponsford. "There was no doubt about it."

"You can explain to the jury your reason for coming to this conclusion?" asked the Coroner. "As simply as possible, if you please."

"There's no necessity to be otherwise than perfectly simple," observed Ponsford. "But may I make the explanation in my own way? I have said that I phoned for Dr. Reeves-Norton. He came very soon, and he and I went to Mill House. I took him up to Mally Brewster's room. She had not regained consciousness, and she died soon after our arrival."

"In your presence?" asked the Coroner.

"Yes. Now, if you please, I will explain my reasons (Dr. Reeves-Norton can give his own) for stating that this woman died as the result of a violent blow on the head from some heavy, blunt instrument, and that she did not have any fall downstairs. I was convinced of the truth of what I am going to say as soon as I had made my first somewhat hurried examination, but positively convinced when Dr. Reeves-Norton and I made a second and thorough one. And first as regards what I unhesitatingly say was the result of a violent blow. This was a large bruise – what would commonly be called a lump – some three inches long by two wide over the left eye-brow – that is, on the left temple. Such a bruise, I knew, was indicative of an injury to the skull which would cause subdural hæmorrhage."

A juror made signal of interruption.

"We don't understand them last terms, Mr. Coroner," he said. "Happen the doctor'll make 'em clear?"

"Yes," said Ponsford. "They mean that the victim's skull sustained a fracture and that there was hæmorrhage – or bleeding—" he smiled explanatorily at the jury – "from beneath the dura mater."

The same juryman interrupted:

"Couldn't we have less of the London talk, Doctor?"

There was a murmur of assent from the other jurors.

"I am sorry," said Ponsford. "To put it plainly, then, the dura mater is the covering or membrane beneath the bony skull. The dura forms what might be called a capsule for the brain. In this case the bleeding took place beneath that covering, indicating that great force had been employed to cause the injury."

"Then the nature of the injury is such that it could not, in your opinion, be caused by a simple fall downstairs?" asked the Coroner.

"No. I do not myself see how this particular injury could have been caused by that particular fall. I may say that it is the third of its kind that I have had occasion to study in the last few weeks. It very closely resembled the two wounds upon the head of the late James Martenroyde, one or both of which a jury sitting under you, sir, found to have caused his death."

At these words a buzz of bewildered excitement filled the cold little schoolroom and I realised, from the sudden jetting of a score of small clouds of white steam all round me, that even those who had not let their surprise become vocal had exhaled it in a silent chorus.

The Coroner, though obviously sharing the shock which the doctor's announcement had occasioned, was not one to be thrown easily off his balance.

"You have made a strange and rather disturbing statement, Doctor," he said, "and one of which notice will have to be taken in the proper place. But, for the moment, as we are dealing with the question of the deceased's bodily condition being not consistent with a fall downstairs, I must ask you if this, quite possibly coincidental, resemblance of which you have spoken is the sole reason you have to advance."

"Not at all, sir," answered Ponsford. "Setting the resemblance between the wounds entirely aside, I have two very good reasons for my opinion."

"Will you state them, Doctor?"

"Well, first consider the way in which the deceased was lying. She was found, on the testimony of Mrs. Martenroyde and of Mr. Ramsden Martenroyde, lying quite flat and straight, half in and half out of the doorway into the living room, her head and shoulders inside the room and the rest of her in the passage. Now if she had struck her head against either lintel, the blow would have arrested her course and twisted her round so that she lay in a huddle across the door. And if she had hit the bottom pedestal of the banister, as suggested by Mrs. Martenroyde, her feet might have come to rest a little way through the door, but it would have been even less possible for her body to have entered the room headfirst. Also there is nothing else at all, as the jury have seen for themselves, which she could have encountered in her fall which might have caused the fatal local injury."

"I see; and your second reason?"

"My second reason is that the deceased sustained no injury whatsoever save the fatal one referred to. There is not a single bruise, not even the faintest discoloration of the skin on any part of the body. If, as has been suggested – I say suggested because no one witnessed the accident – Mally Brewster, holding a tray in both hands, missed her footing at the top of the fifteen-foot staircase, then she might very likely have pitched headforemost down the first part of it, but she would have been bound to strike it lower down and to have made severe contact with some of the remaining stairs. Bruises and, taking the deceased's age into consideration, broken bones would have been inevitable. To miss the entire staircase, this old woman would have had to poise herself at the top, jump high in the air, and dive down. And such an inconceivable and suicidal manœuvre would have resulted almost certainly in a broken neck rather than a fractured skull."

"That sounds reasonable enough, Doctor," remarked the Coroner after a moment's thought. "Are there any . . ."

But his voice was drowned in a growling murmur from the jury and spectators alike, and an unidentified male voice was distinctly audible, saying: "Went t' same way as Martenroyde, poor owd lass. Happen she knew too much."

"Silence!" thundered the Coroner, and I was astonished to hear so great a voice proceeding from so small a man. "Any further noise or interruption and I will have the court cleared. Are there any questions?"

The room immediately quieted, and while Cordukes rose and inspected a small sheaf of notes in his hand, I stole a glance at Mrs. Martenroyde. But she was staring in front of her, with her high colour scarcely heightened. A cold north light caught her face from one of the little windows, and it seemed to me that she had aged some twenty years in half as many days.

"In your opinion, then, Doctor," asked Cordukes formally, "the injury could not have been caused by the fall downstairs?"

"In my opinion, no."

"You are quite convinced that there would necessarily be bruises on the corpse had it fallen?"

"Quite convinced."

"And there were none?"

"None at all. Not even a darkening at the knees and elbows, the parts where one would naturally expect it."

"Thank you."

Scarcely had the police lawyer sunk back on to his chair, when Pybus was on his feet, and it was easy to see from the set look on his somewhat ferret-like face that his questions were likely to be no mere formalities.

"You say 'naturally,' Doctor," he snapped. "What precisely do you mean by that vague and much abused term?"

"I mean," answered Ponsford, and there was an angry edge on his powerful voice, "that the necessary presence of bruises may be inferred from the nature of the thing falling and that of the thing fallen upon, and this apart from masses of empirical experience of what happens to people when they do fall downstairs."

At the promise of lost tempers given by these first exchanges between doctor and lawyers the room filled with that inevitable silent applause which marks either the slackening or quickening of attention on the part of an audience. But as this consisted, apart from a few indistinguishable murmurs, only in a universal stirring and shifting of position, the Coroner could hardly take official exception to it. Scarcely waiting for it to die down, Pybus continued:

"In other words, you are generalising from experience and founding a charge of foul play – trying, in fact, to put a rope round somebody's neck – simply because something you think should be there is not there?"

"Something I know should be there."

"Something you know should be there? Is that not rather an extraordinary word in the mouth of a man of science? Surely the whole history of medical practice is one of the discovery of exceptions to accepted generalised rules, and the isolation by this means of, let us say, some new disease for the doctors to cure?"

"It is not only a question of medical practice, it is a question of gravity, and of angles, and of the relative density of matter."

"Let us put it this way, then: at least you will admit that, in the course of your practice in a small Yorkshire village—"

"I haven't been here all my life, let me tell you."

"I see. I will put my question differently. In the course of your, er, peripatetic practice, you have found plenty of deviations from the normal, from the probable?"

A deep-throated growl was Ponsford's only reply.

"Now consider the case in point. The deceased is an old woman. Evidence goes to show that even in her prime she had not what you would call a quick brain. Recently she had the slow mental and physical reactions of an age approaching senility. She holds a tray full of crockery in her hands. For thirty years she has been trained not to smash things."

A few broad grins greeted this remark, but they were instantly frozen by the glance which the little Coroner let travel inexorably round the room.

"For thirty years she has striven, let us say, not to injure the property of the mistress to whom she is devoted. We have therefore the habits of a lifetime which would lead her to hold on to the tray as long as possible, coupled with the slow mental and physical reactions of her age. I put it to you, Dr. Ponsford, that in these circumstances it is possible for the deceased to have pitched from top to bottom of the staircase without doing more than brush any intervening stairs."

"I do not think it possible at all."

"And, even if you cannot admit the word 'brush,' and insist on a somewhat heavier contact, are there not great individual differences in susceptibility to bruising?"

"There are."

"Thank you, Doctor. Then I submit that the contact might be such that in a subject who might be described as a 'non-bruiser' no mark might have been left."

"I do not agree."

"Yet I put it to you—"

But here the Coroner interrupted:

"May I suggest, Mr. Pybus, that the medical evidence is not yet complete and that this subject could be more profitably pursued when it is complete."

22

DOCTORS AGREE

PYBUS MADE AS IF to protest, then checked himself and, with a stiff bow, resumed his seat, while the Coroner continued:

"I will now call Dr. Reeves-Norton. Dr. Reeves-Norton!"

The Shipton surgeon took the stand with sufficient leisureliness, but from the way he smoothed back his sparse hair and passed a finger round inside his collar, I judged that he did not feel so much at ease as had his robuster colleague.

"You have examined the body of the deceased, Dr. Reeves-Norton?" asked the Coroner, and when the new witness bowed, continued: "Please tell the court the result of your examination."

Thereupon Ponsford's old friend, in a dry, precise voice, deposed that the result of his examination had been the same in every particular as that of his brother medico, and that he had arrived at the same conclusion – namely, that the fatal injury could not have been caused by falling downstairs.

"Any questions?" asked the Coroner, and Cordukes again put his formal inquiry, not as one wishing for information, but rather with the air of a player noting his score.

"In fact," he said, "you are forced to the same conclusion as Dr. Ponsford, that death was the result of a blow delivered by some person on the head of the deceased?"

"No other conclusion seems to me possible."

Cordukes reseated himself with an air of satisfaction, and Pybus, in his eagerness, uttered his first few words before he had fairly got to his feet:

"You were called to his assistance by Dr. Ponsford, is that not so, Doctor?"

"It is so."

"Why?"

"I don't understand you. It was a most ordinary thing for a medical man to wish for a second opinion."

"The opinion of an expert?"

"Well—"

"Let us have this clear. Do you take your stand here as an expert?"

"It is probable that, with my surgical work at the hospital of an important town, I have had more experience than my colleague of the phenomena of violence."

"But do you not claim to be a medico-legal expert?"

"I do not. But—"

"Quite so. Therefore the jury are only being supplied with what I may call a couple of general medical opinions—"

"I do not see what point you are trying to make, Mr. Pybus," interrupted the Coroner.

"I will labour it no further, sir. Now tell me, Dr. Reeves-Norton; the body of the deceased had been moved from the foot of the stairs before you saw it?"

"Of course it had, seeing that it had been moved before the coming of my colleague, whose visit preceded mine. I should have thought—"

"And will you not agree with me that Dr. Ponsford also 'should have thought' – I am asking you as a medical man – before drawing scientific conclusions from unscientific evidence?"

But here the Coroner interrupted again:

"That is an improper question to put to the witness."

"Would it be a proper one to put to you, sir?"

"Scarcely proper, Mr. Pybus; but I do not object to it, since our only object is to ascertain the truth, and I am here as much for your guidance, or for the guidance of anyone concerned, as for that of the jury."

"Thank you, sir. Then will you kindly tell us what weight if any – I was about to bring this matter up when you, er, cut short my examination of Dr. Ponsford – what weight if any is to be attached to deductions drawn by a doctor from the evidence given by Mrs. Martenroyde and her son?"

"It sounds very much as if you were impugning the veracity of the family on whose behalf you are appearing before the court."

"I submit that such is not the case, sir. I am only endeavouring to show the ludicrousness of scientific deduction from unscientifically observed data. Neither of my clients is, I am almost happy to say, a scientist."

"I take your meaning, Mr. Pybus, but I do not agree with it. The evidence of the two witnesses to whom you refer has been admitted as fact, and it is legitimate to draw conclusions from facts."

"I am glad to have your ruling, sir." Then, quickly turning to the witness: "Perhaps you agree? Perhaps you are ready to stake your professional reputation on a deduction from the statements of Mrs. and Mr. Martenroyde – upright and excellent citizens, but, as I have said, no scientists – that it is impossible for the deceased's injury to have been received during a fall?"

"He's too quick, this fellow, for the Coroner," I thought, and indeed the witness had got no further than a hesitating stammer when Pybus was at him again:

"Therefore your whole contention rests on the absence of bruises?"

"Well, no one can swear that anything is impossible. Had I seen the body for myself in situ – But as regards the bruises, even if the deceased made none of the instinctive twisting and snatching movements to break a fall, the breasts and abdomen would have been bruised on the lower stairs."

"But do you not agree with Dr. Ponsford that there is a great deviation in individual susceptibility to bruises?"

"That is so."

"Then I put it to you that if she fell as you suggest—"

"I did not suggest it. On the contrary, I think it unlikely; I merely admit that it is conceivable."

"I beg your pardon, Doctor. I did not mean to offend against the accuracy of the scientific mind. If, then, the deceased fell as you think it conceivable that she may have fallen, I put it to you that her impact with the lower stairs would have been more in the nature of a slither than a bump, and that, if she were not susceptible to bruising, no discoloration of the skin would have been perceptible?"

"It seems to me so unlikely as to be virtually impossible that any skin would show no mark of the impact of the full weight of the body, which would be multiplied by its momentum, against the edges of stairs."

"Virtually impossible? By that do you mean really impossible?"

"Well, inconceivable."

Pybus threw a meaning look at the jury, in order doubtless that this last note of scientific wavering should echo in their minds, bowed to the witness and the Coroner, and resumed his seat.

Thereupon the discomfited surgeon, after half unconsciously glancing round the room as if in search of further enemies, asked the Coroner's leave to quit the court. The latter questioned Beverley and Cordukes with his eye and, receiving no response, gave the required permission. Whereupon Reeves-Norton, his angular frame more angular with pardonable indignation, stalked from the schoolroom, shutting the door behind him none too gently.

After a whispered word or two with Beverley, the Coroner turned to speak to the jury.

"That concludes the evidence, gentlemen. I will now – Yes, Mr. Pybus?"

The lawyer, who had bobbed up from his seat, answered firmly:

"With your permission, sir, I would like to put one or two supplementary questions to Mrs. Martenroyde."

"But you have already had the opportunity of examining Mrs. Martenroyde, and," glancing at his watch, "we're all busy men, you know."

"Yes, but I had not then heard the medical evidence. Counsel for the police elicited a statement from the witness which, taken in conjunction with the hypothesis put forward by the doctors, contains a suggestion most unfair to my client."

"Be more explicit, please."

"My client stated that she was entirely alone in the house at the time of the accident. The medical witnesses state that it is probable to the verge of certainty that death was caused by foul play."

"Very well, then," conceded the Coroner. "Mrs. Martenroyde, please!"

As soon as the enigmatical owner of Hannah's Castle had taken the stand for the second time, Pybus questioned her thus:

"You said, Mrs. Martenroyde, that you were all alone in the house when the deceased met with her accident. Can you be certain of this? Can you be certain that there was no door or window by which some third person might have entered?"

"I couldn't say," replied the witness, "that there mightn't have been a window unsnibbed."

"And you yourself were busy in another part of the house when the accident happened?"

"Ay, I was clattering among my dishes."

"Clattering among your dishes. And in a different part of a large house. Thank you, Mrs. Martenroyde."

Hannah resumed her seat, and the Coroner looked hard at Pybus, as if hoping and expecting that he would do the same. But the lawyer evidently wished there to be no possible misunderstanding as to the conclusion to be drawn from his client's last statement.

"If you will bear with me for a moment longer, sir," he said, "I will make my point quite clear to the jury. Even if conclusive medical evidence can be obtained that the deceased was murdered, there still remains, as you can see from Mrs. Martenroyde's statement, the possibility of the presence in the house of an unknown third party. He could have entered unheard while Mrs. Martenroyde was clattering in the kitchen, and he could have retired unheard while she was absorbed in ministering to the injured woman, fetching restoratives, going out into the street to find a messenger to send to the mill, and so on. In view of Dr. Ponsford's statement that the wound bears a striking resemblance to those which struck down Mr. James Martenroyde, it would seem probable that the second 'murder,' should it ever by expert testimony be proved to be such, was committed by the same hand. Let us hope that if this poor old woman was murdered, the police will be more successful in bringing the murderer to justice than they have so far been in the case of James Martenroyde."

"That is a most improper hope, Mr. Pybus," commented the Coroner, "or, rather, a hope most improperly expressed. Excuse me, gentlemen of the jury, for a moment."

Here he read a note which had been handed along to him and which I had noticed Beverley scribbling during Pybus's last speech.

When he had absorbed its contents, the Coroner said:

"Pray be seated, Mr. Pybus. Should you wish to be heard further, I will grant you an opportunity later. For the moment I call Superintendent Beverley. You want to make a statement on behalf of the police, Superintendent?" he concluded, as my friend took the stand.

"I think it will be fairer to all concerned if I do so," answered Beverley. "There was, as we agreed, sir, nothing to be gained by calling on the police, in the person of myself, as I did not reach the house until after the body had been moved and since the finding of the jury has to be made on medical evidence alone. But, now that Mr. Pybus has raised the subject, I wish to tell the jury that on the morning of the death of Mally Brewster I took the opportunity, while the two doctors were with the body and the three members of the Martenroyde family were talking to Mr. Eddison, of giving the house and grounds a necessarily hasty but sufficiently thorough examination."

"And you made some discovery germane to Mr. Pybus's suggestion of the presence of a third person?"

"I did. I saw no sign, mind you, of such a person's entrance, presence, or exit, but I did satisfy myself that such entrance and exit would have been possible. One of the two French windows in the morning room, on the left side of the house as you face from the road, was slightly ajar, and within three feet of it runs a flagged path incapable of footprints and leading eventually both to the front gate and to the outbuildings at the back of the house. That is all, sir."

"Thank you, Superintendent," said the Coroner, and while Beverley returned to his place, he continued:

"Are you satisfied, Mr. Pybus? Or have you anything else to add which bears on the present case?"

"Only one thing, sir," answered Pybus, as ungraciously as ever. "I wish to ask for an adjournment so that a third and expert opinion – that of Dr. Browning, of Leeds Medical School – may be obtained as to the cause of death."

"What, three medical opinions, Mr. Pybus? This is most unusual."

"It may be unusual," maintained Pybus, "but I have the interests of my client to consider. We have had two medical opinions which might be considered distinctly prejudicial to her, but in reality I submit that they are really only one opinion, that of two friends, quite ordinary practitioners, if I may say so without offence, and seeing, I contend, with the same eyes."

"Very well," acquiesced the Coroner, after a considerable pause for cogitation. "It is a most unusual case, and I therefore adjourn this inquest for three weeks, in order that Dr. Browning may be consulted and that the police may take what steps they think fit."

As Mrs. Martenroyde left the schoolroom and, escorted on each side by one of her sons, embarked upon her return to the Mill House, black looks and harsh murmurs accompanied her. And as she receded, these murmurs swelled into a sort of muffled angry roar, as if to keep pace with her.

The inquest had been adjourned, but the mill hands of Todmanhawe were recording their verdict.

23

THE GUILTY WIFE

ON THE EVENING AFTER the inquest, perhaps the strangest and least satisfactory function of its kind in all my experience, I was sitting with Stephen Eddison and discussing the events of the morning above a bright fire. We had planned an early bed, but lingered to talk over the evidence of the two doctors.

"I suppose it's a foregone conclusion that Dr. Browning will agree with Ponsford and Reeves-Norton?" I asked.

"I should say so," answered Eddison, "though if the case ever comes to trial he might leave a lawyer's loophole as Reeves-Norton did. But it never will. The Coroner's verdict is sure to be murder against some person or persons unknown, and the police will continue to investigate."

"The spectators made it pretty clear what they thought."

"And Pybus had the sense to face that issue and to show that there was no legal case against his client. Poor Mally! I wish that picturesque cap she always wore had been substantial enough to deaden the blow!"

So saying, Eddison drew his chair closer to the blaze and relighted his pipe. Then he continued:

"Yes. It's sad enough, after thirty years. I don't know which murder you are trying to prove on Hannah, but you must admit that thirty years of the mistress-servant relation presumes, to an unbiased audience at least, a mutual devotion telling strongly against the possibility of her mistress brutally murdering Mally."

"Not if Hannah's own life were in danger," I argued. "And why does Mally run away? Because she can't stand seeing James's ghost every night. What is that but her own way of saying that James's murder is somehow connected with the Mill House? Or, if she really thought she saw it, what is that but the reaction of guilty knowledge?"

"Two murders laid at Hannah's door? And not an atom of proof for either. And I can't say I'm sorry. I've known Hannah for thirty years. She has been upright, though never generous; done her duty – though never more than her duty – according to her lights; was an adoring sister and has been a devoted mother."

"Well," said I, "you can't expect me to sympathise with your point of view. I have only known Hannah for a week or two, and in that time I have seen her try to take possession of her bene-factor's house before he was buried, and with an evident enjoy-ment of the good fortune she thought his death had brought her that was simply revolting. Also, and still more revolting, I have heard her blackguard him because it turned out he had not left her his money, and I've seen her give an exhibition of temper which had all the violence of a fishwife's with none of its saving geniality."

"You must remember that she never forgave James for jilting Deborah," countered Eddison. "Still, it was a disgusting exhibi-tion and, I would add, proof of her innocence of any complicity in James's death, were it not that her temper is getting less controllable with age."

"Has she always been something like that?" I asked.

Eddison took a few meditative puffs before replying and then answered judicially: "I must say she has always been liable to outbursts of rage which were abnormal in her social position. There's a queer streak in the family. Deborah was a strange girl. Sometimes she would be quite charming to meet, sometimes

you could get neither word nor smile from her. A melancholy
type, but of course that might have been her disappointment
over James. Sugden is like his mother without her strength. He
has got the worst of both parents, the mother's temper and the
father's weakness. As a child he would fall into black tempers
that made him ill. It was dangerous to his health to cross him
– and he was the youngest – so he never learned self-control.
When he is suddenly transplanted from our dead-alive Todmanhawe to the lights of London, he goes right off the hooks,
as they say. But what was James to do? Ramsden would have
been hopeless in London and was needed at the mill. Sugden
had address, smartness, and readiness of speech."

"Ramsden seems a thoroughly good chap," I ventured.

"Ramsden's pure Martenroyde," he answered; "little of
James's initiative, but all his character."

Eddison had just adjured me to fill up my glass before turning
in and we were both in process of concocting night-caps when
Beverley was announced.

"Come in, come in, Superintendent," said Eddison heartily.
"We were just going to turn in early, having exhausted the topic
of the inquest, but no doubt you have some fresh thoughts for
us."

"I have come to be comforted," growled Beverley, approaching the fire and warming his hands at it. "It's a rough night. Half
a gale, and with wet in it."

"Then make yourself comfortable," urged Eddison, pointing
to the third easy chair, "and join us in a drink. Say when!"

"Never!" said Beverley, as he collapsed into the chair with a
grunt of dissatisfaction, but his eye brightened somewhat when
Eddison handed him a hospitably dark whisky and soda.

"I don't suppose you found the inquest too exhilarating?" I
asked.

"No," replied the Superintendent. "Yet what else could I
expect? But that's not to say I'm pleased. An adjourned inquest

and two murders on my hands, and not a clue to either – at least, not one that comes near to justifying another warrant!"

"But you have your suspicions?"

"Oh, I agree with the spectators. It was pretty clear what they thought. Two murders in one family, so to speak, and done the same way. I can't credit there's no connection."

"But," objected Eddison, "remember that the mill has it in for Mrs. Martenroyde, and we're all mill-folk more or less round here."

"May be. But you can't deny that everything points to her. And that stick she carries round is just the thing to do the damage in both cases."

Not for the first time I felt supremely uncomfortable. It was all very well for Eddison to take a typical lawyer's pleasure in withholding Ann Kitteridge's evidence from the police, but I, though I was equally in honour bound, hated to "hold out," as the Americans say, on a brother detective.

"It looks as if you'd have to call in the Yard," said Eddison at length.

"And they'll be able to do nothing. And they'll put their failure down to being called in when the scent's cold. I know."

"And you'll all have to fall back on the homicidal maniac," chuckled our host, "our dear old friend who leaves no trace of his presence, the murderous lunatic at large. He's saved the face of law and order before now."

"Oh, don't be too funny!" grumbled poor Beverley. "You see my position. My only hope is to get into the Mill House again and see as much of the Mill House people as possible. If there's any clue, it's there. If I could get those three talking off their guard, they might drop something that would give me a lead. Even if none of them committed either of the murders, I swear they know something. But with things left as they are, how am I going to get in? Until Dr. Browning has seen the body, I can do nothing."

He rose impatiently from his chair, went over to the window, drew back the curtains a little, and shivered. "It's a hell of a night, but I suppose I must get out into it." He raised the sash a few inches, and the wind howled into the room.

"Shut down the window," begged Eddison, "and get your coat on, if you must go. Camberwell and I will see you to your car. I hope there's nothing amiss with your headlights. You'll have a dark run into Shipton."

Beverley was in the act of shutting down the window when he paused. Then he threw it wide open and leaned out into the rough wind. Finally he turned back into the room with an exclamation of annoyance.

"It sounds as if you were due for a visitor before you get your beauty sleep," he said. "Someone has just run up to your front door in a mighty excitement, judging by the rumpus she's making. Let's hope it isn't Mrs. John and her walking-stick. I, for one, don't feel equal to her tonight!"

Eddison looked at me apologetically. "I wonder who it can be," he said, glancing at his watch. "It's only just nine, but our talk by the fire has made me so drowsy that no visitor will be very welcome, especially an agitated female."

Even as he spoke, Mrs. Heggus burst headlong into the room, without waiting for the formality of announcement, a wild figure blown to us from a wild night. Her mass of hair was disarranged and falling about her shoulders. She was breathing hard and seemed on the verge of a collapse.

"Who's here?" she called in a loud voice. "Who's here that will help a poor woman to her rights? Happen there's be someone at least to lend me a hand in my troubles."

She stood staring at the three of us, swaying lightly on her feet. Eddison approached her and took her hand. He spoke solicitously to her, but she flung him off.

"Nay, nay – I'm put off no longer with fine soft talk. It's doings I want." She rushed out the words, throwing the hair back impatiently from her forehead and making an imploring gesture. "It's a man I want who will see me right after others have cheated me. Dakin's no use. Poor Dakin's no use! And God forgive me for my ways to him!"

At these words, and to our consternation, she burst into a violent storm of weeping, calling alternately on God and her husband. We gathered round her in dismay as she flung herself into a chair and rocked to and fro in an abandonment of misery. Eddison spoke soothingly to her and motioned us to leave her to him. So Beverley and I retired to the doorway and conferred in whispers, while the woman gradually took command of herself again. The Superintendent told me in a low voice that he thought he had better stay on awhile since this outburst seemed to promise something for him. I replied that apparently his summing up of his Yorkshire friends was correct – they held out longer than most people, but when they did let themselves go, it was without restraint.

"And I may profit by that now!" he whispered grimly. "I'll get something out of this before we're done, you'll see."

"Now then, Mrs. Heggus; now then, Mira," Eddison was saying; "are you able to tell us what's troubling you? You know who these two gentlemen are – Superintendent Beverley and Mr. Camberwell, from London. They called on you the other day, and you took them up to see Prissy Mallison, you mind. Either will help you if he can; and you know well that you can count on me as an old friend to yourself and your husband."

At this mention of Dakin Heggus, Mira seemed likely to start weeping afresh, but a glass from the ever hospitable decanter and the counsels of her host brought back the flash to her eye and calmed her rapid breathing. She sprang to her feet when she had drained her glass, and addressed us all:

"It's sick I am of the Mill House folk – sick to death of 'em! What do they want meddling and muddling and spoiling my life? I was an honest God-fearing woman till Sugden Martenroyde crossed my path, bad success to him! Then he made me wish my poor husband dead – 'our' Sugden, with his grand cunning speech and his smart London ways. God may never forgive me for that; but it's deeds I want now; there's no more time left for weeping. I'll have vengeance on them all from now on, I will."

And then, after tactful solicitation from the three of us, she reseated herself and recited a page of past history.

24

PAST HISTORY

MIRA SPOKE EARNESTLY, AS if to let no detail go unuttered now that she had made up her mind to tell her story; and we listened intently.

Stephen Eddison lay back and bit at his pipe; Beverley sat upright in his chair, with his eyes fixed on the narrator's face, a dog ready to bristle to attention at any scent that might interest the police. I lazed and admired the expressions which flitted across Mira's handsome face.

She told of the beginning of a sorrowful epoch in the lives of her husband and herself, when Dakin was first attacked by the fatal malady that now had him fast in its grip. She had started to chafe at the enforced attendance, the ever strengthening tie of a helpless husband. She asked us to imagine how the long days irked her with no break in their monotony. She pleaded that we should picture her horror at the thought that there would be no release for her as long as her husband lived – her, a young and handsome woman, but two years wedded.

"We'd been gay together for those two years – Dakin and I," she said. "He was a fine chap and a warm man, with a bit of money for us to spend together. We had nowt to spend it on but our own pleasure, for no babes came to us, and we followed our bent without heeding other folk."

She told us how she had loved the carefree life, the jaunts into the neighbouring villages and townships, their thoughts of buying a small car to make their excursions still more pleasant.

"It don't make a gloomy day any better to have a lightsome past to look back upon. Some folk say it do, but I know it don't. When the past has been so short, a body scarce knows they've had it, and what's to come stretches ever boding dark over the hills."

She buried her face in her hands, fighting her emotion.

"We all understand," put in Eddison gently, "how you must have felt when Dakin sickened with this terrible complaint, and all your plans had to be given up."

Mira went on to relate how at first they had "bided" quiet at home, getting one medical opinion after another on Dakin's case. She had taken him farther and farther afield, and he had spent much time in hospitals, while she waited at home, doubting and fearing. The money that went so far when they were buying enjoyment, went not quite so far when they were paying for specialists and electric treatment. She restricted herself to living alone and doing for herself during those enforced separations, in order to save for further invalid expenses; and time hung heavy on her hands.

It was during one of her husband's sojourns in hospital that Sugden Martenroyde came into her life. Whereas before she had merely passed the time of day with him, owing to the unpopularity of his mother, he now began to haunt her home when he was in Todmanhawe. " 'Our' Sugden!" she commented bitterly. "Well, he very soon became 'my' Sugden too!"

At the start he proffered decorous sympathy in her misfortune and pretended to busy himself with inquiries among the doctors of his acquaintance. Next came the suggestion of a few outings together, to take her mind off her loneliness when Dakin was away. Then all talk of Dakin ceased. Sugden's dashing imitation of London words and ways had come as a welcome change, she said, from the dour contact of the neighbours she had never tried to cultivate during her happiness. Sugden seemed occasionally to have plenty of money to spend on presents and for her entertainment. Soon she became his mistress.

"How long ago was that?" interrupted Beverley.

"Let me see, now. We've been married five years come midsummer, and Dakin's been poorly for three of them. It'll be two years gone since I gave myself to Sugden Martenroyde."

"But how did you keep all this from Dakin?" asked Eddison. "He must have been at home a great deal between whiles."

"We contrived," said Mira.

She told us of the shifts to which they had resorted to keep their intrigue hidden; of their perpetual dodging of Mrs. John Martenroyde. The latter was evidently one of those mothers who insist on knowing everything there is to know about their sons. She did not invite their confidence, but tried to force it. Consequently she received no intimate information. Mira also described with remorse how she had so often left Dakin rejoicing in the fact that she took such comfort in her solitary walks on the hillsides round Todmanhawe.

"Now Sugden's done the dirty on me, and I owe him no more faith, though indeed faith was never mine to steal away from Dakin and give to him. Eh, that Sugden! I'll have vengeance on him, come what may!" She shook with indignation, and Eddison spoke gently.

"But, Mira, I don't understand. You say that Sugden has done the dirty on you. How? You can't keep a man of his sort for lover indefinitely, you know."

"I do know. But he needn't flaunt another girl in London where I haven't the chance of getting in a month o' Sundays. Dressing her up, too, and taking her to eat at hotels with the greatest in the land. Louie's no better than me, and both of us no better than we should be."

Eddison looked at me. "Do you remember Colonel Houston and his story of the young ladies at the Grand Transatlantic? This Louie may have been one of them."

I nodded.

"Ay, it's that Sparks lass I mean. She left the mill – lured away, some say – and followed Sugden about in London, pestering him to give her a good name, or a good time. I've done with him, but I don't want her to have him, the slut!" Mira's eyes shone ominously in the firelight. "Sugden, my honest lover! This last six months, while he pretended that he lived only for his visits to Todmanhawe, he was borrowing money off me, which was Dakin's and put aside for treatment, to keep that fancy girl in London."

"Dear, dear!" said Eddison. "This is all most distressing! But why don't you let her have him? Does it upset you so much, Mira, that you have worked yourself free from a cad like that?"

"It is not that," answered Mira. "Trust me to have done with him and all the harm he's wrought. No, it's something I've still to tell ye. May happen it will bring punishment to him and his hellcat of a mother."

Beverley stiffened in his chair.

"Listen," she said, "this piece may be in your line. On the night that James Martenroyde was killed, Sugden came over to see me in a great taking."

"What time was that?" asked Beverley quickly.

"Quarter to eight in the evening or thereabouts, it was. He came in all of a sweat for money. I let him in by the back way so as Dakin wouldn't see him, and he begged and prayed me for a hundred pounds or more. He'd borrowed of me often, though never anything like that, and when I told him that I'd nowt in the house, he carried on something shameful. He thought I could come to his help over some trouble he'd met in London, and he promised faithful to marry me, when Dakin died."

"If that's all," said Beverley in a disappointed voice, when it seemed that Mira's disclosure was over, "your tale's no sort of good to me, Mrs. Heggus. You can't arrest a man because he tries to borrow a hundred pounds, you know."

"And furthermore," interrupted Eddison, "surely all this was some time ago. Why did you tear in to see us in such a state over something that might almost be forgotten by now?"

Mira answered sullenly enough: "I did not know about that Louie then. You see, Bill Heggus, my brother-in-law, before ever he took the train for London this evening, was chatting to Dakin and me all about murder and the Martenroydes. And he mentioned about seeing Louie in London with Sugden, all dressed up to kill, and of Sugden leaving his rooms, and how certainly Louie and he was living together. And, by the living God," she went on shrilly, "I want vengeance on that little swine and on his murdering sow of a mother!"

"Murdering?" queried Beverley. "What do you mean by calling Mrs. Martenroyde a murderess?"

"She murdered James and Mally; they're all saying so."

"That's no good in a court of law, my girl."

"But she tried to murder me too. Threatened to do it and tried."

"What's that?" cried Beverley in obvious excitement.

"Ay," answered Mira heavily. "When Bill Heggus told me of Louie, I flung off hot-foot – oh, I was a fool! – to Mill House."

"And what happened?" It was Eddison who put the question.

"Well, she barred the way when I asked for Sugden – wanted to know my business. And I told her everything. I had a mind to humble her with the knowledge that her precious son had stooped to a woman of the village. She called me a common whore that had ruined her Sugden. I tried to get by her, and she snatched her great stick from the hall rack and aimed a blow at my head. If I hadn't stepped aside she would have caught me, too."

"Any witness?" snapped Beverley.

"I'm thinking that that Sugden was skulking at the back somewhere, but he'd perjure himself to save a headache, that he would."

"Still," cried Beverley, rising from his chair, "that's none so bad! A threat of violence and an attack – there's my excuse for visiting the Mill House; and maybe I'll catch the Martenroydes with their tongues a bit loosened by temper. But I'd like witnesses myself, if I can think of a good reason for bringing anyone with me."

"Well, if you must," grumbled Eddison, "on a night like this, it's easy enough for you to take me. I'm trustee of the Martenroyde estate, and therefore in some sense guardian of the family. It would be natural for me, as their adviser, to be present."

"And I'm retained by Eddison here," I cut in. "You can say I'm there to keep an eye on the police in the Martenroyde interests!"

Eddison and I left Mira ensconced by the fire and followed Beverley to the front door, but there we found him in conversation with a newcomer on the doorstep, who was gabbling feverishly to him and pulling at his coat sleeve in agitation. From the little we could see of this unexpected intruder, she was dressed in finery much bedraggled and had difficulty in keeping the drenched wreck of a fashionable hat attached to her head in the howling wind.

Beverley turned to us. "I say, this is rather a coincidence after our talk just now. I think that this young lady had better come in for shelter too. May we return to the fire a minute?" He took the girl's arm, and we accompanied him back to the hall, half guessing what he meant.

"Go in first, and then there'll be a pair of you," he said, giving the woman a gentle push and opening the door.

Mira Heggus rose in confused surprise at the stranger's entrance.

"Louie Sparks – what do you here?"

25

ASSAULT OF HANNAH'S CASTLE

THE WANING FIRELIGHT FLICKERED over the faces of the two women who had played leading parts in Sugden Martenroyde's trivial life. Upon Mira Heggus with her gypsy beauty and stormy mien, and upon Louie Sparks, whose hair was of a dubious platinum and whose hard little claws were thick with a scarlet that sadly needed either refreshing or abolishing.

Eddison and I had stayed in the shadows, determined to remain nothing but spectators of a scene which might well prove no comedy; while Beverley shuffled uneasily on his feet. "It's taking a risk confronting them," he muttered.

The engagement began briskly enough.

"So Louie Sparks is taking a holiday from the London season," said Mira, without looking at her opponent. "Happen they're spring-cleaning early at Sugden Martenroyde's fine house in Park Lane."

"Ah, so Mira Heggus hasn't forgotten her Sugden!" countered Louie, also looking straight before her. "Village love-story with words and music, music of Dakin's bell. Sugden told me all about that."

"The foul wee tike! But thank God I never nosed all over London after him, like a bought wench."

"Ay, and thank the living God, whatever else I did, I never deserted a helpless husband just because I'd gotten tired of nursing him."

The fight was over. Mira wrung her hands in anguish.

"Oh, Louie, it's God's own truth you say, and I'm a dear sight worse, when all's said and done. You've betrayed nobody but yersen. Oh, you're younger than I am, my poor lass, and my heart aches for you – so pale and clemmed-looking. I'm well filled, if nowt else."

At this Louie winced and fumbled at the waistband of her flimsy skirt.

"Clemmed-looking, you say, Mira Heggus? Then I look what I am indeed. I've had no bite or sup today. My train fare was all I could get together, and I was daft enough to go seeking from him who owes me."

Mira exclaimed in excitement: "Did you go to the Mill House too this night? I'll warrant you had worse then than my greeting, being the second on that cub's trail within an hour or two."

"She called me all the kinds of drab she could lay her tongue to, if that's what you mean. And she said I'd made Sugden embezzle money from the business. She took a crack at me with her stick and chased me out of the door and down the road. I'd no place to flee to but Mr. Eddison's."

"Ay, she's got hell in her, that woman," cried Mrs. Heggus.

"As long as she keeps it in her, that's not my concern," said Beverley, "but when she lets it loose, it's my right and duty to interfere. Come on, you two, and let's get to Mill House before the row's over between Sugden and his mother. For I reckon there's surely been a good one. You stay here with Mrs. Heggus, Louie, my girl, until we come back and decide what's best to do with you. These two gentlemen and I will go and see the Martenroydes."

"Nay," said Mira gently, putting her hand on the other girl's shoulder. "We're sisters in a sort and I'll take Louie home with me and give her sup and shelter. Dakin's heart is so large that he'll find room for her, and maybe that'll be counted for me too. Maybe I'll creep back into his heart as well. The poor lad will never know, on this side of heaven, that I left my corner in it. But punish me that witch and her son, Mr. Policeman! I'd die content if I knew they'd paid their reckoning."

"I can't punish Mrs. John for her threatening, but I can caution her severely – and I will," said Beverley. "Come along quickly, all of you."

"Wait a minute," said Eddison, and he took an old coat from the cupboard and wrapped it round Louie Sparks. Then the little procession left the house and stepped into the teeth of the winter wind and rain.

It was just such a forceful gale from the north-west as had blown on the night James Martenroyde had met his end. Our small party stood undecided for a moment, bracing itself against the gusts; then, with myself in the middle giving an arm to each girl, and Beverley and Eddison arming them on the outsides, we staggered towards the path which led up to Dakin's house. When the lights from the hillside homestead came into view, Mira thanked us for our escort and led Louie Sparks towards the shelter of her dwelling.

Stumbling down the rocky path, we three made our way to the banks of the Scarth with as much speed as we could muster. As we buffeted our way along, Beverley shouted in my ears: "It's my belief that disappointment has made the old woman really daft, dangerously daft. Threats of violence to all and sundry. She'd counted on inheriting the grange and the mill outright."

When at last, drenched and bewildered, we arrived at the old house, we crept silently round the corner of it to the paved yard at the back. There Beverley knocked lightly on the door, and it was opened at once by Ramsden Martenroyde.

His stolid face wore an expression of anxiety, and in answer to Beverley's inquiries for his mother, he told us that she was out, visiting a Mrs. Priest, who was not expected to last till morning. He bade us enter, however, and shelter from the night. "Come your ways, gentlemen," he said, leading us into the front parlour, where a fire was laid but not lit. "I expect I'll be able to aid you in anything, as Mother isn't just handy."

"I'm afraid not, Mr. Martenroyde," said Beverley. "It is my duty to see your mother, for two serious charges have been laid against her; so I hope she won't be long. Also I should like to see your brother, as he has some concern with these charges."

Ramsden sulkily assured us that Sugden had accompanied the old lady, and Beverley answered that he would wait all the same.

Suddenly the Superintendent gave an exaggerated shiver and, stepping through the parlour door, walked heavily to the front door. This he opened and then slammed shut, and afterwards returned cat-foot to the parlour, very gently closing its door.

Immediately, and before Ramsden's rather slow brain could realise Beverley's tactics, high-pitched voices, male and female, became audible from some room in the back of the house, as if an interrupted quarrel were now free to be resumed.

Ramsden swore beneath his breath and excused himself heavily. "Hasn't a man a right to say people are out when they're not wanting visitors?"

"Not to the police," retorted Beverley, "and not in a house where murder has been done and the murderer is yet uncaught."

We accompanied the reluctant Ramsden down the stone passage to the kitchen, where we found Mrs. Martenroyde standing by the range, adjusting a kettle of boiling water over the embers. A bottle of whisky stood on the langsettle by her side, and Sugden leaned against the table glaring at his mother.

Mrs. Martenroyde swung round at our entrance, her eyes congested with fury. "What's the meaning of this damned intrusion?" she cried. "What right have you to force your way into my house, you Beverley, and you, you snake in the grass, you Eddison?"

Eddison answered her soothingly. "I chanced to be with Beverley when two serious charges were made against you, madam, and, as trustee of the Martenroyde interests, I thought it better to come out, even on this rough night, to be at hand if you happened to want advice."

"And how about that?" continued the old lady, pointing at me.

"He is a private inquiry agent, as well you know," replied Eddison, "and after today's inquest I retained him to watch over your interests and to try, for all our sakes, to help to solve these two distressing mysteries."

It almost seemed as if she had not attended to either of his answers; she looked utterly blank for a moment, and then, as if one shutter in her mind had fallen and another opened, became almost a different person.

"Come your ways in, sirs, come your ways in. You're kindly welcome to a seat by the fire and a drop of comfort on this cold night. You must excuse me if I did not greet you at first, but – I was not dressed fit for folks." She indicated her apron and rolled-back sleeves.

We refused the offer of a drink as politely as we could, and I think my friends were as hard put to it as I was to hide their astonishment at this volte-face.

"Well, well, if you won't, you won't. I was just going to make one for mysen. I have it every night, and then I go to sleep as sudden as a babe and dream of nowt. Ay, of nowt."

But as soon as Beverley mentioned the two charges of assault, Hannah's mood shifted again.

"And you take the word of two common trollops against mine, of an adultress and a streetwalker?"

"Whatever their characters, two people do not come entirely independently and make exactly the same complaint without there being grounds for it."

"Complaint, d'ye say? It's me who should make the complaint. They entered my house by force, and I had to do what I could."

"Hadn't they a right to see you?" asked Beverley, suddenly wheeling on Sugden; but it was Hannah who answered:

"This is my house, not Sugden's, and well he'll know that in the future."

Beverley repeated his question and when Sugden, blushing furiously, yelled back: "No!" he continued: "Then do you deny that you lured Louie Sparks up to London with a promise of money? Be careful, you've been seen with her several times, you know."

"If a girl chooses to follow me up to London," replied Sugden sullenly, "am I to blame? I never asked her to come."

"And I suppose it was sheer politeness or an affection for the old village that made you take her out and spend money on her?"

Sugden's reply was drowned by a torrent of indignation on the part of his mother, of which we could distinguish little but repetitions and variations of "common mill-girl," "a son of mine," and "my brass."

"Shut up!" yelled Sugden at last. "These men don't want to hear all our private affairs. Keep your gabbing mouth closed, can't you?"

The old woman – for so indeed she seemed in comparison with the Mrs. John Martenroyde who had motored with me from Shipton only a week or two ago – shook her fist in her son's face. "And now he tells the mother that bore him to hold her tongue! Hear him, please!"

But she soon subsided into inarticulate grumbling, and Beverley went on:

"Do you deny that you borrowed money from Mrs. Dakin Heggus?"

Sugden was taken completely by surprise. He went very white, his lips fell apart, and he made no attempt to answer.

Hannah's volubility made up for her son's silence, however. She burst forth into a stream of bitter denunciation, from which we gathered that he had been writing to her for money, to be spent on business hospitality, which, he said, James was too old-fashioned to sanction, and of which the latter could not be told until he saw its results in the improvement of the London end of the business. "There'll be no more London for you, my fine fellow," she finished. "Henceforth you'll bide in Todmanhawe and in your wretched mother's house. Henceforth you'll be taking commands from our Ramsden. Whining to your mother for brass! And whining to that jack-tart Mira Heggus for brass! And then wasting it all on a Louie Sparks!"

Sugden's fury was really terrible to witness. He leaped towards his mother with an animal growl; but before he could reach her, the three of us, assisted by the ever silent Ramsden, had him under control. It would be hard to say after that whether we were the keener to throw him out of the house to cool his rage, or he to leave it of his own accord. The group around him found itself first in the passage and then at the front door. I think it was Eddison who opened it; certainly it was Sugden who flung himself through it with no help from us. He was standing out in the rain of the pitch-black night, cursing all women in a horrible sort of whisper, when Beverley closed the door upon him. And when we four went back to the kitchen, Hannah Martenroyde sat in her chair by the fire, staring into the glow of the open range, with her great Bible open on her knees. She took no notice at all of our return.

Eddison and I were quite ready to go, but Beverley wished for a few words with the taciturn Ramsden. We were soon ensconced in the parlour, with hot grogs, which we now saw no reason to refuse, to mitigate the change of temperature from the warm kitchen.

When pipes were well alight and first sips taken from steaming glasses, Beverley spoke long and seriously to our host. He had come over that evening, he explained, to warn Hannah in person, but now it was his duty instead to warn the one really responsible member of the family that his mother must not be allowed to threaten and attack people, even in her own house, and that Sugden on his return must be treated to as heavy a dose of the elder brother as Ramsden could compass.

I admired the reasonable way in which Beverley urged his point of view, never hinting at his own suspicions of Hannah, but basing his recommendations on the fact that the police would have to take action in any case of future Martenroyde violence, and that such action, before the two murders were solved, would inevitably prejudice local feeling more and more against the family.

When Beverley had finished, Ramsden, perhaps for the first time in his life, talked without hesitation or apparent reserve of his home life. The minutes slipped by as we heard instance after instance of Sugden's boyish fits of uncontrollable rage, and the more I listened, the more insistently the word "epilepsy" whispered itself in my ear. But, according to Ramsden, soon after he was eighteen, Sugden's rages had not only moderated but become rarer, and when he left for London he was to all seeming a perfectly normal young man.

On the other hand, Ramsden went on to explain, his mother's tempers had broken out at vivid intervals ever since he could remember and had become more frequent since the death of James and her consequent disappointment. Also since then she had unaccountably aged, "crippled down towards the grave," as Ramsden put it.

"That'll be Sugden back," he cried, as a violent knocking on the front door interrupted him. "Damn the young fool, he'll frighten Mother!"

But when the knocking ceased for the moment, it was a woman's voice we heard, shouting: "Let me in! Mr. Beverley, Mr. Eddison, are you there still? For God's sake, let me in!"

26

THE RINGING IN THE NIGHT

RAMSDEN WAS THE FIRST to reach the door, with the rest of us close behind him, and next moment Louie Sparks staggered into the passage. She was panting shrilly and was so near collapse that I had to hold her up while she gasped out her news: murder was like to happen and would we go, would we go?

"Who's being murdered – and where?" demanded Beverley, shaking her gently. "Pull yourself together, lass!"

"It's Mira Heggus – up at the house – Sugden. He'll kill her, I think – he's foaming at the mouth. Oh, my God! He said we two had turned his mother and the world against him – said I'd be the next. Oh, hurry, in Christ's name, gentlemen!"

I had a momentary glimpse of Hannah Martenroyde standing within earshot at the open kitchen door and of Ramsden running towards her. I heard Eddison's murmured: "My place is here, Beverley," and then, without ever having started, it seemed, the Superintendent and I were running and stumbling against the rainy wind through the black night towards the house on the hillside.

As we neared the tragic homestead we could hear the unceasing clangour of a bell, pealing out from an upper window

and making an ugly night more hideous still. I could picture
the poor, helpless husband, frantic with the knowledge that
he could not stir a finger to aid that wife whose willing feet
had so often run to answer the call of his sheep-bell. Beverley
shouted up to stop dinging, as help had come, and ran round
the corner of the house. "In parlour at back," called down Dakin
distractedly; "hurry! Hurry!"

I rushed after Beverley into the Heggus parlour. It was
brightly lighted and seemed to be empty. A small table had been
overturned, the rugs were rucked with trampling, crockery was
scattered over the floor, and a loaf of bread lay where it had
evidently fallen in the fireplace. All this we took in at a glance,
and then our eyes were drawn, as if by a common instinct, to
the corner of the room on the right of the door. A tall, massive
wooden chair was set in the angle, and crumpled down in it was
Mira Heggus, her gypsy beauty distorted by the throes of a tor-
turing death, and the violent marks of Sugden Martenroyde's
last embrace slowly beginning to stain her white neck.

Beverley dropped on his knees and felt the still pulse; then he
rose and looked round. I had not thought him capable of the
passion which showed in his face. "Now then, where is he?" he
growled. "By God, he's daddled me before with his alibis, but
this time – ! Go up to Dakin, Camberwell, and try to break this
gently to him, though I doubt he's certain of the worst already.
Poor soul, this will about be his death, I reckon. I'll have to rout
out the lads and scour the countryside for Master Sugden – 'our'
Sugden – 'my' Sugden now."

But even as he spoke, there happened one of the most discon-
certing experiences of my life. The air of the room was wrung
with a sudden sobbing, as of a child in an abandonment of grief.
We strode in the direction of the sound and craned over the
back of the chair which held the murdered woman. Sitting in
the corner on the floor behind it was Sugden Martenroyde, tears
coursing down from below closed lids, lost fingers pleating and
caressing the hem of Mira's simple skirt; and with those terrible

sobs jerking themselves, as it were, from his weak and twisted mouth.

We had to pull forward the chair with its ghastly burden before we could lift the man behind it to his feet and set him in another chair beside the fireplace. He pawed at Beverley's coat for comfort and, with his eyes half-shut, murmured to us with a most eerie pathos: "Naughty Mira, naughty Mira! She told my mother of me. No more pretty London. No more pretty Mira. Oh, I want to go to bed."

"Well, this is all different, and not so good," said Beverley, and I understood what he meant. "I hate to do it," he added, as he handcuffed the docile killer, "but it's the only way I can be certain of managing him as far as the station. And you must stay and go upstairs."

He led the unprotesting Sugden out of the parlour, while I stayed behind for the moment necessary to cover what remained of Mira Heggus with the striped cotton tablecloth. Then I, too, left the room and, locking the door, gave the key to Beverley.

"Stay with Dakin," he said. "I'll have this fellow safely stowed in jail and call Dr. Ponsford to him. Then I'll be back with the constable; he'll have to stay the night here."

I watched the two go off arm-in-arm in the darkness, and thought, incongruously enough, of a father leading home a child who has been disobedient and is frightened. Then I turned with a sick heart to the Heggus home.

I sighed as I mounted the stairs to Dakin's bedroom, where I found him in his invalid chair with Louie Sparks at his feet. She had evidently followed close behind us from the Mill House and had crept up to share his dreadful uncertainty with the invalid, without daring to break in on us in the parlour.

They gave me a mute questioning look, to which I replied by shaking my head.

"I've lost my girl, then," said Dakin slowly. "She'll come no more to the sound of my old sheep-bell. Willing and cheerful she ever was to answer it, and now – no more!" He knocked the bell off the table with a despairing movement; and I marvelled, not for the first time, how long illness will sap all savage reactions from the most masculine and leave them drained of everything save a most genuine, though theatrical-seeming, pathos.

"Nay, but there are others who will hear the call!" said Louie, placing the bell back within Dakin's reach and putting her hand over his emaciated one.

Then Dakin said in a weak voice: "I couldn't go to help my dear lass in her hour of need, but I know she'll come to me in mine, to guide me, like. And it won't be so long before that hour will strike, I'm thinking."

"You mustn't say that, Dakin!" and Louie looked at him with all the protection in the world showing in her eyes, as if she had at last found justification for herself. "It will be my duty and my pleasure to be your servant now, for Mira in her kindness was meaning to take me in and shelter me."

It was a scene in which I felt myself an intruder, and when footsteps on the gravel outside the window told me that Beverley had returned with the constable, I gave Dakin a silent shake of the hand and left the couple gladly.

27

VOLUME OF EVIDENCE

THE CONSTABLE WAS GIVEN orders to remain in charge until relieved in the morning, and Beverley and I were soon back at the Mill House. We knocked cautiously on the door, and Ramsden let us in and conducted us to the living room, where Eddison nodded over a brisk fire which had been lighted in our absence.

After questioning our faces, Ramsden exclaimed: "Thank God, my mother has gone to bed! It's the worst, isn't it?"

But his gratification was premature, for even as Beverley made an end of his terrible tidings, Hannah Martenroyde, who must have been listening at the door, opened it and tottered into the room. She had made no attempt to undress and still carried the Bible under her arm. She must have been waiting and hearkening in the upper part of the house.

Ramsden, whose colour at Beverley's recital had slowly drained from his honest, moon face, rose and led her to the chair next to his.

"Oh, Ramsden," she said, setting down the book gently on the floor beside her, "you'll no let our Sugden be taken away – you'll have care of him?"

"Nay, Mother," he answered hopelessly. "It's true I've stood by you both in thick and thin, but the time has come when I am powerless to do more. If Sugden has done this terrible thing we'll be lucky if it's an asylum and not a hanging."

Hannah shook him violently by the shoulder. "Ye shall not say that! Ye shall not say it! Dare not take such words on your tongue!" She faced us defiantly. "Ay his brother may utter such a cruel thing, but Sugden's still my son – my pretty son. And he's not really well. If he has killed that good-for-nothing slut, what loss is she or a hundred like her, I should like to know?"

There was naturally no answer to this, and then occurred a very strange thing, or so it seemed to me; perhaps those who know their Yorkshire folk will understand it better than I do.

Hannah Martenroyde relaxed in her chair, and said: "Ramsden lad, give me the Book," and when Ramsden, with a puzzled frown, had picked the Bible up and handed it to her – it was the same one, I noticed, which I had examined on my first and surreptitious visit to the Mill House – she searched among various book-marks and eventually found the page she desired. "I've been reading in the Book while you were gone," she said, "and some of it was a rare comfort. Will you listen to this now? 'Lord, have mercy on my son: for he is lunatick, and sore vexed. . . . And Jesus rebuked the devil; and he departed out of him: and the child was cured from that very hour.' "

She shut the Bible and sat caressing it, with her look fixed on vacancy. Then her face became troubled and she started fumbling with the markers again. "But wasn't there another bit? An evil bit?" she asked disquietedly. "An unkind, evil bit I read to my child tonight? Ay, here it is! You wouldn't put faith in this about our Sugden, would you? 'The abominable, and murderers, and whoremongers . . . and all liars, shall have their part in the lake which burneth with fire and brimstone: which is the second death.' The foul, damned liar of a Book!" she cried, and hurled the volume from her on to the floor. But scarcely had she thrown it when she was on her knees after it. She returned to her seat with it and kissed its black binding all over and crooned over it: "Oh, what have I done to you? Surely, I'm damned, and'll go to hell. But see, I'm kissing you, my guide and stay, as if you were my Sugden. You wouldn't be hard, would you, on an old woman of sorrows, ay, and bitter acquainted with grief?"

Then she fell silent. Ramsden was plainly shocked by this strange little three-act tragedy, and Eddison and Beverley were as plainly uncomfortable and at a loss. But I was paying little attention to any of the four of them. I had been damned slow, as Chaney always says I am, but I had got there at last, as Chaney always says I do. I had solved the mystery of James Marten-royde's murder.

As Ramsden took the Bible gently from his mother's hands, the old woman's face worked painfully, and it was in a beaten voice that she said as she groped her way – as if unseeing – to the door:

"The poor lad! The handsome babe was never quite – quite as we are. They'll not be hanging him. But his old mother – well, she's done now – and she must have her rest." She stumbled out of the room, and soon we could hear her heavy footsteps reverberating through the upper passages of the old house.

Ramsden sighed heavily and passed his hand over his forehead with a bewildered gesture.

"There's times when it's hard for a body to know what to do for the good of all," he said. "To know what should come out into the light of day, and what is best hid up in darkness for ever."

He assured us that he would leave his mother in peace for the rest of the night, and sleep downstairs to keep watch over the house and prevent her leaving it. It was a broken man who closed the front door upon us, and I was the only one who had understood his remark about the light of day.

Eddison insisted that Beverley should sleep at his house, and as the three of us descended the path towards the river I heard both my companions yawning copiously. It was in the dead hour of three o'clock on a winter's morning, when the mind and the moral fibre are at their slackest. The other two were at the end of their tethers, and I doubtless would have felt the same had it not been for the revelation which had been vouchsafed to me. Beverley complained in a very weary voice that he was no nearer to a solution of his first two murders, and when I told him that I would have something to give him in the morning as soon as I had put my thoughts in order, his only answer was: "It's useless driving a sleepy head. I'm glad you've got nothing for me tonight."

But after the others had tumbled into bed, I lay awake for a long time, for the strange truth was making a sort of firework display in my mind. Thank the Lord, it didn't matter that I had withheld Ann Kitteridge's evidence from Beverley! Or perhaps it did matter? Perhaps he'd have seen more in it than I had? Either way, Sugden's slaying of Mira could not have been prevented. That was a comfort. I would make a long-distance call in the morning; and then, if I was right, I would tell Beverley. At last I slept.

28

TWO OF A KIND

"I hope to God she'll be more normal this morning!"

It was Beverley who spoke, pushing aside his empty plate at our late breakfast table and lighting the pipe for which he had reserved his last cup of coffee.

Neither Eddison nor I needed to ask of whom he spoke, and the Superintendent continued between heavy puffs: "It's really damned awkward! I could do without another visit to that house; but I've got to get some sort of a statement from her as to Sugden's mental condition yesterday. And she's pretty 'mental' herself by this time. Besides, after last night, suspicion focuses dead on the Mill House lot again. What's that theory you were getting at when I was walking downhill in my sleep last night? Does it square with a return to that angle?"

"Entirely," I answered. "As a matter of fact, I wanted to put in a long-distance call before I told you. But a visit to the Mill House will do just as well. Better! Because now you can do the discovering yourself and owe nothing to the awkward amateur."

"I believe you really do know something," said Beverley with a friendly smile, as we struggled into our overcoats. "Well, Eddison's your employer, and if he's content to let you give the police a start—"

The weather had changed while we slept, and the sun beat down hearteningly from a clean sky of dark dry blue as we made what was to prove to be our last journey together to that tragic house.

Arriving, we were greeted by Ramsden, and guessed from his stricken manner and rigid expression that something further had gone amiss since we had left him such a short time ago. On Beverley's inquiry for Mrs. Martenroyde, Ramsden told us that his mother had gone, just gone.

"Gone? What do you mean by that?" asked Beverley sharply. "But, man, you promised faithfully that on no condition would you allow her to leave the house! I must insist upon your mother being produced at once. You mustn't obstruct the police a second time, you know."

Ramsden beckoned us to the bottom of the stairs and pointed upwards: "Last night there was such a to-do in the old house that it could be heard a mile around. This morning – listen! D'ye hear ought?"

We held our breath and strained to catch any noise in that still house, but no sound greeted our ears save the melancholy beat of an unseen clock.

"Ay!" and Ramsden waved us upwards. "Ye'll never hear her voice scolding again. She's gone. I've just found her gone."

"Suicide!" ejaculated Beverley. "I might have known it! Why didn't you watch her? She'd have been able to live a peaceful life again, with Sugden out of the way."

"Say no more till ye've seen."

Ramsden thereupon led us upstairs and along the gallery. As we made our way through the accumulation of old furniture that cumbered up this passage, I remembered my clandestine visit to that floor and could almost hear the ghost of that groan which had come to me near the door of the locked bedroom up the next flight. In a flash, as a final confirmation of my overnight's surmise, I recalled that the door through which the body of Mally Brewster had been carried to her own bed was on the first floor. In spite of the bright sunshine outside, the tortuous stairs up which we next climbed were in shadow, and we stumbled blindly behind Ramsden as he threw open the door of the small room at the head of the stairs.

A shaft of morning brightness entering through a window in the roof illumined the chamber now disclosed and struck down upon two still figures stretched upon a double bed.

"Look now," said Ramsden, "and say whether this is one of those things which should have been told before or whether I was right to hold my tongue."

Beverley strode forward to the bed, and Eddison and I tiptoed after him into the tiny chamber. There lay Mrs. John Martenroyde, hand in hand with her frailer and younger-seeming counterpart, two waxen images from the same mould, the one bruised and coarsened by outside contacts, and the other, in spite of snow-white hair, looking curiously girlish in death – twin sisters of sorrow and despair.

"That's Aunt Deborah," said Ramsden simply. "She lost her wits with being jilted by Uncle James this long time since."

"Of course you knew that your aunt was living concealed in the house with you. You couldn't avoid doing so," said Beverley grimly.

"Ay – Sugden and I both knew," answered Ramsden. "But what we did not know was that she had escaped the night that Uncle James was killed. God forgive her, Mother only told me that early this morning."

"That's just as well for you," said Beverley, as he began curiously to examine the room. "There's such a thing as being accessory after the fact. What did they take, I wonder. Something violent enough. Is there any disinfectant about?"

Ramsden pointed to an old Kruschen salts jar on the small washstand. A few crystals of cyanide of potassium still adhered to the bottom of it. He had had no idea, he told us, that there had been any of the poison left over after the destruction of the wasps's nests in the autumn. He had examined the bottle carefully when they had finished, found it empty, and buried it in the garden. Mrs. Martenroyde must, however, have had in mind this means of ending her problem even then, for he remembered her questioning him minutely on the action of cyanide. She was quite normal at the time, seeming interested in the subject from an impersonal point of view, and he could remember having consulted a small book on poisons which he possessed, in order to clear up some point she had raised. She must in some way have secreted a few sufficient fragments, given some to her usually docile sister that morning, and ended her life with the remainder.

The story we heard from Ramsden in that doleful chamber came to us doubtless in much the same words as he himself had received it from his mother when he reached manhood. The heavy, groping, honest speech, which considerably heightened the tragedy for the three of us who listened, could not be effectively reproduced on paper. I give the gist of the tale merely.

John Stead had always been a "queer" man, and after his wife's death he became queerer. He survived her by two years, the last six months of which he spent in the county asylum, where he died in 1893. Ramsden knew nothing of the scientific diagnosis made of the old man's condition; nothing in fact, save that his derangement had violence in it.

The eighteen-year-old orphans were not unduly cast down, it seems, by their father's misfortune, and at the time when Hannah Stead married John Martenroyde, she and Deborah were the acknowledged belles of the neighbourhood. They were handsome, animated girls, and the spirit which had later developed into cantankerousness in Mrs. Martenroyde, gave delightful high spirits to Deborah's greater gentleness. She was popular and did not lack for suitors of the humbler sort. Her heart, however, was soon set upon James Martenroyde and for a year or two after Hannah's marriage it was accepted in the locality that these two would be making a match of it. Then time went on without any announcement to this effect being made, and upon the early death of Hannah's husband, James had definitely cooled off towards the lively twin. Whether it was because he found himself suddenly saddled with the upkeep of the sister-in-law and her two sons or whether certain inherited traits in Hannah's character were already becoming apparent, Ramsden could not say; but I, remembering his remark to me: "John never made out – I don't know how it was – or happen I do know," had suddenly a clear enough picture of a normal, clean-strained, ambitious man gradually recognising the taint in the stock which attracted him and, without a word spoken, putting temptation from him and turning to his mill for consolation.

Beverley had been prowling gently round the room during this recital, looking at all the pathetic comforts provided for its inmate, and now drew our attention to a small what-not near the head of the bed. It bore a certain tragic resemblance to a shrine; a large photograph of James Martenroyde occupied the centre of the top shelf, and this was surrounded by three withered flowers, a broken fan, and various girlish trifles of another day. "Look!" said he, pointing to a home-made dance program, scrawled over with "James" in bold characters. "He certainly danced with her enough to make her conspicuous, didn't he? And look at this!" He took up a yellowing portrait showing the two in the stiff attitudes of courtship as imagined by a village photographer. "They must have gone some ways towards marriage to have had this taken. She must have thought herself secure of him."

Ramsden continued his story.

At first, evidently, Deborah had appeared to take her jilting with melancholy philosophy and had busied herself in helping Hannah look after the house and the children. After their installation by James in the Mill House, however, a change had come over her. She appeared to realise that her suitor had finally thrown her over and she started to brood in solitude. She would sometimes go down to the village and listen eagerly to any titbits of gossip concerning James, especially if such gossip coupled his name with that of any other woman. Also it was noticed by the villagers that she frequented the society of Prissy Mallison.

Hannah, beset by the cares of her family, had not the wit to notice the change in Deborah's condition until too late, though she always, then and thereafter, was the actively loving one of the pair. Then came the firing of the mill. Deborah had confessed to this piece of incendiarism and had threatened to take James's life if she ever heard that he was thinking of giving her a more human rival.

After the fire Hannah realised that she must either hand her sister over to the asylum authorities or keep her secreted for all time about the house, and when she herself was absent, in that room hidden away at the top of the gallery stairs. She chose the latter course; and as her sons were then of an age to understand the meaning of an oath, had made them swear not to tell that their relative was concealed in the Mill House. Thenceforward they had helped their mother to attend the stricken woman and control her when necessary, maintaining the strictest watch to prevent her escaping to work further harm at Todmanhawe Grange or Mill. Ramsden said it told hardly on Hannah's temper, but that she had persevered faithfully in her self-imposed task.

She gave out that Deborah had taken a post as companion at Chorlton in Lancashire, and soon after engineered a telegram reporting her death in that place. The family went into mourning, and then, to give colour to the state of siege obtaining in Hannah's Castle, its owner had caused it gradually to be whispered through the village that her own brain had begun to give way on one point: that she refused to believe that her sister, who had always taken the lead in social matters, was dead and had sworn that there would not be open house again until its hostess returned. The secret was then considered safe, for Mally Brewster was of the family-retainer type of servant, who would rather die than give her employers away.

"But how ever did she escape to murder James?" asked Beverley.

"The night Uncle was killed," answered Ramsden, "she got round Mally Brewster. It was during one of her sane intervals, and she told so sad a tale to Mally about being quite recovered and in need of an evening stroll, that Mally gave in, the poor old fool."

"Poor old fool indeed!" agreed Eddison. "She little knew that she sealed her own death-warrant that night."

"When Auntie got back – raving and dishevelled – Mally was in a rare taking. And then, to her horror, she discovered that there was blood on Mother's walking-stick. She wiped it off and was too terrified to say anything. Mother only got it out of her after we brought Mally back from Shawes."

After that the two old women had quaked in their shoes and confined Deborah closer and closer yet.

"That clears up several points," said Beverley. "I had become certain that it was Hannah whom the old witch saw by the church on the nights of the two crimes. Of course it was Deborah in her sister's white mackintosh, the one so like Sugden's!"

"And it clears up a much more difficult point!" I said to myself, remembering Ann Kitteridge's recognition of the woman she had seen leaving the conservatory and heard talking to herself as she hurried away as Hannah Martenroyde. Well, there would be no gain to myself or Ann or Beverley if I told of that now.

Aloud I said: "So it wasn't Hannah who listened at the conservatory door on the night of my introduction to James Martenroyde! We were all wrong as to the motive, too – it was a slow-fire *crime passionnel*. Whereas we thought fear of Sugden's safety had driven Hannah to murder, it was the jealous realisation of a poor old mad brain that her lover was finally unfaithful to her that prompted Deborah to kill. I remember Martenroyde was showing me photographs of Miss Houston and expatiating on her comeliness when I heard those sounds behind the door."

"To hear him praising another woman would have been the last touch," said Ramsden gloomily, reaching for a small book that lay among the treasures on the what-not.

"Why did Mally run away that time?" asked Eddison.

"As far as I could gather from Mother this morning – she was so worked up that it wasn't too easy to follow all she told me – Mally's conscience started to trouble her for keeping what she knew to herself. She thought James's ghost came to her in the night and told her that if she stayed on at the Mill House, Deborah would frighten her into letting her loose again, and there would be more murder done."

"Then Mally was brought back here for obvious reasons, and there was more murder," said Beverley. "Who killed Mally herself, Deborah or Hannah?"

"Deborah," answered Ramsden. "I'd honestly thought it was an accident, but poor Mother told me this morning, and I believe her. After James's murder we were much stricter with Aunt Debbie, and her anger was mainly roused against old Mally, who had to do most of the guarding. On that morning, through Mally forgetting to lock the bedroom door, she had escaped downstairs again and was actually at the front door with the stick in her hand when Mally saw and tried to stop her. After the blow had been struck, my aunt was docile enough, thinking, Mother believed, that she had killed James's betrothed. After she had taken her back to her room and locked her in, Mother dragged poor Mally along to the bottom of the stairs and smashed down the tray of crockery beside her. And it must have happened that way, Superintendent."

"It sounds plausible, and, anyway, it's the only explanation we'll ever get," replied Beverley. "A very remarkable woman – your mother! What have you there, Martenroyde?"

"It's a diary Auntie seems to have kept," answered Ramsden. "I was dipping into it just before you came. Happen you would like to read it?"

"Thank you," and Beverley took the small book. "It may give us a background against which to understand the case."

On that we left the two distracted old sisters to the first enjoyment of their release. Beverley locked the bedroom door, and the four of us went downstairs.

29

THE LAST OF THE MARTENROYDES

BEVERLEY HAD MUCH TO do. Dr. Ponsford must be summoned to view the bodies, and arrangements for their removal had to be made. Also Sugden had to be transferred from the local police station to Shipton. Ramsden said that he would accompany the Superintendent to see whether he could convey any cheer or comfort to his distraught brother. Eddison and I volunteered to stay at the Mill House during their absence, and settled ourselves in the living room.

"A strange, strange story!" said Eddison. "To think of that warped existence working itself out up here for all these years, while the little life of Todmanhawe revolved unsuspecting down below! Well, I expect the facts of this morning have upset your theory of last night, whatever it was?"

"On the contrary," I answered, "my theory – one without detail, as I freely admit – has been amply and tragically borne out this morning. I had intended first thing to put a phone call through to Chorlton in Lancashire, and I should have been very much surprised if the local authorities had not confirmed my supposition that no Deborah Martenroyde had ever lived or died there."

"Why so?" asked Eddison, who was evidently deeply interested.

"I'll try to give you the stages of my complete befogging and subsequent enlightenment in their proper order. First, you must realise that to a stranger like myself, arriving here to be faced by a murder connected with two houses, the mystery of the state of siege in which one of those houses was kept, the mystery of Hannah's Castle, was bound to seem a very real one, whether connected with the murder or not. But for you Todmanhawe folk it had long ceased to seem more than an eccentricity, which had been once explained, and the explanation already half forgotten. Remember that it occurred to no one, until I questioned Avis, to tell me of Hannah's belief that her dead sister was not really dead.

"To me a house with the entry denied to the outside world naturally suggested a house of concealment, and, since the whole house had been placed out of bounds, the concealment of some living thing, almost certainly of some living person. It must have been as much to set my mind at rest on this point, though I hardly realised the fact at the time, as to investigate the surroundings of Hannah Martenroyde, my prime suspect, that I paid my surreptitious visit to the Mill House.

"Have you ever noticed that the order in which facts or supposed facts reach the brain is as important to the correctness or incorrectness of our interpretation of them as the facts themselves? When I came to the entry in the family Bible recording the death of Deborah, I took it merely as further proof of what I had heard of Hannah's twin, and the crossing out of that entry fitted in with what Avis and you and others had told me of Hannah's delusion. I went on with the investigation of the house with my mind perfectly satisfied on the subject of Deborah. But if I had ever heard of her before I looked at the Bible, I guarantee that those entries would have lit a flaming question-mark in my brain concerning her: an unknown Martenroyde, whose death was first affirmed and then denied, and the home of the Marten-

roydes shut to the outside world! I would have come away with
the intention of making exhaustive inquiries. Rest assured, at
least, that I would not have so complacently put down the groan
I heard to the old servant suffering in her sleep. In fact, this is the
only case I have ever come across where knowledge on the part
of the detective has considerably postponed the solution of the
problem."

"Yes, yes, I see that," said Eddison. "But what was it that put
you on to the truth last night?"

"That rather horrible business of the Bible," I replied; "Hannah apologising to the book and fearing for her immortal soul
because she'd maltreated it. It suddenly flashed across me that
the death entry and its deletion, if they had been made considerably later than any who saw them were intended to suppose,
were capable of another explanation and one more in keeping
with Hannah's superstitious attitude. It was quite possible, of
course, that she had entered the death on hearing of it, but it
seemed to me unlikely that she would have defaced the volume
later in order to correct what at times she took to be a mis-state-
ment. This would have meant her ordered and her disordered
mind working together, and a consistency between fact and
delusion which is rare in cases of monomania. I remembered
that both entry and deletion had been in black ink, which,
if of good quality, never gives its age away. No, it was much
more likely that a woman with such limited cunning and such
faith in the Bible as a support would have made it tell a lie for
her – the death entry, set down, I suppose, just after James's
murder, to fool any investigator, as it fooled me, into the belief
that the murderess had been dead for many years. Then days
pass, suspicion seems to be getting no nearer the little room
upstairs, the book lie weighs more and more heavily, and, by
way of apology, she erases it, probably only a few hours before
I examined the entries. Mally had not been murdered then, you
must remember."

"Excellent, Camberwell!" exclaimed Eddison when I had finished. "But, as your employer, I cannot help being glad that you were prevented from bringing your case to a close while those two poor sisters were still alive."

"No more glad than I am!" I answered, and from the bottom of my heart I meant it.

Eddison now took up the volume which Beverley had brought downstairs. It was not a diary in the ordinary sense, but a thick, squat account book. The entries were sporadic; months and even years had passed without comment.

"The writing is young and firm at the beginning," said Eddison. "And here's the first entry, dated January 1897. Listen!

> *'Attended dance at Shipton Town Hall last night, wearing my rose muslin made over again. Could not help hearing kind remarks on appearance from all sides. He was not there, and I felt like Robin's forlorn lady in the old song. But I know he dreams of me, as I do of him. Life in this dreary village would not be tolerable else. Did he not call me his "dewy Deborah" three weeks ago? That seems a long time, but I must be patient. I had thought he would speak at this dance, but Hannah was not so sure. Hannah is a good sister, but just now taken up with John Martenroyde.'*

Then later in the same year:

> *James walked home with me behind John and Hannah. He remarked how fine it was to watch their newly wedded happiness and looked fondly at me. I felt there was meaning in his eye and that he was nerving himself. Hannah and I are so much alike that he must realise that the same*

bliss would be his . . . but he said nothing more.
Dear diary, you shall be the first to be told when he
asks me to be his wife. Every girl goes through these
extremes of hope and fear, but they are especially
hard on a girl of spirit like myself.'"

Hereafter Eddison turned over the leaves in silence, and only
when he found some significant entry read it aloud. "There's
this," he said. "At the end of 1904:

'The doctor now tells Hannah that there is no hope
she will keep John. She will be left with two helpless
children and I fear nothing in the way of mon-
ey provided. John was never a saver. Will James
help? He has been so sad and quiet of late in my
company. I cannot rally him as I used. He seems
to detest my high spirits as much as he used to
admire them, and indeed they are a trifle forced
nowadays. Cannot he see that I am wearing myself
out waiting for him? Will he ever speak now?'

And a few days later:

'Today buried John. James round at Hannah's af-
ter, looking into business matters. There will be
little or nothing for her and the children. I would
that I had a bit of money of my own for her, but my
best years are gone in waiting for James. It humbles
me to the dust to write this.'

And a month later:

'Today sees us installed at the Mill House, an old dwelling which James has put into repair for us. He is making himself responsible for the future of my sister and her boys. Will he never make himself responsible for me? Is he waiting till I am more sedate and old? Hannah and I are turning thirty now, and James has lost my prime.'

I don't know how much later the next entry is:

'Today had another long talk with Mother Mallison. She gave me comforting words and said that my lover would come to me at the end. Got Hannah to put it into his teacup when he called this afternoon.'

From now on, the writing becomes less and less decipherable. This entry must date from three years ago, as you will see:

'I know now that he has never loved me. He has given his heart to the mill, and tonight I go to settle accounts with my rival. I have all ready. The fool! He valued a thing of bricks and mortar above the living body of Deborah Stead. He may regret his choice tomorrow when the hillsides at last have peace from the clacking of his wheels.'

The writing, as I say, is getting worse and worse; but here's one page almost schoolgirlish clear. Just a piece of poetry:

'O western wind, when wilt thou blow
That the small rain down can rain?

Christ, that my love were in my arms
And I in my bed again!'

There are only two more entries:

'Today Hannah told me that I am not right in the
head and that my storms of fury against James are
a sign of failing reason. It is not to be wondered
at. She says I must be kept close and see no one,
or I shall be taken off to prison. But I'd like to see
James sometimes, so that I could hate him more;
I love him too much when I never see him.'

And here's the last:

'Oh, the days, the endless days! Hannah is kind
and good . . . she has always loved me almost
oppressively . . . but surely death would be better
than only seeing her and Mally. The boys come
so seldom. I have just lain on my back for an hour
upon my bed stretching wide my arms to the
ceiling. James! James! Hannah says he will come
to me soon. She promises he will come. But my
head is clear tonight, I think I will go to meet him.
Shall I?'

And it breaks off so on a question mark." Eddison blew his
nose loudly. "A few blotted tears, and then some pages torn right
across."

Two days afterwards, the tragic old twins were buried in Todmanhawe churchyard in a single grave, adjacent to that of Mally
Brewster. The whole village was there to pay its last respects,
and a few early spring flowers returned to earth with them.

"Poor Mrs. John! We didn't understand her trouble!" was the tribute I heard paid by one of the mill lassies; it will serve as Todmanhawe's epitaph.

I walked back to the Mill House with Ramsden and questioned him as to his plans for the future. With his steady eyes on the grey surface of the ruffling Scarth – as though indeed he were already seeing new horizons – he told me that he intended to leave for Canada almost at once. He had mill-owning friends there from whom he could buy a partnership. There could be no more happiness for him in England. Our path took us along the wide-stretching front of the mill. Through the open windows we heard the steady murmur of the machinery. Death lay behind us in the churchyard by the river, but Martenroyde's mill was throbbing with life and its spindles were still running.

Q.E.D.
by Lynn Brock

There's Death in the Churchyard
by William Gore

Murder of the Ninth Baronet
by J.S. Fletcher

Dead Man Manor
by Valentine Williams

The Man in the Dark
by John Ferguson

The Dressing Room Murder
by J.S. Fletcher

*Glory Adair and the
Twenty-First Burr*
by Victor Lauriston

The Tunnel Mystery
by J.C. Lenehan

Murder on the Marsh
by John Ferguson

The Fatal Five Minutes
R.A.J. Walling

*The Crime
of a Christmas Toy*
Henry Herman

Death of an Editor
Vernon Loder

Death on May Morning
Max Dalman

The Hymn Tune Mystery
George A. Birmingham

The Middle of Things
JS Fletcher

The Essex Murders
Vernon Loder

The Boat Race Murder
R. E. Swartwout

Who Killed Alfred Snowe?
J. S. Fletcher

Murder at the College
Victor L. Whitechurch

*The Yorkshire
Moorland Mystery*
J. S. Fletcher

Fatality in Fleet Street
Christopher St. John Sprigg

The Doctor of Pimlico
William Le Queux

The Charing Cross Mystery
J. S. Fletcher

Fatality in Fleet Street ePub & PDF
FREE when you sign up for our
infrequent Newsletter.

Made in the USA
Columbia, SC
14 October 2023

24447531R00143